Poul Anderson

The Star Fox

Panther

Granada Publishing Limited
Published in 1968 by Panther Books Ltd
Frogmore, St Albans Herts AL2 2NF
Reprinted 1975

First published in Great Britain by Victor
Gollancz Ltd 1966
Copyright © Poul Anderson 1964, 1965
These stories have appeared in a slightly
different form in *The Magazine of Fantasy &
Science Fiction*, Copyright © Mercury Publications
Inc 1965
Made and printed in Great Britain by
Cox & Wyman Ltd, London, Reading and Fakenham
Set in Intertype Times

Zoom in with Hugo Award-winning Poul Anderson on any of his far-flung alien planets and some of the most unnerving, mind-stretching adventures in the whole of SF await you.

'There are beleaguered colonists to rescue, naval battles in space, aliens beautiful and uncouth and a gripping account of a stranding on a planet with a hydrogen atmosphere.

I would sign on again in the Spaceship **Star Fox**' – *Daily Telegraph*

Also by Poul Anderson in Panther Books

Time and Stars
Trader to the Stars
After Doomsday
The Corridors of Time
The Trouble Twisters

À François Bordes:
Merci . . . et au revoir!

Part One

MARQUE AND REPRISAL

CHAPTER ONE

'Le roi a fait battre tambour'
Le roi a fait battre tambour—'

Gunnar Heim halted in midstride. He stood a while, turning his head in search of the voice that had risen out of the dark.

'Pour voir toutes ces dames.
Et la première qu'il a vue—'

It was some distance off, almost lost in the background of machine rumble to landward of the docks. But only one man was likely to be making his mock with that sinister old ballad, in San Francisco on this night.

'Lui a ravi son âme.
Rataplan! Rataplan! Rataplan-plan-plan-plan!'

Heim started after the sound. He could still move fast and softly when he wanted to. In a moment his ears picked up the ring and snarl of a guitar played in anger.

'Rataplan! Rataplan! Rataplan-plan-plan-plan!'

Warehouses bulked black on his right. At this hour not very long before dawn, the city had dimmed; there was only a reddish haze above the roofs, and the remote luminous heap of the palace towers on Nob Hill. To the left a cargo submarine lay like a sleek moon-scaled dragon, but no longshore robots or men were at work around it. The bay was ebony and a shimmer of glade. Kilometers distant, the hills on the eastern shore made a wall besprinkled with artificial stars. The real stars were wan, and so was the defense satellite that climbed rapidly into view – as if all suns had withdrawn from a planet gone strengthless. Luna stood at half phase near the zenith. He could not see the light-spot of Apollo City on the dark side, through the damp autumn air.

Heim rounded a shed by the pier and saw the minstrel. He sat on a bollard, looking out across the water, a man more small and shabby than expected. His fingers leaped across the twelve strings as if attacking an enemy, and the moon gleamed off tears on his face.

Heim paused in the shadow of the wall. He ought not to interrupt. They had related, in the Spaceman's Rest, that the buck was drunk and wild. 'And when he'd spent his last millo, he wanted to sing for booze,' the bartender said. 'I told him we didn't want none of that here. He said he'd sung his way through a dozen planets and what was wrong with Earth that nobody wanted to listen to him. I said the strip show was coming on the 3V in a minute and that's what the customers wanted, not any of his foreign stuff. So he yelled about singing to the stars or some such pothead notion. I told him go ahead, get out before I threw him out. And out he went. That was about an hour ago. Friend of yours?'

'Maybe,' Heim said.

'Uh, you might go look for him then. He could get into trouble. Somebody might go for an expensive gutbucket like he was hauling.'

Heim nodded and tossed off his beer. The Welfare section of any large city was bad to be alone in after nightfall. Even the police of Western countries made little effort to control those whom the machines had displaced before birth. They settled for containing that fury and futility in its own district, well away from the homes of people who had skills the world needed. On his walkabouts through the subculture of the irrelevant men, Heim carried a stun pistol. He had had use for it on occasion.

They knew him locally, though. He had told them he was a retired spaceman – anything nearer the truth would have been unwise – and before long he was accepted as a genial drinking or gambling companion, less odd than many of the floaters who drifted in and out of their indifferent purview. He waved at several acquaintances, some feral and some surrendered to hopelessness, and left the bar.

Since the minstrel had probably headed for the Embarcadero, Heim did too. His stride lengthened as he went. At first there had been no sense of mission about finding the fellow. It had merely been an excuse to go on yet another slumming trip. But the implications grew in his mind.

And now that his search was ended, the song caught at him and he felt his pulse accelerate. This stranger might indeed have the truth about that which had happened among yonder constellations.

> '—La reine a fait faire un bouquet
> De belles fleurs de lyse.
> Et la senteur de ce bouquet
> A fait mourir marquise.'

As the older tale, also of tyranny, treachery, and death, crashed to its end, Heim reached a decision.

> 'Rataplan! Rataplan! Rataplan-plan-plan-plan!
> Rataplan! Rataplan! Rataplan-plan-plan-plan!'

Silence followed, except for the lapping of water and the ceaseless throb of that engine which was the city. Heim trod forth.

'Good evening,' he said.

The minstrel jerked where he sat, drew a ragged breath, and twisted about. Heim spread his hands, smiling. 'I'm harmless,' he said. 'Was just admiring your performance. Mind if I join you?'

The other wiped at his eyes, furiously. Then the thin sharp face steadied into a considering look. Gunnar Heim was not one you met unperturbed, in such an area. He was nigh two meters tall, with breadth to match. His features were blunt and plain, an old scar zigzagging across the brow, under reddish-brown hair that in this forty-sixth year of his age was peppered with gray. But he was decently clad, in the high-collared tunic and the trousers tucked into soft half-boots that were the current mode. The hood of his cloak was thrown back. His weapon did not show.

'Well—' The minstrel made a spastic shrug. 'This is a public place.' His English was fluent, but bore a heavier accent than his French.

Heim took a flat bottle of whisky from his pocket. 'Will you drink with me, sir?'

The minstrel snatched it. After the first swallow he gusted, 'Ahhh!' Presently: 'Forgive my bad manners. I needed that.' He raised the flask. '*Isten éltesse,*' he toasted, drank again, and passed it back.

'*Skål.*' Heim took a gulp and settled himself on the wharf next to the bollard. What he had already drunk buzzed in him, together with a rising excitement. It was an effort to stay relaxed.

The minstrel came down to sit beside him. 'You are not American, then?' he asked. His tone wavered a bit; he was obviously trying to make unemotional conversation while the tears dried on his high cheekbones.

'I am, by naturalization,' Heim said. 'My parents were Norwegian. But I was born on Gea, Tau Ceti II.'

'What?' The hoped-for eagerness sprang into the singer's countenance. He sat up straight. 'You are a spaceman?'

'Navy, till about fifteen years ago. Gunnar Heim is my name.'

'I . . . Endre Vadász.' The agile fingers disappeared in Heim's handshake. 'Hungarian, but I have spent the last decade off Earth.'

'Yes, I know,' Heim said with care. 'I saw you on a news program recently.'

Vadász's lips writhed. He spat off the dock.

'You didn't get a chance to say much during the interview,' Heim angled.

'No. They were cautious to mute me. "So you are a musician, Mr. Vadász. You have worked your way by any means that came to hand, from star to star, bearing the songs of Mother Earth to the colonists and the non-humans. *Isn't* that interesting!" ' The guitar cried out under a stroke.

'And you wanted to tell about New Europe, and they kept steering you from the subject. I wondered why.'

'The word had come to them. From your precious American authorities, under pressure from the big brave World Federation. It was too late to cancel my announced appearance, but I was to be gagged.' Vadász threw back his head and laughed, a coyote bark under the moon. 'Am I paranoid? Do I claim I am being persecuted? Yes. But what if the conspiracy against me is real? Then does my sanity or lunacy make any difference?'

'M-m-m.' Heim rubbed his chin and throttled back the emotions within himself. He was not an impetuous man. 'How can you be sure?'

'Quinn admitted it, when I reproached him afterward. He said he had been told the station might lose its license if it, ah, lent itself to allegations which might embarrass the Federation in this difficult time. Not that I was too surprised. I had had talks with officials, both civil and military, since arriving on Earth. The kindest thing any one of them said was that I must be mistaken. But they had seen my proofs. They knew.'

'Did you try the French? They'd be more likely to do something, I should think.'

'Yes. In Paris I got no further than an assistant under-secretary. He was frightened of my story and would not refer me to anyone higher who might believe. I went on to Budapest, where I have kin. My father arranged for me to see the foreign minister himself. He was at least honest with me. New Europe was no concern of Hungary, which could in any event not go against the whole Federation. I left his office and walked for many hours. Finally I sat down in the dark by the Freedom Memorial. I looked at Imre Nagy's face, and it was only cold bronze. I looked at the figures of the martyrs, dying at his feet, and knew why no one will listen to me. So I got very drunk.' Vadász reached for the bottle. 'I have been drunk most of the time since.'

Now we ask him! flared in Heim. His voice would not remain calm any longer; but Vadász didn't notice. 'Your story, I gather from what bits and pieces have leaked past this unofficial official censorship – your story is that the people are not dead on New Europe. Right?'

'Right, sir. They fled into the mountains, every one of them.'

'The Haute Garance,' Heim nodded. He had all he could do merely to nod. 'Good guerrilla country. Lots of cover, most never mapped, and you can live off the land.'

'You have been there!' Vadász set the bottle down and stared.

'Pretty often, while in the Navy. It was a favourite spot to put in for overhaul and planet leave. And then I spent four months in a stretch on New Europe by myself, recovering from this.' Heim touched the mark on his forehead.

Vadász peered close through the dappled moonlight. 'Did the Aleriona do that to you?'

'No. This was over twenty years ago. I bought it while we

were putting down the Hindu-German trouble on Lilith, which you're probably too young to remember. The skirmishes with Alerion didn't begin till later.' Heim spoke absently. For this moment the drive and ferocity in him were overlaid by—

Red roofs and steep narrow streets of Bonne Chance, winding down along the River Carsac to the Baie des Pêcheurs, which lay purple and silver to the world's edge. Lazy days, drinking Pernod in a sidewalk café and lapping up the ruddy sunshine as a cat laps milk. When he got better, hunting trips into the highlands with Jacques Boussard and Toto Astier ... good bucks, open to heart and hand, a little crazy as young men ought to be. Madelon—

He shook himself and asked roughly, 'Do you know who is, or was, in charge?'

'A Colonel de Vigny of the planetary constabulary. He assumed command after the *mairie* was bombed, and organized the evacuation.'

'Not old Robert de Vigny? My God! I knew him.' Heim's fist clenched on the concrete. 'Yes, in that case the war is still going on.'

'It cannot last,' Vadász mumbled. 'Given time, the Aleriona will hunt everyone down.'

'I know the Aleriona too,' Heim said.

He drew a long breath and looked at the stars. Not toward the sun Aurore. Across a hundred and fifty light-years, it would be lost to his eyes; and it lay in the Phoenix anyway, walled off from him by the heavy curve of Earth. But he could not look straight at the minstrel while he asked, 'Did you meet one Madelon Dubois? That'd be her maiden name. I expect she's long married.'

'No.' Vadász's drink-slurred voice became instantly clear and gentle. 'I am sorry, but I did not.'

'Well—' Heim forced a shrug. 'The chances were way against it. There's supposed to be half a million people on New Europe. Were the ... the casualties heavy?'

'I heard that Coeur d'Yvonne, down in Pays d'Or, was struck by a hydrogen missile. Otherwise – no, I do not believe so. The fighting was mostly in space, when the Aleriona fleet disposed of the few Federation Navy ships that happened to be near. Afterwards they landed in force, but in uninhabited areas at first, so that except for a couple of raids with nothing worse than lasers and chemical bombs, the other towns had time to

12

evacuate. They had been called on to surrender, of course, but de Vigny refused and so many went off with him that the rest came too.'

Damn it, I have got *to keep this impersonal. At least till I know more.* 'How did you escape? The newscasts that mentioned you when you first arrived were vague about it. Deliberately, I suppose.'

Vadász made the bottle gurgle. 'I was there when the attack came,' he said, thickly again. 'The French commandeered a merchant vessel and sent it after help, but it was destroyed when scarcely above the atmosphere. There was also a miner in from Naqsa.' He got the non-human pronunciation nearly right. 'You may know that lately there has been an agreement, the Naqsans may dig in Terre du Sud for a royalty. So far off, they had seen nothing, knew nothing, and cloud cover above Garance would keep them ignorant. After a radio discussion, the Aleriona commander let them go, I daresay not wanting to antagonize two races at once. Of course, the ship was not allowed to take passengers. But I had earlier flitted down for a visit and won the captain's fancy – that a human should be interested in *his* songs, and even learn a few – so he smuggled me aboard and kept me hidden from the Aleriona inspectors. De Vigny thought I could carry his message – hee, hee!' Vadász's laugh was close to hysteria. Fresh tears ran out of his eyes. 'From Naqsa I had to, what you call, bum my way. It took time. And was all, all for nothing.'

He laid the guitar across his knees, strummed, and sang low.

> ' "*Adieu, ma mie, mon coeur,*
> *Adieu, ma mie, adieu, mon coeur,*
> *Adieu, mon espérance—*" '

Heim took the bottle, then abruptly set it down so hard that it clanked. He jumped to his feet and began pacing. His shadow wove back and forth across the minstrel, his cloak fluttered against the moonlight on the water.

'*Nej, ved fanden!*' he exploded.

'Eh?' Vadász blinked up at him.

'Look, do you say you have proof?'

'Yes. I have offered to testify under drugs. And de Vigny gave me letters, photographs, a whole microfilm packet with every bit of information he could scrape together. But no one on Earth will admit it is genuine. Few will even look at it.'

13

'I will,' Heim said. The blood roared in his ears.

'Good. Good. Right here, the package is.' Vadász fumbled in his soiled tunic.

'No, wait till later. I'll take your word for now. It fits in with every other scrap of fact I've come across.'

'So I have convinced one man,' Vadász said bitterly.

'More than that.' Heim drew a long breath. 'Look, friend, with due respect for you – and I respect anyone who's had the guts to go out and make his own kind of life – I'm not a raggedy-ass self-appointed troubadour. I'm boss and chief owner of Heimdal.'

'The nuclear motor makers?' Vadász shook his head, muzzily. 'No. *Non. Nein. Nyet.* You would never be here. I have seen your motors as far from home as the Rigel Domain.'

'Uh, huh. Damn good motors, aren't they? When I decided to settle on Earth, I studied the possibilities. Navy officers who've resigned their commissions and don't want to go into the merchant fleet have much too good a chance of ending down among the unemployables. But I saw that whoever was first to introduce the two-phase control system the Aleriona invented would lock gravs on the human market and half the non-human ones. And ... I'd been there when Tech Intelligence dissected an Aleriona ship we captured in the set-to off Achernar. My father-in-law was willing to stake me. So today I'm – oh, not one of the financial giants. But I have ample money.

'Also, I've kept in touch with my Academy classmates. Some of them are admirals by now. They'll pay attention to my ideas. And I'm a pretty good contributor to the Libertarian Party, which means that Twyman will listen to me too. He'd better!'

'No.' The dark tousled head moved from side to side, still drooping. 'This cannot be. I cannot have found someone.'

'Brother, you have.' Heim slammed a fist into his palm with a revolver noise. A part of him wondered, briefly, at his own joy. Was it kindled by this confirmation that they were not dead on New Europe? Or the chance that he, Gunnar Heim, might personally short-circuit Alerion the damned? Or simply and suddenly a purpose, after five years without Connie? He realized now the emptiness of those years.

No matter. The glory mounted and mounted.

He bent down, scooped up the bottle with one hand and

14

Vadász with the other. '*Skål!*' he shouted to Orion the Hunter, and drank a draught that made the smaller man gape. 'Whoo-oo! Come along, Endre. I know places where we can celebrate this as noisily as we damn please. We shall sing songs and tell tales and drink the moon down and the sun up and then we shall go to work. Right?'

'Y-yes—' Still dazed, Vadász tucked his guitar under an arm and wobbled in Heim's wake. The bottle was not quite empty when Heim began 'The Blue Landsknechts', a song as full of doom and hell as he was. Vadász hung the guitar from his neck and chorded. After that they got together on 'La Marseillaise', and 'Die Beiden Grenadiere', and 'Skipper Bullard', and about that time they had collected a fine bunch of roughneck companions, and all in all it turned out to be quite an evening.

CHAPTER TWO

1700 hours in San Francisco was 2000 in Washington, but Harold Twyman, senior senator from California and majority leader of United States representatives in the Parliament of the World Federation, was a busy man whose secretary could not arrange a sealed-call appointment any earlier on such short notice as Heim had given. However, that suited the latter quite well. It gave him time to recover from the previous night without excessive use of drugs, delegate the most pressing business at the Heimdal plant to the appropriate men, and study Vadász's evidence. The Magyar was still asleep in a guest room. His body had a lot of abuse to repair.

Shortly before 1700 Heim decided he was sufficiently familiar with the material Robert de Vigny had assembled. He clicked off the viewer, rubbed his eyes, and sighed. An assortment of aches still nibbled at him. Once – Lord, it didn't seem very long ago! – he could have weathered twenty times the bout he'd just been through, and made love to three or four girls, and been ready to ship out next morning. *I'm at the awkward age,* he thought wryly. *Too young for antisenescence treatment to make any difference, too old for – what?*

Nothing, by Satan! I simply sit too much these days. Let me get away for a bit and this paunch I'm developing will melt off.

He sucked in his stomach, reached for a pipe, and stuffed the bowl with unnecessary violence.

Why not take a vacation? he thought. Go into the woods and hunt; he had a standing invitation to use Ian McVeigh's game preserve in British Columbia. Or sail his catamaran to Hawaii. Or order out his interplanetary yacht, climb the Lunar Alps, tramp the Martian hills; Earth was so stinking cluttered. Or even book an interstellar passage. He hadn't seen his birthplace on Gea since his parents sent him back to Stavanger to get a proper education. Afterwards there had been Greenland Academy, and the Deepspace Fleet, and Earth again, always too much to do.

Sharply before him the memory rose: Tau Ceti a ball of red gold in the sky; mountains coming down to the sea as they did in Norway, but the oceans of Gea were warm and green and haunted him with odours that had no human name; the Sindabans that were his boyhood playmates, laughing just like him as they all ran to the water and piled into a pirogue, raised the wingsail and leaped before the wind; campfire on an island, where flames sprang forth to pick daoda fronds and the slim furry bodies of his friends out of a night that sang; chants and drums and portentous ceremonies; and – and—

No. Heim struck a light to his tobacco and puffed hard. *I was twelve years old when I left. And now Far and Mor are dead, and my Sindabans grown into an adulthood which humans are still trying to understand. I'd only find an isolated little scientific base, no different from two score that I've seen elsewhere. Time is a one-way lane.*

Besides – his gaze dropped to the micros on his desk – *there's work to do here.*

Footfalls clattered outside the study. Glad of any distraction, Heim rose and walked after them. He ended in the living room. His daughter had come home and flopped herself in a lounger.

'Hi, Lisa,' he said. 'How was school?'

'Yechy.' She scowled and stuck out her tongue. 'Old Espinosa said I gotta do my composition over again.'

'Spelling, eh? Well, if you'd only buckle down and learn—'

'*Worse'n* correcting spelling. Though why they make such a fuss about that, *me* don't know! He says the semantics are upwhacked. Old pickleface!'

Heim leaned against the wall and wagged his pipe stem at

her. ' "Semantics" is a singular, young'un. Your grammar's no better than your orthography. Also, trying to write, or talk, or think without knowing semantic principles is like trying to dance before you can walk. I'm afraid my sympathies are with Mr. Espinosa.'

'But Dad!' she wailed. 'You don't *realize*! I'd have to do the whole paper again from *go*!'

'Of course.'

'I *can't*!' Her eyes, which were blue like his own – otherwise she was coming to look heartbreakingly like Connie – clouded up for a squall. 'I got a date with *Dick*— Oh!' One hand went to her mouth.

'Dick? You mean Richard Woldberg?' Lisa shook her head wildly. 'The blaze you don't,' Heim growled. 'I've told you damn often enough you're not to see that lout.'

'Oh, Dad! J-j-just because—'

'I know. High spirits. I call it malicious mischief and a judge that Woldberg Senior bought, and I say any girl who associates with that crowd is going to get in trouble. Nothing so mild as pregnancy, either,' Heim realized he was shouting. He put on his court-martial manner and rapped: 'Simply making that date was not only disobedience but disloyalty. You went behind my back. Very well, you're confined to quarters for a week whenever you're not in school. And I expect to see your composition tomorrow, written right.'

'I hate you!' Lisa screamed. She flung out of the lounger and ran. For a second the bright dress, slender body, and soft brown hair were before Heim's gaze, then she was gone. He heard her kick the door of her room, as if to make it open for her the faster.

What else could I do? he cried after her, but of course there was no reply. He prowled the long room, roared at a maid who dared come in with a question, and stalked forth to stand on the terrace among the roses, glaring across San Francisco.

The city lay cool and hazed under a lowering sun. From here, on Telegraph Hill, his view ranged widely over spires and elways, shining water and garden islands. That was why he had picked this suite, after Connie died in that senseless flyer smash and the Mendocino County house got too big and still. In the past year or so Lisa had begun to whine about the address being unfashionable. But the hell with her.

No. It was only that fourteen was a difficult age. It had to be

17

only that. And without a mother— He probably should have remarried, for Lisa's sake. There'd been no lack of opportunity. But at most the affairs had ended as . . . affairs . . . because none of the women were Connie. Or even Madelon. Unless you counted Jocelyn Lawrie, but she was hopelessly lost in her damned peace movement and anyway— Still, he could well be making every mistake in the catalogue, trying to raise Lisa by himself. Whatever had become of the small dimpled person to whom he was the center of the universe?

He glanced at his watch and swore. Past time to call Twyman.

Back in the study he had a wait while the secretary contacted her boss and sealed the circuit. He couldn't sit; he paced the room, fingering his books, his desk computer, his souvenirs of the lancer to whose command he had risen. Hard had it been to give up *Star Fox*. For a year after his marriage, he'd remained in the Navy. But that wouldn't work out, wasn't fair to Connie. He stroked a hand across her picture, without daring to animate it right now. *Not hard after all, sweetheart. Well worth everything.*

The phone chimed and the secretary said, 'The senator is on the line, sir.' Her image gave way to Twyman's distinguished gray head. Heim sat down, on the edge of the chair.

'Hello, Gunnar,' Twyman said. 'How's everything?'

'*Comme ci, comme ça,*' Heim answered. 'A little more *ci* than *ça*, I think. How's with you?'

'Rushed damn near to escape velocity. The Aleriona crisis, you know.'

'Uh-huh. That's what I wanted to talk about.'

Twyman looked alarmed. 'I can't say much.'

'Why not?'

'Well . . . well, there really isn't much to say yet. Their delegation has only been here for about three weeks, you remember, so no formal discussions have commenced. Diplomacy between different species is always like that. Such a fantastic lot of spadework to do, information exchange, semantic and xenological and even epistemological studies to make, before the two sides can be halfway sure they're talking about the same subjects.'

'Harry,' said Heim, 'I know as well as you do that's a string of guff. The informal conferences are going on right along. When Parliament meets with the Aleriona, you boys on the inside will have everything rigged in advance. Arguments

18

marshaled, votes lined up, nothing left to do but pull the switch and let the machine ratify the decision you've already made.'

'Well, ah, you can't expect, say, the Kenyan Empire representatives to understand something so complex—'

Heim rekindled his pipe. 'What are you going to do, anyhow?' he asked.

'Sorry, I can't tell you.'

'Why not? Isn't the Federation a "democracy of states"? Doesn't its Constitution guarantee free access of information?'

'You'll have as much information as you want,' Twyman snapped, 'when we start to operate on an official basis.'

'That'll be too late.' Heim sighed. 'Never mind. I can add two and two. You're going to let Alerion have New Europe, aren't you?'

'I can't—'

'You needn't. The indications are everywhere. Heads of state assuring their people there's no reason to panic, we're not going to have a war. Politicians and commentators denouncing the 'extremists'. Suppression of any evidence that there might be excellent reason to go to war.'

Twyman bristled. 'What do you mean?'

'I've met Endre Vadász,' Heim said.

'Who? – oh, yes. That adventurer who claims— Look, Gunnar, there is some danger of war. I'm not denying that. France especially is up in arms, demonstrations, riots, mobs actually tearing down the Federation flag and trampling on it. We'll have our hands full as is, without letting some skizzy like him inflame passions worse.'

'He's not a skizzy. Also, Alerion's whole past record bears him out. Ask any Navy man.'

'Precisely.' Twyman's voice grew urgent. 'As we move into their sphere of interest, inevitably there've been more and more clashes. And can you blame them? They were cruising the Phoenix region when men were still huddled in caves. It's theirs.'

'New Europe isn't. Men discovered and colonized it.'

'I know, I know. There are so many stars— The trouble is, we've been greedy. We've gone too far, too fast.'

'There are a lot of stars,' Heim agreed, 'but not an awful lot of planets where men can live. We need 'em.'

'So does Alerion.'

'Ja? What use is a people-type world to them? And even on

19

their own kind of planet, why didn't they ever colonize on anything like our scale, till we came along?'

'Response to our challenge,' Twyman said. 'What would you do if an alien culture started grabbing planetary systems as near to Sol as Aurore is to The Eith?' He leaned back. 'Oh, don't get me wrong. The Aleriona are no saints. They've sometimes been fiends, by our standards. But we have to inhabit the same cosmos with them. War is unthinkable.'

'Why?' drawled Heim.

'What? Gunnar, are you out of your brain? Haven't you read any history? Looked at the craters? Understood how close a call the Nuclear Exchange was?'

'So close a call that ever since the human race has been irrational on the subject,' Heim said. 'But I've seen some objective analyses. And even you must admit that the Exchange and its aftermath rid us of those ideological governments.'

'An interstellar war could rid us of Earth!'

'Twaddle. A planet with space defenses like ours can't be attacked from space by any fleet now in existence. Every beam would be attenuated, every missile intercepted, every ship clobbered.'

'That didn't work for New Europe,' Twyman said. He was getting angry.

'No, of course not. New Europe didn't have any space fortresses or home fleet. Nothing but a few lancers and pursuers that happened to be in the vicinity – when Alerion's armada came.'

'Don't be ridiculous, Gunnar. The affair was simply another clash, one that got out of hand.'

'So the Aleriona say,' Heim murmured. 'If that's the truth, how come none, not one, of our vessels escaped?'

Twyman ignored him. 'We'll never be sure who fired the first shot. But we can be sure the Aleriona wouldn't have missiled New Europe if our commander hadn't tried to pull his ships down into atmosphere for a toadhole maneuver. What other conceivable reason was there?'

If New Europe really was missiled, Heim thought. *But it wasn't.*

The senator checked indignation, sat silent for a bit, and went on almost mildly. 'The whole episode illustrates how intolerable the situation has become, how matters are bound to escalate if we don't halt while we still can. And what do we want to fight for? A few wretched planets? We need only let Alerion's traditional sphere alone, and the rest of the galaxy is open to us. Fight for revenge? Well, you can't laugh off half a million dead human beings, but the fact remains that they are dead. I don't want to send any more lives after theirs.'

'Okay,' Heim said with equal quietness, 'What do you figure to do?'

Twyman studied him before answering: 'You're my friend as well as a political backstop. I can trust you to keep your mouth shut. And to support me, I think, once you know. Do I have your promise?'

'Of secrecy ... well ... yes. Support? That depends. Say on.'

'The details are still being threshed out. But in general, Alerion offers us an indemnity for New Europe. A very sizable one. They'll also buy out our other interests in the Phoenix. The exact terms have yet to be settled – obviously they can't pay in one lump – but the prospect looks good. With us out of their sphere, they'll recognize a similar one for humans around Sol, and keep away. But we aren't building any walls, you understand. We'll exchange ambassadors and cultural missions. A trade treaty will be negotiated in due time.

'There. Does that satisfy you?'

Heim looked into the eyes of a man he had once believed honest with himself and said: No.'

'Why not?' Twyman asked most softly.

'From a long-range viewpoint, your scheme ignores the nature of Alerion. They aren't going to respect our sphere any longer than it takes them to consolidate the one you want to make them a present of. And I do mean a present – because until a trade treaty is agreed on, which I predict will be never, how can we spend any of that valuta they so generously pay over?'

'Gunnar, I know friends of yours have died at Aleriona hands. But it's given you a persecution complex.'

'Trouble is, Harry,' Heim stole from Vadász, 'the persecution happens to be real. You're the one living in a dream. You're so obsessed with avoiding war that you've forgotten every other consideration. Including honor.'

'What do you mean by that?' Twyman demanded.

'New Europe was not missiled. The colonists are not dead. They've taken to the hills and are waiting for us to come help them.'

'That isn't so!'

'I have the proof right here on my desk.'

'You mean the documents that – that tramp forged?'

'They aren't forgeries. It can be proved. Signatures, finger-prints, photographs, the very isotope ratios in film made on New Europe. Harry, I never thought you'd sell out half a million human beings.'

'I deny that I am doing so,' Twyman said glacially. 'You're a fanatic, *Mister* Heim, that's all. Even if it were true what you say ... how do you propose to rescue anyone from a planet occupied and space-guarded? But it isn't true. I've spoken to survivors whom the Aleriona brought here. You must have seen them yourself on 3V. They witnessed the bombardment.'

'Hm. You recall where they were from?'

'The Coeur d'Yvonne area. Everything else was wiped clean.'

'So the Aleriona say,' Heim retorted. 'And doubtless the survivors believe it too. Any who didn't would've been weeded out during interrogation. I say that Coeur d'Yvonne was the only place hit by a nuke. I say further that we can fight if we must, and win. A space war only; I'm not talking the nonsense about "attacking impregnable Alerion" which your tame commentators keep putting into the mouths of us "extremists", and Earth is every bit as impregnable. I say further that if we move fast, with our full strength, we probably won't have to fight. Alerion will crawfish. She isn't strong enough to take us on ... yet. I say further and finally that if we let down those people out there who're trusting us, we'll deserve everything that Alerion will eventually do to us.' He tamped his smol-dering pipe. 'That's my word, Senator.'

Twyman said, trembling: 'Then my word, Heim, is that we've outgrown your kind of sabertooth militarism and I'm not going to let us be dragged back to that level. If you're blasé enough to quote what I've told you here in confidence, I'll des-troy you. You'll be in the Welfare district, or correction, within a year.'

'Oh, no,' Heim said. 'I keep my oaths. The public facts can speak for themselves. I need only point them out.'

'Go ahead, if you want to waste your money and reputation. You'll be as big a laughingstock as the rest of the warhawk crowd.'

Taken aback, Heim grimaced. In the past weeks, after the

news of New Europe, he had seen what mass media did to those who spoke as he was now speaking. Those who were influential, that is, and therefore worth tearing down. Ordinary unpolitical people didn't matter. The pundits simply announced that World Opinion Demanded Peace. Having listened to a good many men, from engineers and physicists to spacehands and mechanics, voice their personal feelings, Heim doubted if world opinion was being correctly reported. But he couldn't see any way to prove that.

Conduct a poll, maybe? No. At best, the result would frighten some professors, who would be quick to assert that it was based on faulty statistics, and a number of their students, who would organize parades to denounce Heim the Monster.

Propaganda? Politicking? A Paul Revere Society? ... Heim shook his head, blindly, and slumped.

Twyman's face softened. 'I'm sorry about this, Gunnar,' he said. 'I'm still your friend, you know. Regardless of where your next campaign donation goes. Call on me any time.' He hesitated, decided merely to add 'Good-by,' and switched off.

Heim reached into his desk for a bottle he kept there. As he took it forth, his gaze crossed the model of *Star Fox* which his crew had given him when he retired. It was cast in steel retrieved from that Aleriona battlewagon into which the lancer put an atomic torpedo at Achenar.

I wonder if the Aleriona make trophies of our wrecks.

Hm. Odd. I never thought about it before. We know so little of them. Heim put his feet on the desk and tilted the bottle to his lips. *Why don't I corner one of their delegation and ask?*

And then he choked on his drink and spluttered; his feet thumped to the floor, and he never noticed. The thought had been too startling. *Why not?*

CHAPTER THREE

THE ceiling glowed with the simulated light of a red dwarf sun, which lay like blood on leaves and vines and slowly writhing flowers. A bank of Terrestrial room instruments – phone, 3V, computer, vocascribe, infotrieve, service cubicle, environmental control board – stood in one corner of the jungle

23

with a harsh incongruity. The silence was as deep as the purple shadows. Unmoving, Cynbe waited.

The decompression chamber finished its cycle and Gunnar Heim stepped out. Thin dry atmosphere raked his throat. Even so, the fragrances overwhelmed him. He could not tell which of them – sweet, acrid, pungent, musky – came from which of the plants growing from wall to wall, reaching to the ceiling and arching down again in a rush of steel-blue leaves, exploding in banks of tawny, crimson, black, and violet blossoms. The reduced gravity seemed to give a lightness to his head as well as his frame. Feathery turf felt like rubber underfoot. The place was tropically warm; he sensed the infrared baking his skin.

He stopped and peered about. Gradually his eyes adjusted to the ember illumination. They were slower to see details of shapes so foreign to Earth.

'*Imbiac dystra?*' he called uncertainly. 'My lord?' His voice was muffled in that tenuous air.

Cynbe ru Taren, Intellect Master of the Garden of War, fleet admiral, and military specialist of the Grand Commission of Negotiators, trod out from beneath his trees. 'Well are you come, sir,' he sang. 'Understand you, then, the High Speech?'

Heim made the bowing Aleriona salute of a ranking individual to a different-but-equal. 'No, my lord, I regret. Only a few phrases. It's a difficult language for any of my race to learn.'

Cynbe's beautiful voice ranged a musical scale never invented by men. 'Wish you a seat, Captain Heim? I can dial for refreshment.'

'No, thank you,' the human said, because he didn't care to lose whatever psychological advantage his height gave him, nor drink the wine of an enemy. Inwardly he was startled. *Captain* Heim? How much did Cynbe know?

There would have been ample time to make inquiries, in the couple of days since this audience was requested. But one couldn't guess how interested an Aleriona overlord was in a mere individual. Very possibly Heim's wish had been granted at Harold Twyman's urging, and for no other reason. The senator was a strong believer in the value of discussion between opponents. *Any discussion. We may go down, but at least we'll go down talking.*

'I trust your trip hither was a pleasant one?' Cynbe cantillated.

'Oh ... all right, my lord, if, uh, one doesn't mind traveling with sealed eyelids after being thoroughly searched.'

'Regrettable is this necessity to keep the whereabouts of our delegation secret,' Cynbe agreed. 'But your fanatics—' The last word was a tone-and-a-half glissando carrying more scorn than Heim would have believed possible.

'Yes.' The man braced himself. 'In your civilization, the populace is better ... controlled.' *I haven't quite the nerve to say 'domesticated', but I hope he gets my meaning.*

Cynbe's laughter ran like springtime rain. 'You are a marksman, Captain.' He advanced with a movement that made cats look clumsy. 'Would your desire be to walk my forest as we discuss? You are maychance not enrolled with the few humans who set ever a foot upon Alerion.'

'No, my lord, I'm sorry to say I haven't had the pleasure. Yet.'

Cynbe halted. For a moment, in the darkling light, they regarded each other. And Heim could only think how fair the Aleriona was.

The long-legged, slightly forward-leaning body, 150 centimetres tall, its chest as deep and waist as spare as a greyhound's, the counterbalancing tail never quite at rest, he admired in abstraction. How the sleek silvery fur sparkled with tiny points of light; how surely the three long toes of either digitigrade foot took possession of the ground; how graciously the arms gestured; how proudly the slim neck lifted. The humans were rare who could have dressed like Cynbe, in a one-piece garment of metallic mesh, trimmed at throat and wrists and ankles with polished copper. It revealed too much.

The head, though, was disturbing. For the fur ended at the throat, and Cynbe's face – marble-hued, eyes enormous below arching brows, nose small, lips vividly red, wide cheekbones and narrow chin – could almost have been a woman's. Not quite: there were differences of detail, and the perfection was inhuman. Down past the pointed ears, along the back and halfway to the end of the tail, rushed a mane of hair, thick, silken fine, the color of honey and gold. A man who looked overly long at that face risked forgetting the body.

And the brain, Heim reminded himself.

A blink of nictitating membrane dimmed briefly the emerald of Cynbe's long-lashed feline eyes. Then he smiled, continued his advance, laid a hand on Heim's arm. Three double-jointed

25

fingers and thumb closed in a gentle grip. 'Come,' the Aleriona invited.

Heim went along, into the murk under the trees. 'My lord,' he said in a harshened tone, 'I don't want to waste your time. Let's talk business.'

'Be our doings as you choose, Captain.' Cynbe's free hand stroked across a phosphorescent branch.

'I'm here on behalf of the New Europeans.'

'For the mourned dead? We have repatriated the living, and indemnified they shall be.'

'I mean those left alive on the planet. Which is nearly all of them.'

'Ah-h-h-h,' Cynbe breathed.

'Senator Twyman must have warned you I'd bring the subject up.'

'Truth. Yet assured he the allegation is unbelieved.'

'Most of his side don't dare believe it. Those who do, don't dare admit it.'

'Such accusations could imperil indeed the peace negotiations.' Heim wasn't sure how much sardonicism lay in the remark. He stumbled on something unseen, cursed, and was glad to emerge from the bosket, on to a little patch of lawn starred with flowers. Ahead rose the inner wall, where some hundred books were shelved, not only the tall narrow folios of Alerion but a good many ancient-looking Terrestrial ones. Heim couldn't make out the titles. Nor could he see far past the archway into the next room of the suite; but somewhere a fountain was plashing.

He stopped, faced the other squarely, and said: 'I have proof that New Europe was not scrubbed clean of men – in fact, they retreated into the mountains and are continuing resistance to your occupation force. The evidence is in a safe place' – *Goodness, aren't we melodramatic?* – 'and I was planning to publicize it. Which would, as you say, be awkward for your conference.'

He was rather desperately hoping that the Aleriona didn't know the facts of life on Earth well enough to understand how forlorn his threat was. Cynbe gave him no clue. There was only an imperturbable upward quirk of mouth, and: 'Seeming is that you have decided upon another course, Captain.'

'That depends on you,' Heim answered. 'If you'll repatriate those people also, I'll give you the evidence and say no more.'

Cynbe turned to play with a vine. It curled about his hand

and reached its blossoms towards his face. 'Captain,' he sang presently, 'you are no fool. Let us assume your belief is truth. We shall speak of a folk in wrath under the mountain peaks. How shall they be made come to our ships?'

'They're fighting because they expect help. If representatives of the French government told them to return here, they would. The parley can be arranged by radio.'

'But the entity France, now, would it so co-operate?'

'It'd have no choice. You know even better than I, a majority of the Federation doesn't want to fight over New Europe. About the only thing that could provoke such a war is the plight of the settlers. Let them come back unharmed and . . . and you'll have your damned conquest.'

'Conceivable that is.' Light rippled red down Cynbe's locks when he nodded. His gaze remained with the blooms. 'But afterward?' he crooned. 'Afterward?'

'I know,' Heim said. 'The New Europeans would be living proof you lied – not only about them, but about the entire battle. Proof that things didn't happen because someone got trigger happy, but because you planned your attack.' He swallowed a nasty taste. 'Well, read Terrestrial history, my lord. You'll find we humans don't take these matters as seriously as we might. Lies are considered a normal part of diplomacy, and a few ships lost, a few men killed, are all in the day's work. If anything, this concession of yours will strengthen the peace party. "Look," they'll say, "Alerion isn't so bad, you can do business with Alerion, our policies saved those lives and avoided an expensive war." Unquote.'

Now the muliebrile face did turn about, and for a while the eyes lay luminous upon Heim. He felt his pulse grow thick. The sound of the fountain seemed to dwindle and the hot red dusk to close in.

'Captain,' Cynbe sang, almost too low to hear, 'The Eith is an ancient sun. The Aleriona have been civilized for beyond a million of your years. We sought not far-flung empire, that would crack an order old and stable; but our Wanderers ranged and our Intellects pondered. Maychance we are wiser in the manifold ways of destiny than some heedless newcomer. Maychance we have read your own inwardness more deeply than have you yourselves.

' "Afterward" did I say. The word carries another freight when echoed through a million of years. My regard was to no gain for a decade, a generation, a century. I speak beyond.

'Between these walls, let truth be what you have claimed. Then let truth also be that Alerion cannot hithersend five hundred thousand of individuals to leaven their race with anger.

'Had they yielded, the case were otherwise. We would have told Earth this battle was one more incident than tolerable and now we must have our own sphere where no aliens fare. But any of your colonists enwished to stay might do so, did they become subject to Alerion. We would offer inspection, that Earth might be sure they were not oppressed. For such little enclaves are significanceless; and Alerion has ways to integrate them into civilization: ways slow, as you look upon time, ways subtle, ways quite, quite certain.

'The colonists yielded not, I say between these walls. Even could we capture them alive, in so much wilderness – and we cannot – even then could they not become subject to Alerion. Not as prisoners, forever dangerous, forever an incitement that Earth deliver them. Yet if the entity France commanded them home: in their nerves, that were betrayal of folk who had not surrendered, and they must strive for a Federation government of males more brave. I look in the future and I see how they shame the others of you – yes, yes, Captain, such intangibles make your history, you are that kind of animal. Truth, there would not be war to gain back Europe Neuve. Those bones grow dry before leaders as I speak of come to power. But when the next debatable issue arises – ah-h-h.'

So there is to be a next issue, Heim thought. *Not that he's told me anything I hadn't already guessed. I wonder, though, when the second crisis is scheduled. Maybe not in my lifetime. But surely in Lisa's.*

His voice came out flat and remote, as if someone else spoke: 'Then you're not going to admit the colonists are alive. What will you do? Hunt them down piecemeal?'

'I command space fleets, Captain, not groundlings.' Astonishingly, Cynbe's lashes fluttered and he looked down at his hands. The fingers twined together. 'I have said more than needful, to you alone. But then, I am not Old Aleriona. My type was bred after the ships began their comings from Earth. And ... I was at Achernar.' He raised his eyes. '*Star Fox* captain, as Earth's men do, will you clasp my hand farewell?'

'No,' said Heim. He turned on his heel and walked towards the compression chamber.

CHAPTER FOUR

His escort of Peace Control troopers unsealed his eyes and let him off the official flyer at Port Johnson in Delaware. They'd taken longer on whatever circuitous route they followed than he had expected. There was barely time to make his appointment with Coquelin. He hurried to the beltway headed for the civilian garages, elbowed aboard through the usual crowd, and found he must stand the whole distance.

Fury had faded during the hours he sat blind, exchanging banalities with the earnest young officer of his guards ('Weather Reg really muffed the last hurricane, don't you think?' ... 'Yes, too bad about New Europe, but still, we've outgrown things like imperialism and revenge, haven't we? Anyhow, the galaxy is big.' ... 'I sure envy you, the way you've traveled in space. We get around in this job, of course, but seems like the places and people on Earth get more alike every year.') or thinking his own thoughts. He hadn't really expected to accomplish anything with the Aleriona. The attempt was nothing but a duty.

Grayness remained in him. *I don't see what I can do in Paris either.*

A shabby man, unnecessarily aggressive, pushed him. He controlled his temper with an effort – he hated crowds – and refrained from pushing back. You couldn't blame the poor devil for being hostile to one whose good clothes revealed him a member of the technoaristocracy.

That's why we've got to move into space, he told himself for the thousandth time. *Room. A chance to get out of this horrible huddle on Earth, walk free, be our own men, try out new ways to live, work, think, create, wonder. There was more happiness on New Europe, divided among half a million people, than these ten billion could ever imagine.*

What is it in them – fear? inertia? despair? plain old ignorance? – makes them swallow that crock about how the rest of the universe is open to us?

Because it was a crock. Habitable planets aren't that common. And most of those that exist have intelligent natives; a good many of the rest have already been colonized by others.

29

Heim did not want his race forced to the nearly ultimate immorality of taking someone else's real estate away.

Though more was involved in the Phoenix affair. A loss of nerve; throughout history, yielding to an unjustifiable demand for the sake of a few more years of peace has been the first step on a long downward road. An admission of the essentially vicious principle of 'interest spheres'; there should not be any boundaries in space. And, to be sure, appalling fatuity: a blank refusal to read the record which proved Alerion's intentions toward Earth, a positive eagerness to give the enemy the time and resources he needed to prepare for his next encroachment,

But what can a man do?

Heim claimed his flyer at the garage and fretted while TrafCon stalled about sending him aloft. Quite a time passed before the pattern of vehicle movement released him. He went on manual for a while, to have the satisfaction of personally getting away. The gravitrons in this Moonraker were custombuilt, with power to lift him far into the stratosphere. Otherwise the flyer was nothing special; he was fairly indifferent to creature comforts. He set the autopilot for Orly, took a long hot bath, got some whale from the freezer and made himself a 'burger for lunch, and bunked out for a couple of hours.

The clock woke him with the 'Light Cavalry Overture' and handed him a mug of coffee. He changed into fresh clothes – somewhat formal, gold on the collar and down the pants – while the flyer slanted in for a landing. Momentarily he debated whether to go armed, for he would be carrying Vadász's package. But no, that might start more argument than it was worth. If he failed here too, he doubted if there would be any further use for New Europe's appeal. No action would be possible, except to get roaring drunk and afterwards consider emigration to an especially remote planet.

Entering the Douane office, he showed his ID and got a thirty-day permit. France, being less crowded than most countries, was rather stuffy about letting people in. But this official was balm and unguents from the moment he saw Heim's name. 'Ah, yes, yes, monsieur, we 'ave been told to expect ce pleasure of your company. A car is waiting for you. Does monsieur 'ave any baggage 'e wishes carried? No? *Bien*, cis way, please, and 'ave a mos' pleasant visit.'

Quite a contrast with what Endre Vadász must have experienced. But he was only a musician of genius. Gunnar Heim headed a well-known manufacturing concern and was son-in-law to Curt Wingate, who sat on the board of General Nucleonics. If Gunnar Heim requested a private interview with Michel Coquelin, minister of extraterrestrial affairs and head of French representatives in the World Parliament, why, of course, of course.

Even so, he had crowded his schedule. Twyman had leaned backwards to oblige him about seeing Cynbe; nevertheless, the peacemongers were fairly sure to have agents keeping tabs on him, and if he didn't move fast they might find ways to head him off.

The car entered Paris by ground. Blue dusk was deepening into night. The trees along the boulevards had turned their leaves, red and yellow splashed against Baron Haussmann's stately old walls or scrittling among the legs of pretty girls as they walked with their men. The outdoor cafés had little custom at this season. Heim was as glad of that. Paris could have made him remember too many things.

The car stopped at the Quai d'Orsay and let him out. He heard the Seine lap darkly against its embankment, under the thin chill wind. Otherwise the district was quiet, with scant traffic, the whirr of the city machines nearly lost. But sky-glow hid the stars.

Gendarmes stood guard. Their faces were tense above the flapping capes. All France was tensed and bitter, one heard. Heim was conducted down long corridors where not a few people were working late, to Coquelin's office.

The minister laid aside a stack of papers and rose to greet him. 'How do you do,' he said. The tone was weary but the English flawless. That was luck; Heim's French had gotten creaky over the years. Coquelin gestured at a worn, comfortable old-style chair by his desk. 'Please be seated. Would you like a cigar?'

'No, thanks, I'm a pipe man.' Heim took his out.

'I too.' Coquelin's face meshed in crow's feet and calipers when he smiled; he sat down and began to load a still more disreputable briar. He was short but powerfully built, square of countenance, bald of dome, with very steady brown eyes. 'Well, Mr. Heim, what can I do for you?'

'Uh . . . it concerns New Europe.'

'I thought so.' The smile died.

'In my opinion—' Heim decided he was being pompous. 'M.

31

Coquelin,' he said, 'I believe Earth ought to do whatever is necessary to get New Europe back.'

Coquelin's look went over his guest's features, centimeter by centimeter, while he started his pipe. 'Thank you for that,' he said at length. 'We have felt lonely in France.'

'I have some material here that might help.'

The least intake of breath went through Coquelin's teeth. 'Proceed, if you please.'

He sat altogether expressionless, smoking, never glancing away, while Heim talked. Only once did he interrupt: 'Cynbe? Ah, yes, I have met him. The one they have quartered at— No, best I not say. Officially I am not supposed to know. Go on.'

In the end he opened the packet, slipped a few films into the viewer on his desk, read, and nodded. The stillness quivered near breaking point. Heim puffed volcano-like, stared out the window into darkness, shifted his bulk so the chair groaned, and listened to his own heartbeat.

Finally Coquelin muttered, 'There have been rumors about this.' After another silence: 'I shall see that you and Vadász join the Légion d'Honneur. Whatever happens.'

'What will?' Heim asked. His jaws ached with being clamped together.

Coquelin shrugged. 'Nothing, probably,' he said, dull-voiced. 'They are determined to buy what they call peace.'

'Oh. Yes, you'd know. So I can tell you I also know the plan.'

'That Alerion shall have Europe Neuve? Good, we can speak freely. I am naturally honor bound not to reveal what is being decided until my fellow committeemen agree, and it would be a futile act with disastrous political consequences if I broke that promise. So I am most glad to have an outside listener.' Coquelin passed a hand across his eyes. 'But there is little we can say, no?'

'There's plenty!' Heim exclaimed. 'Come the formal meeting, you can show this stuff to Parliament, with scientific proof it's genuine. You can ask them how anyone can hope to get re-elected after selling out so many human beings.'

'Yes, yes.' Coquelin stared at his pipe bowl, where the fire waxed and waned, waxed and waned. 'And some will say I lie. That my evidence is forged and my scientists are bribed. Others will say alas, this is terrible, but – half a million people? Why, a few missiles striking population centers on Earth could kill twenty times that many, a hundred times; and we had no right to be in the Phoenix; and nothing matters except to make friends with Alerion, for otherwise we must look for decades of war; so we can only weep for our people out there, we cannot help them.' His grin was dreadful to see. 'I daresay a monument will be raised to them. Martyrs in the cause of peace.'

'But this is ridiculous! Earth can't be attacked. Or if it can, then so can Alerion, and they won't provoke that when we have twice their strength. A single flotilla right now could drive them out of the Auroran System.'

'Half the Navy has been recalled for home defense. The other half is out in the Marches, keeping watch on the Aleriona fleet, which is also maneuvering there. Even some of the admirals I have consulted do not wish to spare a flotilla for Aurore. For as you must know, monsieur, the numbers available on either side are not large, when a single nuclear-armed vessel has so much destructive capability.'

'So we do nothing?' Heim grated. 'Why, at the moment even one ship could – could make serious trouble for the enemy. They can't have any great strength at Aurore as yet. But give them a year or two and they'll make New Europe as unattackable as Earth.'

'I know.' Coquelin swiveled around, rested his elbows on his desk, and let his head sink between his shoulders. 'I shall argue. But . . . tonight I feel old, Mr. Heim.'

'My God, sir! If the Federation won't act, how about France by herself?'

'Impossible. We cannot even negotiate as a single country with any extraterrestrial power, under the Constitution. We are not allowed any armed force, any machine of war, above the police level. Such is reserved for the Peace Control Authority.'

'Yes, yes, yes—'

'In fact—' Coquelin glanced up. A muscle twitched in one cheek. 'Now that I think about what you have brought me, these documents, I do not know if I should make them public.'

'What?'

'Consider. France is furious enough. Let the whole truth be known, including the betrayal, and I dare not predict what might happen. It could well end with Peace Control troops occupying us. And, yes, that would hurt the Federation itself, even more than France. One must put loyalty to the Federation above anything else. Earth is too small for national sovereignty. Nuclear weapons are too powerful.'

Heim looked at the bent head, and the rage in him seemed about to tear him apart. 'I'd like to go out myself!' he shouted.

'That would be piracy,' Coquelin sighed.

'No ... wait, wait, wait.' The thought flamed into being. Heim sprang to his feet. 'Privateers. Once upon a time there were privately owned warships.'

'Eh, you have read a little history, I see.' Some life came back to Coquelin. He sat straighter and watched the huge, restless figure with eyes again alert. 'But I have read more. Privateering was outlawed in the nineteenth century. Even countries not signatory to that pact observed the prohibition, until it came to be regarded as a part of international law. Admitted, the Federal Constitution does not mention so archaic a matter. Still—'

'Exactly!' Heim roared; or was it the demon that had come to birth in his skull?

'No, no, flout the law and the Peace Control forces arrive. I am too old and tired, me, to stand trial before the World Court. To say nothing of the practical difficulties. France cannot declare war by herself. France cannot produce nuclear weapons.' Coquelin uttered a small sad chuckle. 'I am a lawyer by past profession. If there were a, you say loophole? – I could perhaps squirm through. But here—'

Word by word, Heim said: 'I can get hold of the weapons.'

Coquelin leaped in his seat. '*Qu'est-ce que vous dites?*'

'Off Earth. I know a place. Don't you see – Alerion has to put space defenses in orbit around New Europe, or she can't hold it against any determined attack.' Heim was leaning on the desk now, nose to nose with the other, talking like a machine gun. 'New Europe has only a limited industry. So the Aleriona will have to bring most of the stuff from home. A long supply line. One commerce raider – what'd that do to their bargaining position? What'd it do for our own poor buffaloed people? *One ship!*'

'But I have told you—'

'You told me it was physically and legally impossible. I can prove the physical possibility. And you said you were a lawyer.'

Coquelin rose too, went to the window, and stared long out across the Seine. Heim's pace quivered the floor. His brain

34

whirled with plans, data, angers, hopes; he had not been so seized by a power since he bestrode his bridge at Alpha Eridani.

And then Coquelin turned about. His whisper filled the silence: *'Peut-être—'* and he went to the desk and began punching keys on an infotrieve.

'What are you after?' Heim demanded.

'Details of the time before quite every country had joined the Federation. The Moslem League did not recognize that it had any right as a whole to deal with them. So during the troubles, the Authority was charged with protecting Federation interests in Africa.' Coquelin gave himself entirely to his work. Once, though, he met Heim's eyes. His own danced in his head. *'Mille remercîments, mon frère,'* he said. 'It may be for no more than this night, but you have given me back my youth.'

CHAPTER FIVE

ENDRE VADÁSZ took the lid off the kettle, inhaled a sumptuous odor, gave the contents a stir, and re-covered them. 'Almost done, this,' he said. 'I had better make the salad. Have you the materials ready?'

Lisa Heim blushed. 'I ... I'm afraid I'm not so good at slicing cucumbers and stuff,' she said.

'Poof to that.' Vadász scooped the disorderly pile of greens into a bowl. 'For a cadet, you do very well. ... Find me the seasonings, will you? One must needs be an engineer to operate this damned machine shop you call a kitchen. ... As I was saying, small one, when I so rudely interrupted myself, we shall yet win you to your cook and bottle washer (j.g.) rating. Charge, a boar's head erased with an apple gules in its mouth, field barry of six vert and or. That's for cabbage and clotted cream.'

Lisa giggled and hopped onto the table, where she swung her legs and watched Vadász with embarrassing warmth. He had only tried to be good company to his host's daughter while her father was away. He gave the herbs and spices more attention than was really necessary.

'My mother taught me a Spanish saying,' he remarked, 'that it takes four men to make a salad: a spendthrift for the oil, a philosopher for the seasonings, a miser for the vinegar, and a madman for the tossing.'

Lisa giggled again, 'You're cute.'

'Er – here we go.' Vadász got to work, singing.

There was a rich man and he lived in Jerusalem.
Glory, hallelujah, hi-ro-de-rung!
He wore a top hat and his clothes were very spruce-iung.
Glory, hallelujah, hi-ro-de-rung!
Hi-ro-de-rung! Hi-ro-de-rung!
Skinna-ma-rinky doodle doo, skinna-ma-rinky doodle doo,
Glory, hallelujah, hi-ro-de-rung!

'Is that a real old song too?' Lisa asked when he paused for breath. He nodded. 'I just love your songs,' she said.

'*Now outside his gate there sat a human wreckiung,*' Vadász continued hastily.

Glory, hallelujah, hi-ro-de-rung!
He wore a bowler hat in a ring around his neckiung.
Glory, hallelujah, hi-ro-de-rung!

Lisa grabbed a skillet and spoon to beat out time as she joined him in the chorus.

Hi-ro-de-rung! Hi-ro-de-rung!
Skinna-ma-rinky doodle doo, skinna-ma-rinky doodle doo,
Glory, hallelujah, hi-ro-de-rung!

'*Now the poor man asked for a piece of bread and cheese-*
iung.
Glory, hallelujah, hi-ro-de-rung!
The rich man said, "I'll send for the police-iung."
Glory, hallelujah, hi-ro-de-rung!

'Hi-ro-de-rung! Hi-ro-de-rung!' chimed in a bull basso. Gunnar Heim stormed through the door.

'*Skinna-ma-rinky doodle doo, skinna-ma-rinky doodle doo* ('Daddy!' 'Gunnar!').

'*Glory, hallelujah, hi-ro-de-rung!*' He snatched Lisa off the table, tossed her nearly to the ceiling, caught her, and began to whirl her around the floor. Vadász went merrily on. Heim took

36

the chorus while he stamped out a measure with the girl, who squealed.

'Now the poor man died and his soul went to Heaviung.
Glory, hallelujah, hi-ro-de-rung!
He danced with the angels till a quarter past eleviung.
Glory, hallelujah, hi-ro-de-rung!
Hi-ro-de-rung! Hi-ro-de-rung!
Skinna-ma-rinky doodle doo, skinna-ma-rinky doodle doo,
Glory, hallelujah, hi-ro-de-rung!'

'Oh, Daddy!' Lisa collapsed in a laughing fit.

'Welcome home,' Vadász said. 'You timed yourself well.'

'What's going on here, anyway?' Heim inquired. 'Where are the servants? Why put a camp stove in a perfectly good kitchen?'

'Because machines are competent enough cooks but will never be chefs,' Vadász said. 'I promised your daughter a goulash, not one of those lyophilized glue-stews but a genuine handmade *Gulyás* and sneeze-with-joy in the spices.'

'Oh. Fine. Only I'd better get me—'

'Nothing. A Hungarian never sets the table with less than twice as much. You may, if you wish, contribute some red wine. So, once more, welcome home, and it is good to see you in this humor.'

'With reason.' Heim rubbed his great hands and smiled like a happy tiger. 'Yes, indeedy.'

'What have you done, Daddy?' Lisa asked.

' 'Fraid I can't tell you, *jente min*. Not for a while.' He saw the first symptoms of mutiny, chucked her under the chin, and said, 'It's for your own protection.'

She stamped her foot. 'I'm not a child, you know!'

'Come, now; come, now,' interrupted Vadász. 'Let us not spoil the mood. Lisa, will you set a third place? We are eating in the high style, Gunnar, in your sunroom.'

'Sure,' she sighed. 'If I can have the general intercom on, vid and audio both. Can I, please, Daddy?'

Heim chuckled, stepped out to the central control panel, and unlocked the switch that made it possible to activate any pickup in the apartment from any other room. Vadász's voice drifted after him:

'Now the rich man died and he didn't fare so welliung.

Glory, hallelujah, hi-ro-de-rung!
He couldn't go to Heaven so he had to go to Helliung.
Glory, hallelujah—'

and on to the end.

When Heim came back, he remarked in an undertone, because she'd be watching and listening, 'Lisa doesn't want to miss a second of you, eh?'

The finely molded face turned doleful. 'Gunnar, I didn't mean—'

'Oh, for crying in the beer!' Heim slapped Vadász on the back. 'You can't imagine how much I'd rather have her in orbit around you than some of that adolescent trash. Everything seems to be turning sunward for me.'

The Magyar brightened. 'I trust,' he said, 'this means you have found a particularly foul way to goosh our friends of Alerion.'

'Shh!' Heim jerked a thumb at the intercom screen. 'Let's see, what wine should I dial for your main course?'

'Hey, ha, this is quite a list. Are you running a hotel?'

'No, to be honest, my wife tried to educate me in wines but never got far. I like the stuff but haven't much of a palate. So except when there's company, I stay with beer and whisky.'

Lisa appeared in the screen. She laughed and sang.

'Now the Devil said, "This is no hoteliung.
Glory, hallelujah, hi-ro-de-rung!
This is just a plain and ordinary helliung."
Glory, hallelujah, hi-ro-de-rung!'

Vadász put thumb to nose and waggled his fingers. She stuck out her tongue. They both grinned, neither so broadly as Heim.

And supper was a meal with more cheer, more sense of being home, than any he could remember since Connie died. Afterward he could not recall what was said – banter, mostly – it had not been real talk but a kind of embracement.

Lisa put the dishes in the service cubicle and retired demurely to bed; she even kissed her father. Heim and Vadász went downramp to the study. He closed the door, took Scotch from a cabinet, ice and soda from a coldbox, poured, and raised his own glass.

Vadász's clinked against it. 'And a voice valedictory . . .' the minstrel toasted. 'Who is for Victory?

'Who is for Liberty? Who goes home?'

'I'll drink to that,' said Heim, and did, deeply. 'Where's it from?'

'One G. K. Chesterton, a couple of centuries ago. You have not heard of him? Ah, well, they no longer care for such unsophisticated things on Earth. Only in the colonies are men so naïve as to think victories are possible.'

'Maybe we can make 'em change their minds here, too.' Heim sat down and reached for a pipe.

'Well,' Vadász said, in a cool tone but with a kind of shiver through his slim form, 'now we come to business. What has happened, these last several days while I fretted about idle?'

'I'll begin from the beginning,' Heim said. He felt no compunction about revealing what Twyman had admitted, since this listener could be trusted. His acquaintance with Vadász, though brief, had been somewhat intense.

The Magyar wasn't surprised anyway. 'I knew they had no intention to get New Europe back when none would hear me.'

'I found a buck who would,' Heim said, and went on with his account. As he finished, Vadász's jaw fell with a nearly audible clank.

'A privateer, Gunnar? Are you serious?'

'Absodamnlutely. So's Coquelin, and several more we talked with.' Heim's mirth had dissolved. He drew hard on his pipe, streamed the smoke out through dilated nostrils, and said:

'Here's the situation. One commerce raider in the Phoenix can make trouble out of all proportion to its capabilities. Besides disrupting schedules and plans, it ties up any number of warships, which either have to go hunt for it or else run convoy. As a result, the Aleriona force confronting ours in the Marches will be reduced below parity. So if then Earth gets tough, both in space and at the negotiations table – we shouldn't have to get very tough, you see, nothing so drastic that the peacemongers can scream too loud – one big naval push, while that raider is out there gobbling Aleriona ships – we can make them disgorge New Europe. Also give *us* some concessions for a change.'

'It may be. It may be.' Vadász remained sober. 'But how can you get a fighting craft?'

'Buy one and refit it. As for weapons, I'm going to dispatch a couple of trusty men soon, in a company speedster, to Staurn – you know the place?'

39

'I know of it. Ah-ha!' Vadász snapped his fingers. His eyes began to glitter.

'Yep. That's where our ship will finish refitting. Then off for the Auroran System.'

'But . . . will you not make yourself a pirate in the view of the law?'

'That's something which Coquelin is still working on. He says he thinks there may be a way to make everything legal and, at the same time, ram a spike right up the exhaust of Twyman and his giveaway gang. But it's a complicated problem. If the ship does have to fly the Jolly Roger, then Coquelin feels reasonably sure France has the right to try the crew, convict them, and pardon them. Of course, the boys might then have to stay in French territory, or leave Earth altogether for a colony – but they'll be millionaires, and New Europe would certainly give them a glorious reception.'

Heim blew a smoke ring. 'I haven't time to worry about that,' he continued. 'I'll simply have to bull ahead and take my chances on getting arrested. Because you'll understand how Coquelin and his allies in the French government – or in any government, because not every nation on Earth has gone hollowbelly – well, under the Constitution, no country can make warlike preparations. If we did get help from some official, that'd end every possibility of legalizing the operation. We'd better not even recruit our men from a single country, or from France at all.

'So it depends on me. I've got to find the ship, buy her, outfit her, supply her, sign on a crew, and get her off into space – all inside of two months, because that's when the formal talks between Parliament and the Aleriona delegation are scheduled to begin.' He made a rueful face. 'I'm going to forget what sleep's like.'

'The crew—' Vadász frowned. 'A pretty problem, that. How many?'

'About a hundred, I'd say. Far more than needful, but the only way we can finance this venture is to take prizes, which means we'll need prize crews. Also . . . there may be casualties.'

'I see. Wanted, a hundred skilled, reliable spacemen, Navy experience preferred, for the wildest gamble since Argilus went courting of Witch Helena. Where do you find them? . . . Hm, hm, I may know a place or two to look.'

'I do myself. We can't recruit openly for a raider, you real-

40

ize. If our true purpose isn't kept secret to the last millisecond, we'll be in the calaboose so fast that Einstein's ghost will return to haunt us. But I think, in the course of what look like ordinary psych tests, I think we can probe attitudes and find out who can be trusted with the truth. Those are the ones we'll hire.'

'First catch your rabbit,' Vadász said. 'I mean find a psychologist who can be trusted!'

'Uh-huh. I'll get Wingate, my father-in-law, to co-opt one. He's a shrewd old rascal with tentacles everywhere, and if you think you and I are staticked about Alerion, you should listen to him for a while.' Heim squinted at the model of *Star Fox*, shining across the room. 'I don't believe ordinary crewmen will be too hard to find. When the Navy appropriation was cut, three years ago, a good many fellows found themselves thumb-twiddling on planet duty and resigned in disgust. We can locate those who came to Earth. But we may have trouble about a captain and a chief engineer. People with such qualifications don't drift free.'

'Captain? What do you mean, Gunnar? You'll be captain.'

'No.' Heim's head wove heavily back and forth. A good deal of his bounce left him. 'I'm afraid not. I want to – God, how I want to! – but, well, I've got to be sensible. Spaceships aren't cheap. Neither are supplies, and especially not weapons. My estimates tell me I'll have to liquidate all my available assets and probably hock everything else, to get that warship. Without me to tend the store, under those conditions, Heimdal might well fail. Lord knows there are enough competitors who'll do everything they can to make it fail. And Heimdal, well, that's something Connie and I built – her father staked us, but she worked the office end herself while I bossed the shop, those first few tough years. Heimdal's the only thing I've got to leave my daughter.'

'I see.' Vadász spoke with compassion. 'Also, she has no mother. You should not risk she lose her father too.'

Heim nodded.

'You will forgive me, though, if I go?' Vadász said.

'Oh, *ja, ja,* Endre, I'd be a swine to hold you back. You'll even have officer rank: chief steward, which means mainly that you oversee the cooking. And you'll bring me back some songs, won't you?'

Vadász could not speak. He looked at his friend, chained to

41

possessions and power, and there ran through his head

> Now the moral of the story is riches are no
>   joke-iung.
> Glory, hallelujah, hi-ro-de-rung!
> We'll all go to Heaven, for we all are stony
>   broke-iung.
> Glory, hallelujah, hi-ro-de-rung!

But the rhythm got into his blood, and he realized what Heim had done and what it meant, leaped to his feet, and capered around the study shouting his victorious music aloud till the walls echoed.

> 'Hi-ro-de-rung! Hi-ro-de-rung!
> Skinna-ma-rinky doodle doo, skinna-ma-rinky
>   doodle doo,
> Glory, hallelujah, hi-ro-de-rung!'

CHAPTER SIX

FROM WORLDWEEK:

31 October

Gunnar Heim, principal owner of the American firm Heimdal Motors, has purchased the starship *Pass of Balmaha* from British Minerals, Ltd. The transaction astonished shipping circles by its speed. Heim made a cash offer that was too good to turn down, but insisted on immediate occupancy.

He has announced that he plans to send an expedition in search of new worlds to colonize. 'We seem to have lost out in the Phoenix,' he told 3V interviewer John Phillips. 'Frankly, I am shocked and disgusted that no action has been taken in response to Alerion's attack on New Europe. But I can't do much about it except try to find us some new place – which I hope we'll have the nerve to defend.'

As large and powerful as a naval cruiser, Glasgow-built *Pass of Balmaha* was originally intended to prospect for ores. But no deposits were found sufficiently rich to pay the cost of inter-stellar shipment when the Solar System still has workable mines. The ship has therefore been in Earth orbit for the past four years. Sir Henry Sherwin, chairman of the board of British Minerals, told Phillips, 'We're overjoyed to get rid of that white elephant, but I must confess I feel a bit guilty about it.'

7 November

U.S. Senator Harold Twyman (Libn., Calif.), high-ranking member of the Federal pre-formal negotiations team conferring with the delegation from Alerion, issued a statement Thursday denying rumors of a planned sellout of New Europe.

'Certainly we are already talking business with them,' he said. 'And that, by the way, is a slow and difficult process. The Aleriona are alien to us, biologically and culturally. In the past we have had far too little contact with them, and far too much of what we did have was hostile. You don't get understanding out of a battle. Some of the finest xenologists on Earth are working day and night, trying to acquire a knowledge in depth that we should have gotten three decades ago.

'But we do know that the Aleriona share some things with mankind. They too are rational beings. They too wish to live. Their ancient civilization, which achieved a million years of stability, can teach us a great deal. And no doubt we can teach them something. Neither can do this, however, until we break the vicious circle of distrust, competition, fight, and retaliation.

'That's why the Deepspace Fleet has been ordered not to fire except in self-defense. That's why we aren't crowding the government of Alerion – if it *is* anything like what we understand by a government – to get out of the Auroran System. That's why we are taking our time with the honorable delegation: who, remember, came to us on Alerion's own initiative.

'Under the Constitution, only Parliament as a whole is empowered to negotiate with non-human states. Certainly the Executive Committee will observe this law. But you can't expect a body as large, diverse, and busy as Parliament to do the spadework in a case so intricate. Its duly appointed representatives were given that duty. We hope in a few more weeks to have a complete draft treaty ready for submission. At that time we shall be prepared to meet every conceivable objection to it. Meanwhile, however, it would be too great a handicap for us to operate in a glare of publicity.

'But we do not, repeat not, plan to betray any vital interest of the human race. Negotiation is a mutual process. We shall have to give a little as well as take a little. The Aleriona realize this too, perhaps better than some members of our own young and arrogant species. I am confident that, in the last analysis, all men of good will are going to agree that we have opened a new and hopeful era of cosmic history. The people of New Europe have not died in vain.'

14 November

Retired Vice Admiral Piet van Rinnekom, 68, was set upon by about twenty men as he neared his house in Amsterdam on Monday evening, and badly beaten. When the police arrived, the assailants fled shouting taunts of 'Warmonger!' They appeared to be of mixed nationality. Van Rinnekom has been an outspoken opponent of what he describes as 'appeasement of Alerion', and is the author of the so-called Manhood Petition, whose backers are trying to gather one billion signatures in favor of Earth using force, if necessary, to regain New Europe. Most sociologists consider this sheer lunacy.

His condition is listed as serious.

At his Chicago office, Dr. Jonas Yore, founder and president of World Militants for Peace, issued the following statement: 'Naturally this organization regrets the incident and hopes for Admiral van Rinnekom's recovery. But let us be honest. He has only gotten a taste of the very violence he advocated. The issue before us is one of life and death. WMP stands for life. Unhappily, a great many uninformed people have let their emotions run away with them and are crying for blood with no thought of the consequences. WMP exists to fight this tendency, to fight for sanity, to give atavism its deathblow, by any means required. We make no threats. But let the militarists beware.'

21 November

Last Tuesday mankind throughout the Solar System watched an unprecedented event. Cynbe ru Taren, a member of the Aleriona delegation to Earth, appeared on an official 3V broadcast and answered questions put to him by Crown Prince Umberto of Italy, who represented the World Federation.

The questions were selected from an estimated forty million sent in by people around the globe, with Cynbe choosing a dozen from the final list. As he remarked, with a grim humor he displayed throughout the interview, 'Thirteen bears for you an unhappy freight. It numbered either that one who betrayed or that one who was slain.'

In general, he repeated statements already made about the New Europe tragedy. How did it happen? 'Our ships were on maneuvers. Near Aurore did they pass, for Alerion recognizes no other claim of sovereignty in the Phoenix. Maychance the Terrestrial chief believed this was attack, for truth is we had many. When fired on, we made response, with more than he may have awaited. His remnants entered atmosphere for an outflank with radiation protection. That it might save itself, our closest detachment launched weapons of multiple megatonnage. Grief, the settled fringe of that continent they named Pays d'Espoir was lineally beneath. At orbital height the warheads kindled a firestorm. Terrible it ran, from end to end of that coast. When we could land, we found none alive, and but few in the southern region, where also a missile struck. Those we have hitherbrought, with our own mourning. Yet their Thirteenth-the-Betrayer was that captain who took them not into account when he plunged.'

Why does Alerion now keep possession? 'Naught but woe came ever from this intermingling. Time and again have humans ordered us from planets we discovered thousands of years agone, whose peace is now broken with machines and alien feet. And truth, we have often felt need to forbid places, even force them evacuated of the first few men. Races that knew us long grow latterly hostile to us, unrestful by what men have told and sold them. Resources we need are taken away. From such has come tension, which unseldom bursts in battle. Long past is that hour we should have ended it.'

Why doesn't Alerion let an inspection team from Earth visit New Europe? 'As we understand the symbolism of your culture, this were an admission of weakness and wrongness. Too, we cannot hazard espionage, or yet a suicide mission with nuclear bombs ensmuggled. I say never your Parliament would such plot, but you have individuals who are otherwise, some in high command. Maychance later, when faith has been achieved . . .'

28 November
The Aleriona Craze, already well established in North

45

America, gained so much momentum from delegate Cynbe ru Taren's recent 3V appearance that in the past week it has swept like a meteorite through the upper-class teen-agers of most countries. Quite a few in Welfare have caught the fever too. Now girls blessed with naturally blonde long hair flaunt it past their sisters waiting in line to buy wigs and metal mesh jerkins – like their brothers. No disciplinary measure by parents or teachers seems able to stop the kids warbling every word they utter. You need ear seals not to be assaulted by the minor-key caterwaulings of 'Alerion, Alerion' from radio, juke, and taper. The slithering Aleriona Ramble has driven even the Wiggle off the dance floors. On Friday the city of Los Angeles put an educational program on the big screen at La Brea Park, a rebroadcast of the historic interview; and police fought three hours to halt a riot by five thousand screaming high-schoolers.

In an effort to learn whether this is a mere fad or a some-what hysterical expression of the world's sincere desire for peace, our reporters talked with typical youngsters around the globe. Some quotes:

Lucy Thomas, 16, Minneapolis: 'I'm just in hyperbolic orbit about him. I play the show back even when I'm asleep. Those eyes – they freeze you and melt you at the same time. Yee-ee!'

Pedro Fraga, 17, Buenos Aires: 'They can't be male. I won't believe they are.'

Machiko Ichikawa, 15, Tokyo: 'The Samurai would have understood them. So much beauty, so much valor.'

Simon Mbulu, 18, Nairobi: 'Of course, they frighten me. But that is part of the wonder.'

In Paris, Georges de Roussy, 17, threatened surlily: 'I don't know what's gotten into those young camels. But I'll tell you this. Anybody *we* saw in that costume would get her wig cut off, and her own hair with it.'

No comment was available from the still hidden delegates.

5 December

Lisa Heim, 14, daughter of manufacturer and would-be exploration entrepreneur Gunnar Heim of San Francisco, disappeared Wednesday. Efforts to trace her have so far been unsuccessful, and police fear she may have been kidnapped. Her father has posted a reward of one million American dollars for 'anything that helps get her back. I'll go higher than this in ransom if I have to,' he added.

CHAPTER SEVEN

UTHG-A-K'THAQ twisted his face downward as far as he could, which wasn't much, and pointed his four chemosensor tendrils directly at Heim. In this position the third eye on top of his head was visible to the man, aft of the blowhole. But it was the front eyes, on either side of those fleshy feelers, that swiveled their gray stare against him. A grunt emerged from the lipless gape of a mouth: 'So war, you say. We 'rom Naqsa know lit-tle ow war.'

Heim stepped back, for to a human nose the creature's breath stank of swamp. Even so, he must look upward; Uthg-a-K'thaq loomed eighteen centimeters over him. He wondered fleetingly if that was why there was so much prejudice against Naqsans.

The usual explanation was their over-all appearance. Uthg-a-K'thaq suggested a dolphin, of bilious green-spotted yellow, that had turned its tail into a pair of short fluke-footed legs. Lumps projecting under the blunt head acted as shoulders for arms that were incongruously anthropoid, if you overlooked their size and the swimming-membranes that ran from elbows to pelvis. Except for a purse hung from that narrowing in the body which indicated a sort of neck, he was naked, and grossly male. It wasn't non-humanness as such that offended men, said the psychologists, rather those aspects which were parallel but different, like a dirty joke on *Homo sapiens*. Smell, slobbering, belching, the sexual pattern—

But mainly they're also space travelers, prospectors, colonizers, freight carriers, merchants, who've given us stiff competition, Heim thought cynically.

That had never bothered him. The Naqsans were shrewd but on the average more ethical than men. Nor did he mind their looks; indeed, they were handsome if you considered them functionally. And their private lives were their own business. The fact remained, though, most humans would resent even having a Naqsan in the same ship, let alone serving under him. And ... Dave Penoyer would be a competent captain,

47

he had made lieutenant commander before he quit the Navy, but Heim wasn't sure he could be firm enough if trouble of that nasty sort broke out.

He dismissed worry and said, 'Right. This is actually a raiding cruise. Are you still interested?'

'Yes. Hawe you worgotten that horriwle den you wound me in?'

Heim had not. Tracking rumors to their source, he had ended in a part of New York Welfare that appalled even him. A Naqsan stranded on Earth was virtually helpless. Uthg-a-K'thaq had shipped as technical adviser on a vessel from the planet that men called Caliban, whose most advanced tribe had decided to get into the space game. Entering the Solar System, the inexperienced skipper collided with an asteroid and totaled his craft. Survivors were brought to Earth by the Navy, and the Calibanites sent home; but there was no direct trade with Naqsa and, in view of the crisis in the Phoenix where his world also lay, no hurry to repatriate Uthg-a-K'thaq. *Damnation, instead of fooling with those Aleriona bastards, Parliament ought to be working out a distressed-spaceman covenant.*

Bluntly, Heim said, 'We haven't any way of testing your mind in depth as we can for our own sort. I've got to trust your promise to keep quiet. I suppose you know that if you pass this information on, you'll probably get enough of a reward to buy a ride home.'

Uthg-a-K'thaq burbled in his blowhole. Heim wasn't sure whether it represented laughter or indignation. 'You hawe my word. Also, I am wothered awout Alerion. Good to strike at them. And, *suq*, will there not we loot to share?'

'Okay. You're hereby our chief engineer.' *Because the ship has got to leave soon, and you're the only one I could get who knows how to repair a Mach Principle drive.* 'Now about details—'

A maid's voice said over the intercom, which was set for one-way only: 'Mail, sir.'

Heim's heart shuddered, as it daily did. 'Excuse me,' he said. 'I'll be back. Make yourself comfortable.'

Uthg-a-K'thaq hissed something and settled his glabrous bulk on the study couch. Heim jogged out.

Vadász sat in the living room, bottle to hand. He hadn't spoken much or sung a note in the past few days. The house was grown tomb silent. At first many came; police, friends, Curt Wingate and Harold Twyman arrived at the same hour and clasped hands; of everyone Heim knew well only Jocelyn Lawrie had remained unheard from. That was all a blur in his memory; he had continued preparations for the ship because there was nothing else to do, and he scarcely noticed when the visits stopped. Drugs kept him going. This morning he had observed his own gauntness in an optex with faint surprise – and complete indifference.

'Surely the same null,' Vadász mumbled.

Heim snatched the stack of envelopes off the table. A flat package lay on the bottom. He ripped the plastic off. Lisa's face looked forth.

His hands began to shake so badly that he had trouble punching the animator button. The lips that were Connie's opened. 'Daddy,' said the small voice. 'Endre. I'm okay. I mean, they haven't hurt me. A woman stopped me when I was about to get on the elway home. She said her bra magnet had come loose and would I please help her fix it. I didn't think anybody upper-class was dangerous. She was dressed nice and talked nice and had a car there and everything. We got in the car and blanked the bubble. Then she shot me with a stunner. I woke up here. I don't know where it is, a suite of rooms, the windows are always blanked. Two women are staying with me. They aren't mean, they just won't let me go. They say it's for peace. Please do what they want.' Her flat speech indicated she was doped with antiphobic. But suddenly herself broke through. 'I'm so lonesome!' she cried, and the tears came.

The strip ended. After a long while Heim grew aware that Vadász was urging him to read a note that had also been in the package. He managed to focus on the typescript.

Mr. Heim:

For weeks you have lent your name and influence to the militarists. You have actually paid for advertisements making the false and inflammatory claim that there are survivors at large on New Europe. Now we have obtained information which suggests you may be plotting still more radical ways to disrupt the peace negotiations.

If this is true, mankind cannot allow it. For the sake of humanity, we cannot take the chance that it might be true.

Your daughter will be kept as a hostage for your good

behavior until the treaty with Alerion has been concluded, and for as long thereafter as seems wise. If meanwhile you publicly admit you lied about New Europe, and do nothing else, she will be returned.

Needless to say, you are not to inform the police of this message. The peace movement has so many loyal supporters in so many places that we will know if you do. In that event we will be forced to punish you through the girl. If on the other hand you behave yourself, you will continue to receive occasional word from her.

Yours for peace and sanity.

He had to read three or four times before it registered.

'San Francisco meter,' Vadász said. He crumpled the plastic and hurled it at the wall. 'Not that that means anything.'

'*Gud i himlen.*' Heim stumbled to a lounger, fell down, and sat staring into the unspeakable. 'Why don't they go straight after me?'

'They have done so,' Vadász answered.

'Personally!'

'You would be a risky target for violence. A young and trusting girl is easier.'

Heim had a feeling that he was about to weep. But his eyes remained two coals in his skull. 'What can we do?' he whispered.

'I don't know,' Vadász said like a robot. 'So much depends on who they are. Obviously not anyone official. A government need only arrest you on some excuse.'

'The Militants, then. Jonas Yore.' Heim rose and walked toward the exit.

'Where are you going?' Vadász grabbed his arm. It was like trying to halt a landslip.

'For a gun,' Heim said, 'and on to Chicago.'

'No. Hold. Stop, you damned fool! What could you do except provoke them into killing her?'

Heim swayed and stood.

'Yore may or may not know about this,' Vadász said. 'Certainly no one has definite information about your plans, or they would simply tip the Peace Control. The kidnappers could be in the lunatic fringe of the Militants. Emotions are running so high. And that sort must needs be dramatic, attack people in the street, steal your daughter, strut their dirty little

50

egos – yes, Earth has many like them in the upper classes too, crazed with uselessness. Any cause will serve. "Peace" is merely the fashionable one.'

Heim returned to the bottle. He poured a drink, slopping much. *Lisa is alive,* he told himself. *Lisa is alive. Lisa is alive.* He tossed the liquor down his gullet. 'How long will she be?' he screamed.

'Hey?'

'She's with fanatics. They'll still hate me, whatever happens. And they'll be afraid she can identify them. Endre, help me!'

'We have some time,' Vadász snapped. 'Use it for something better than hysterics.'

The glow in Heim's stomach spread outward. *I've been responsible for lives before*, he thought, and the old reflexes of command awoke. *You construct a games theoretical matrix and choose the course with smallest negative payoff*.

His brain began to move. 'Thanks, Endre,' he said.

'Could they be bluffing about spies in the police?' Vadász wondered.

'I don't know, but the chance looks too big to take.'

'Then . . . we cancel the expedition, renounce what we have said about New Europe, and hope?'

'That may be the only thing to do.' It whirred in Heim's head. 'Though I do believe it's wrong also, even to get Lisa home.'

'What is left? To hit back? How? Maybe private detectives could search—'

'Over a whole planet? Oh, we can try them, but— No, I was fighting a fog till I got the idea of the raider, and now I'm back in the fog and I've got to get out again. Something definite, that they won't know about before too late. You were right, there's no sense in threatening Yore. Or even appealing to him, I guess. What matters to them is their cause. If we could go after *it*—'

Heim bellowed. Vadász almost got knocked over in the big man's rush to the phone.

'What in blue hell, Gunnar?'

Heim unlocked a drawer and took out his private directory. It now included the unlisted number and scrambler code of Michel Coquelin's sealed circuit. And 0930 in California was – what? 1730? – in Paris. His fingers stabbed the buttons.

51

A confidential secretary appeared in the screen. '*Bureau de – oh, M. Heim.*'

'*Donnez-vous moi M. le Minister tout de suite, s'il vous plaît.*' Despite the circumstances, Vadász winced at what Heim thought was French.

The secretary peered at the visage confronting him, sucked down a breath, and punched. Coquelin's weary features came to view.

'Gunnar! What is this? News of your girl?'

Heim told him. Coquelin turned gray. 'Oh, no,' he said. He had children of his own.

'Uh, huh,' Heim said, 'I see only one plausible way out. My crew's assembled now, a tough bunch of boys. And you know where Cynbe is.'

'Are you crazy?' Coquelin stammered.

'Give me the details: location, how to get in, disposition of guards and alarms,' Heim said. 'I'll take it from there. If we fail, I won't implicate you. I'll save Lisa, or try to save her, by giving the kidnappers a choice: that I either cast discredit on them and their movement by spilling the whole cargo; or I get her back, tell the world I lied, and show remorse by killing myself. We can arrange matters so they know I'll go through with it.'

'I cannot – I—'

'This is rough on you, Michel, I know,' Heim said. 'But if you can't help me, well, then I'm tied. I'll have to do exactly what they want. And half a million will die on New Europe.'

Coquelin wet his lips, stiffened his back, and asked: 'Suppose I tell you, Gunnar. What happens?'

CHAPTER EIGHT

'SPACE yacht *Flutterby,* GB-327-RP, beaming Georgetown, Ascension Island. We are in distress. Come in, Georgetown. Come in, Georgetown.'

The whistle of cloven air lifted toward a roar. Heat billowed through the forward shield. The bridge viewports seemed aflame and the radar screen had gone mad. Heim settled firmer into his harness and fought the pilot console.

'Garrison to *Flutterby*.' The British voice was barely audible as maser waves struggled through the ionized air enveloping that steel meteorite. 'We read you. Come in *Flutterby*.'

'Stand by for emergency landing,' David Penoyer said. His yellow hair was plastered down with sweat. 'Over.'

'You can't land here. This island is temporarily restricted. Over.' Static snarled around the words.

Engines sang aft. Force fields wove their four-dimensional dance through the gravitrons. The internal compensators held steady, there was no sense of that deceleration which made the hull groan; but swiftly the boat lost speed, until thermal effect ceased. In the ports a vision of furnaces gave way to the immense curve of the South Atlantic. Clouds were scattered woolly above its shiningness. The horizon line was a deep blue edging into space black.

'The deuce we can't,' Penoyer said. 'Over.'

'What's wrong?' Reception was loud and clear this time.

'Something blew as we reached suborbital velocity. We've a hole in the tail and no steering pulses. Bloody little control from the main drive. I think we can set down on Ascension, but don't ask me where. Over.'

'Ditch in the ocean and we'll send a boat. Over.'

'Didn't you hear me, old chap? We're hulled. We'd sink like a stone. Might get out with spacesuits and life jackets, or might not. But however that goes, Lord Ponsonby won't be happy about losing a million pounds' worth of yacht. We've a legal right to save her if we can. Over.'

'Well – hold on, I'll switch you to the captain's office—'

'Nix. No time. Don't worry. We won't risk crashing into Garrison. Our vector's aimed at the south side. We'll try for one of the plateaux. Will broadcast a signal for you to home on when we're down, which'll be in a few more ticks. Wish us luck. Over and out.'

Penoyer snapped down the switch and turned to Heim. 'Now we'd better be fast,' he said above the thunders. 'They'll scramble some armed flyers as soon as they don't hear from us.'

Heim nodded. During those seconds of talk *Connie Girl* had shot the whole way. A wild dark landscape clawed up at her. His detectors registered metal and electricity, which must be at Cynbe's lair. Green Mountain lifted its misty head between him and the radars at Georgetown. He need no longer use only

53

the main drive. *That* had been touch and go!

He cut the steering back in. The boat swerved through an arc that howled like a wolf. A tiny landing field carved from volcanic rock appeared in the viewports. He came down in a shattering blast of displaced air. Dust vomited skyward.

The jacks touched ground. He slapped the drive to Idle and threw off his harness. 'Take over, Dave,' he said, and pounded for the main airlock.

His score of men arrived with him, everyone space-suited. Their weapons gleamed in the overhead illumination. He cursed the safety seal that made the lock open with such sadistic slowness. Afternoon light slanted through. He led the way, jumped off the ramp before it had finished extruding, and crouched in the settling dust.

There were three buildings across the field, as Coquelin had said: a fifteen-man barracks, a vehicle shed, and an environmental dome. The four sentries outside the latter held their guns in a stupefied fashion, only approximately pointed at him. The two men on a mobile GTA missile carrier gaped. Georgetown HQ had naturally phoned them not to shoot if they detected a spacecraft. The rest of the guard were pouring from quarters.

Heim counted. Some weren't in sight yet. . . . He lumbered toward them. 'Emergency landing,' he called. 'I saw your field—'

The young man with Peace Control lieutenant's insignia, who must be in charge, looked dismayed. 'But—' He stopped and fumbled at his collar.

Heim came near. 'What's wrong?' he asked. 'Why shouldn't I have used your field?'

That was a wicked question, he knew. Officially PCA didn't admit this place existed.

The Aleriona overlords who comprised the delegation could not be housed together. They never lived thus at home; to offer them less than total privacy would have been an insult, and perhaps risky of all their lives. So they must be scattered around Earth. Ascension was a good choice. Little was here nowadays except a small World Sea Police base. Comings and goings were thus discreet.

'Orders,' the lieutenant said vaguely. He squinted at the argent spear of the yacht. 'I say, you don't look damaged.'

You could fake a name and registry for *Connie Girl*, but not unsoundness. The last couple of men emerged from barracks. Heim raised his arm and pointed. 'On her other side,' he said. He chopped his hand down and clashed his faceplate shut.

Two men in the airlock stepped back. The gas cannon they had hidden poked its nose out. Under fifty atmospheres of pressure, the anesthetic aerosol boiled forth.

A sentry opened fire. Heim dove for dirt. A bullet splintered rock before his eyes. The yellow stream gushed overhead, rumbling. And now his crew were on their way, with stunners asnicker. No lethal weapons; he'd hang before he killed humans doing their duty. But this was an attack by men who had seen combat against men whose only job had been to prevent it. Death wasn't needed.

The short, savage fight ended. Heim rose and made for the dome. Zucconi and Lupowitz came behind, a ram slung between them on a gravity carrier. Around the field, *Connie Girl*'s medical team started to check the fallen Peacemen and give what first aid was indicated.

'Here,' said Heim into his suit radio. Zucconi and Lupowitz set down the ram and started the motor. Five hundred kilos of tool steel bashed the dome wall at sixty cycles. The narcotic fog clamored with that noise. The wall smashed open. Heim leaped through, into the red sun's light.

A dozen followed him. 'He's somewhere in this mess,' Heim said. 'Scatter. We've got maybe three minutes before the cops arrive.'

He burst into the jungle at random. Branches snapped, vines shrank away, flowers were crushed underfoot. A shadow flitted – Cynbe! Heim plunged.

A laser flame sizzled. Heim felt the heat, saw his combat breastplate vaporizing in coruscant fire. Then he was upon the Aleriona. He wrenched the gun loose. *Mustn't close in – he'd get burned on this hot metal.* Cynbe grinned with fury and whipped his tail around Heim's ankles. Heim fell, but still Cynbe hung on. His followers arrived, seized their quarry, and frogmarched away the Intellect Master of the Garden of War. Outside, Cynbe took a breath of vapor and went limp.

I hope the biomeds are right about this stuff's being harmless to him, Heim thought.

He ran onto the field and had no more time for thought. A couple of PCA flyers were in the sky. They swooped like hawks. Their guns pursued Heim's crew. He saw the line of explosions stitch toward him, heard the crackle and an over-head whistle through his helmet. 'Open out!' he yelled. His throat was afire. Sweat soaked his undergarments. 'Let 'em see who you're toting!'

The flyers screamed about and climbed.

They'll try to disable my boat. If we can't get away fast – The ramp was ahead, hell-road steep. A squadron appeared over Green Mountain. Heim stopped at the bottom of the ramp. His men streamed past. Now Cynbe was aboard. Now everyone was. A flyer dove at him. He heard bullets sleet along the ramp at his heels.

Over the coaming! Someone dogged the lock. *Connie Girl* stood on her tail and struck for the sky.

Heim lay where he was for some time.

Eventually he opened his helmet and went to the bridge. Space blazed with stars, but Earth was already swallowing them again. 'We're headed back down, eh?' he asked.

'Right-o,' Penoyer answered. The strain had left him, his boyish face was one vast grin. 'Got clean away, above their ceiling and past their radar horizon before you could say fout.'

Then a long curve above atmosphere, but swiftly, racing the moment when Peace Control's orbital detectors were alerted, and now toward the far side of the planet. It had been a smooth operation, boded well for the privateer. If they carried it the whole way through, that was.

Heim lockered his suit and got back steadiness from the routine of an intercom check with all stations. Everything was shipshape, barring some minor bullet pocks in the outer plates. When Lupowitz reported, 'The prisoner's awake, sir,' he felt no excitement, only a tidal flow of will.

'Bring him to my cabin,' he ordered.

The boat crept downward through night. Timing had been important. The Russian Republic was as amiably inept about TrafCon as everything else, and you could land undetected after dark on the Siberian tundra if you were cautious. Heim felt the setdown as a slight quiver. When the engines ceased their purr, the silence grew monstrous.

Two armed men outside his cabin saluted in triumph. He went through and closed the door.

Cynbe stood near the bunk. Only his tailtip stirred, and his hair in the breeze from a ventilator. But when he recognized

56

Heim, the beautiful face drew into a smile that was chilling to see. 'Ah-h-h,' he murmured.

Heim made the formal Aleriona salute. '*Imbiac*, forgive me,' he said. 'I am desperate.'

'Truth must that be' – it trilled in his ears – 'if you think thus to rouse war.'

'No, I don't. How could I better disgrace my side of the argument? I just need your help.'

The green eyes narrowed. 'Strange is your way to ask, Captain.'

'There wasn't any other. Listen. Matters have gotten so tense between the war and peace factions on Earth that violence is breaking out. Some days ago my daughter was stolen away. I got a message that if I didn't switch sides, she'd be killed.'

'Grief. Yet what can I do?'

'Don't pretend to be sorry. If I backed down, you'd have a distinct gain, so there was no point in begging your assistance. Now, no matter what I myself do, I can't trust them to return her. I had to get a lever of my own. I bribed someone who knew where you were, recruited this gang of men, and – and now we'll phone the head of the organized appeasement agitators.'

Cynbe's tail switched his heels. 'Let us suppose I refuse,' said the cool music.

'Then I'll kill you,' Heim said without rancor. 'I don't know if that scares you or not. But your delegation meets Parliament in another week. They'll be handicapped without their military expert. Nor are things likely to proceed smoothly, after such a stink as I can raise.'

'Will you not terminate my existence in every case, Captain, that I never denounce you?'

'No. Cooperate and you'll go free. I simply want my daughter back. Why should I commit a murder that'll have the whole planet looking for the solution? They'd be certain to find me. The general type of this vessel is sufficient clue, since I've no alibi for the time of the kidnapping.'

'Yet have you not said why I shall not accuse you.'

Heim shrugged. 'That'd be against your own interest. Too sordid a story would come out. A father driven wild by the irresponsible Peace Militants, and so forth. I'd produce my documents from New Europe in open court. I'd testify under neoscop what you admitted when last we talked. Oh, I'd fight dirty. Sentiment on Earth is delicately balanced. Something like my trial could well tip the scales.'

Cynbe's eyes nictitated over. He stroked his chin with one slim hand.

'In fact,' Heim said, 'your best bet is to tell PCA you were taken by an unidentified bunch who wanted to sabotage the treaty. You persuaded them this was the worst thing they could do, from their own standpoint, and they let you go. Then insist that our own authorities hush the entire affair up. They will, if you say so, and gladly. A public scandal at this juncture would be most inconvenient.' Still the Aleriona stood hooded in his own thoughts. 'Cynbe,' said Heim in his softest voice, 'you do not understand humans. We're as alien to you as you are to us. So far you've juggled us pretty well. But throw in a new factor, and what are all your calculations worth?'

The eyes unveiled. 'Upon you I see no weapon,' Cynbe crooned. 'If I aid you not, how will you kill me?'

Heim flexed his fingers. 'With these hands.'

Laughter belled forth. '*Star Fox* captain, let us seek the radiophone.'

It was late morning in Chicago. Jonas Yore's Puritan face looked out of the screen with loathing. 'What do you want, Heim?'

'You know about my girl being snatched?'

'No. I mean, I'm sorry for her if not for you, but how does it concern me? I have no information.'

'I got word the kidnappers are skizzies in the peace faction. Wait, I don't accuse you of having any part in it. Every group has bolshies. But if you passed the word around quietly, personal calls to your entire membership list, directly or indirectly you'd get to them.'

'See here, you rotten—'

'Turn on your recorder. This is important. I want to present Delegate Cynbe ru Taren.' In spite of everything, Heim's heart came near bursting.

The Aleriona glided into pickup range. 'My lord!' Yore gasped.

'In honor's name did Captain Heim appeal me-ward,' Cynbe sang. 'A bond is between us that we did battle once. Nor may my ancient race drink of shame. Is not yonder child returned, we must depart this planet and invoke that cleansing which is in open war. Thus do I command your help.'

58

'M-m-my lord – I— Yes! At once!'

Heim switched off the set. The air whistled from his lungs and his knees shook. 'Th-th-thanks,' he stuttered. 'Uh . . . uh . . . as soon as Vadász lets me know she's arrived, we'll take off. Deliver you near a town.'

Cynbe watched him for a time before he asked: 'Play you chess, Captain? Of Earth's every creation, there is the one finest. And well should I like that you not have her enminded a while.'

'No, thanks,' Heim said. 'You'd win on fool's mate every time. I'd better see about getting our false identification removed.'

He was glad of the winter cold outside.

They were almost through when Cynbe appeared in the airlock, etched black across its light. His tone soared: 'Captain, be swift. The wandersinger calls from your home. She is again.'

Heim didn't remember running to the phone. Afterward he noticed bruises on shin and shoulder. But he did lock the radio-room door.

Lisa looked at him. 'Oh, Daddy!'

'Are you all right?' he cried. His hands reached out. The screen stopped them.

'Yes. They . . . they never hurt me. I got doped. When I woke up, we were parked here in town. They told me, take an elway from there. I was still dopey and didn't pay any attention – no number – Please hurry home.'

'I'll – ja. Two, three hours.'

The remnants of the drug left her more calm than him. 'I think I know how it happened, Daddy. I'm awful sorry. That night you and Endre talked about your – you know – well, you'd forgot to turn off the general intercom switch. I listened from my room.'

He remembered how slinky and mysterious she had acted in the following couple of weeks. He'd put that down to an attempt at impressing Vadász. Now the knowledge of his carelessness hit him in the belly.

'Don't,' she asked. 'I never told. Honest. Only when Dick and some other kids teased me 'cause I wouldn't go in for that stupid Aleriona stuff, I got mad and told them one human was worth a hundred of those crawlies and my father was going to prove it. I never said more. But I guess word got back to somebody, 'cause those women kept asking me what I'd meant. I told them I was just bragging. Even when they said they'd beat

59

me, I told them it was just a brag, and I guess they believed that because they never did beat me. Please don't be too mad, Daddy.'

'I'm not,' he said harshly. 'I'm more proud than I deserve. Now go to bed and rest. I'll be home as fast as I can.'

'I missed you so much.'

She switched off. Then Heim could weep.

Connie Girl purred aloft, and down again a kilometer outside Krasnoe. Heim escorted Cynbe to the ground. It was frozen, and rang underfoot. A few lights shone from outlying houses, dim compared to the winter stars.

'Here.' Awkwardly, Heim proffered a heated cloak. 'You'll want this.'

'My thanks,' blew from under the frost-cold locks. 'When your authorities fetch me, I shall tell as you suggested. Wisest for Alerion is thus; and for I, who would not see you further hurt.'

Heim stared at the thin snowcrust. It sparkled like Cynbe's fur. 'I'm sorry about what I did,' he mumbled. 'It was no way to treat you.'

'No more of anger in-dwells.' Cynbe's song dropped low. 'I knew not humans hold their young so dear. Well may you fare.'

'Good-by.' This time Gunnar Heim shook hands.

The boat took off afresh, found orbital height, and went toward Mojave Port along a standard trajectory. As far as the world was concerned, she had gone out to check on the loading of the star cruiser. Heim was surprised to note how calmly he could now wait to see his daughter again.

And when it'd be for such a short time, too. The ship must depart in a few more days, with him her captain.

That had to be, he saw. The evil had grown so mighty that he dared not challenge it with less than his whole strength: which was found among the stars, not on this sick Earth. Nor would he be worthy to be Lisa's father, if he sent men against that thing whose creatures had tried to devour her, and did not go himself.

She'd be safe in Wingate's care. As for the Heimdal company, it might or might not survive without him, but that really made no difference. Lisa's grandfather would provide for her, whatever happened. *And don't forget the chance of prize money!*

60

Laughter welled in Heim. *Maybe I'm rationalizing a selfish, atavistic desire to raise hell. Okay, what if I am? This is the way it's going to be.*

CHAPTER NINE

THEY had celebrated an early Christmas. The tree glittered forlorn in the living room. Outside, a surf of rain drove against the windows.

'It's so awful,' Lisa said. 'That there has to be war.'

'There doesn't, pony,' Heim answered. 'In fact, that's what we're trying to prevent.'

She regarded him in bewilderment.

'If we don't stand up to Alerion,' Heim said, 'there'll be trouble and more trouble, worse each time, and we'll forever lose, until at last Earth is driven into a corner. And when it's cornered, the human race always does fight, with everything it's got. Planet against planet – that would be the real Ragnarok. What we have to do is show them right now that we aren't going to be pushed. Then we and they can talk business. Because space truly is big enough for everybody, as long as they respect each other's right to exist.' He put on his cloak. 'We'd better start.'

They went downshaft in silence to the garage, and entered his flyer – himself, his daughter, her grandfather, two hard-looking men who must keep watch over her until this affair had been outlived, and Vadász. Out the doors they glided, and rose through storm. The hull shivered and resounded. But when they got into the upper lanes, blue stillness encompassed them, with clouds below like snow mountains.

Wingate lit a cigar and puffed, his nutcracker face squinched together. Finally he barked, 'I hate these good-by waits, sitting around wishing you could think of something to say. Let's tune in Parliament.'

'Not worth while,' Heim replied. 'They expect a full week of preliminary debate before they invite the Aleriona delegation. Every two-cent politician wants to make sure he's heard at least once.'

'But according to the news yesterday, France came out near

the top of the alphabetical draw. Coquelin will probably start to speak any minute.'

'He'll – oh, go ahead.' Heim was chiefly conscious of the slight form huddled between him and Vadász.

The time was not much later in Mexico City than here, but you couldn't tell that from inside the Capitol. The view swept across the Chamber of Council, faces and faces and faces, white, brown, black, amber, their eyes zeroed on the rostrum as the speaker for Finland stepped down. President Fazil knocked with his gavel; through that waiting quiet, the sound was like nails being driven into a coffin. Wingate, whose Spanish was not the best, dialed for English translation.

'—the honorable spokesman for France, M. Michel Coquelin.'

Heim set the 'pilot and leaned back to watch. The square shape trudged down the aisle deliberately, almost scornfully, and took a stance at the lectern. The camera zoomed in on a countenance shockingly aged, but one which might have been cast in iron.

'Mr. President, distinguished delegates, ladies and gentlemen. I shall not detain you long at this point. The world knows the French feeling about New Europe. My country wishes to make her position entirely clear and to advance a certain argument. Since this is sure to precipitate considerable discussion, I request leave to defer my address until the other honorable spokesmen have finished theirs.'

'You see?' Heim said. 'He has to gain time for us to get clear. It was bad luck that France came on so early in the session, but he'll handle it.'

'What's he going to say, anyhow, Daddy?' Lisa asked. 'He *can't* let you be called pirates!'

Heim grinned. 'You'll find out.'

'Mr. President! Point of order.' The camera wheeled around and closed in on Harold Twyman. He had jumped to his feet and looked angry. 'In so grave a matter, a departure from precedence must be approved in the form of a motion.'

Coquelin raised his brows. 'I fail to see why there should be any objection to France yielding precedence,' he said.

'Mr. President, distinguished members of this body,' Twyman rapped, 'the honorable spokesman for France has warned us that he intends a surprise. This is a time for serious discussion, not for debater's tricks. If we find ourselves forced to rebut an unexpected assertion, our meeting with the honorable delegates of Alerion may easily be postponed another week. There has already been too much delay. I insist that this chamber vote upon whether to let M. Coquelin play with us or not.'

'Mr President—' The Frenchman's retort was cut off. Fazil slammed his gavel and said:

'The chair finds the point well taken, if perhaps somewhat heatedly expressed. Does anyone wish to make a motion that the French statement be deferred until every other national spokesman has finished his remarks?'

'Oh, oh,' Vadász muttered. 'This does not look good.'

Heim reached out and adjusted the 'pilot for top speed. The engine hum strengthened. Above it he heard a member of the Argentine group say, 'I so move,' and a Dutchman, 'I second.'

'It has been moved and seconded—'

'What if they don't let him?' Lisa wailed.

'Then we've got to go like bats out of Venus,' Heim said.

Coquelin began to speak in favor of the motion. After a few minutes, Vadász clicked his tongue and said admiringly: 'Never did I hear anything so long-winded. That man is an artist.'

'Um,' Wingate grunted. 'He may antagonize 'em.'

'Obviously,' said Heim in a bleak tone, 'he doesn't expect to win, no matter what.'

Debate droned back and forth. The flyer left the storm behind and fled over a huge wrinkled landscape. Far to the east gleamed the Sierra peaks. *We could lose all that beauty someday*, Heim thought.

Mojave Field sprawled into view. He slanted down on the beam and saw *Connie Girl* poised in the open. Garaging, formalities of clearance, the long walk across concrete under a glaring sun – was the light what blinded him?

They stopped at the ramp. 'Well,' said Wingate gruffly, 'you can't waste time. God ride with you, Son.' He let the handclasp die.

Lisa came into Heim's arms. 'Daddy, Daddy, I'm sorry, I c-c-can't help bawling.'

'Blaze to that.' He ruffled her hair and held her close against his chest. 'We'll be back, you know. Rich and famous and a million stories to tell.' He swallowed. 'You ... you've been ... you are a good girl. I couldn't have asked for a finer girl. So long. Plain old *på gensyn*.'

He gave her to Vadász, who embraced her very lightly and bestowed a kiss on the wet cheek. '*Isten veled*,' the Magyar said low. 'I shall bring you home a song.'

Hastily, then, they mounted the ramp, stood waving while it retracted, and saw the lock close before them.

'Thanks, Endre,' Heim said. He turned on his heel. 'Let's get cracking.'

The yacht could have sprung straight into orbit. But better not show unseemly haste. Heim took her up according to the beams. The sky darkened and stars awoke, until blackness was a jewel box. Vadász fiddled with the com controls and eventually succeeded in getting a satellite relay from Mexico.

Debate on a procedural motion was not unlimited. The voting started before *Connie Girl* had made rendezvous. A roll call tolled overwhelming defeat.

'Mr. President,' Coquelin's voice lifted from the 3V, blurred, small as an insect's, 'this is a strange development. France had looked for the normal courtesies. Since I am required to make my country's basic policy statement today, I will. However, I note the time is near mid-day, and I warn the distinguished representatives that I shall be speaking at some length. Accordingly, I suggest that first we adjourn for lunch.'

'The chair so rules,' Fazil conceded. 'This meeting will resume at 1400 hours sharp.' His gavel clubbed down.

'An artist, I tell you,' Vadász laughed.

'A couple hours isn't much time to get under way, with a crew new to the ship,' Heim reminded him.

The great torpedo shape hove in sight and waxed as he closed until it filled his bow vision. As yet she was uncamouflaged, and sunlight lay furious on the stern assembly; drive units, Mach rings, boathouses, turrets, hatches cast long shadows on the metal flanks.

'Yacht *Connie Girl* calling cruiser *Fox II*. We are coming in. Please stand by. Over.'

Wingate had argued about the change of cognomen. 'I know what your old command meant to you, Gunnar,' he said. 'But you'll get enough people mad without taking the name of a Navy ship.'

'I'm not, exactly,' Heim said. 'Last I heard, foxes were still in the public domain. Besides, I damn well figure to rub people's noses in what the Navy ought to be doing. What it wants to do, in fact.'

Number Four boathouse stood open for him. He cradled the yacht – she was about the size of a regular auxiliary – and fretted while airpumps filled the shell. The corridors beyond were bustle and clangor. He'd had the men aboard for assignments and instruction, but nonetheless he wished terribly there had been time for a shakedown cruise.

First Officer Penoyer saluted on the bridge. 'Welcome, sir.' Until Dave greeted him so, he had not really remembered how alone the captain is. 'Full roster present. Work proceeding. Estimated time of acceleration, 2300 hours GMT.'

'Knock at least an hour off that,' Heim said.

'Sir?'

'You heard me.' Heim sat down and riffled through the manual of operations. 'Here, for instance. The C.E. doesn't have to check out the internal field compensators again. If they fail, we'll accelerate at no more than one-point-five gee; once in free fall, we can stand weightlessness till they're fixed. Not that I expect any trouble in his department anyway. He's good. Have him proceed directly to tuning the pulse manifolds. The more carefully that job is done, the nearer Sol we can go FTL.'

'Aye, aye, sir.' With noticeable distaste, Penoyer flicked the intercom and spoke to Uthg-a-K'thaq. Heim continued his search for corners that might be cut.

And somehow, in some typically human left-handed fashion, the job was done. At 2145 klaxons hooted, orders echoed, atoms flamed in fusion generators, and gravitational forces laid hold of space. Slowly, smoothly, with a deep purr felt less within the ears than the bones, *Fox II* slipped her moorings to Earth and departed orbit.

Heim stood on the bridge and watched his world recede. Still she dominated heaven, vast and infinitely fair, clouds and seas and a sapphire rim of sky. He had observed the continents in their nights and days as he rounded her: Africa, whence man came; Asia, where first he was more than a savage; Europe, where he outgrew myth and measured the stars; Australia, long-sought dream; Antarctica of the heroes. But he was happy that his last sight as he drove starward was of America, where the law was first written that all men are free.

Doubts and fears, even homesickness, had fallen away. He was committed now, and joy dwelt within him.

'Stations report condition satisfactory,' Penoyer announced after a while.

'Very good. Carry on.' Heim found the intercom and called the steward's department. 'Endre? D'you have things in hand so they can get along without you for a spell? ... Okay, come onto the bridge. And bring your guitar. We'll want a song or two.'

The Magyar's voice was troubled. 'Captain, have you been listening to Parliament?'

'Uh ... no. Too busy. Good Lord, they started fresh more than an hour ago, didn't they?'

'Yes. We're picking up the beam to Mars. I have watched and – well, they did not let Coquelin delay. He tried, with a long introductory speech, and the chair ruled he must keep to the point. Then he tried to introduce the evidence about New Europe, and someone objected, and they decided to vote on whether that was germane now. The roll is still being called, but already he has a majority against him.'

'Oh-oh.' Heim was not shaken, on this day when he commanded anew a ship for Earth. But the need for action stabbed through his nerves. 'Mr. Penoyer,' he directed, 'signal for maximum acceleration and order all hands to emergency stations.'

The mate gulped and obeyed. 'Have Sparks shunt that debate to our 3V,' Heim went on. 'Mr. Vadász, please come to the bridge.' His chuckle was flat. 'Yes, bring your guitar.'

'What's the problem, sir?' Penoyer asked in unease.

'You'll see,' Heim replied. 'France is about to throw a nuke into the whole machine. Our plan was to have *Fox* well away by then. Now we'll need luck as well as brains and beauty.'

The screen flickered to fuzzy motion. Coquelin was nearly drowned out by the risen rumble of engines. Earth dwindled among the stars and Luna's pocked face grew nearer.

'—this assembly is determined to give my country not one centimeter. As you like, ladies and gentlemen. I wished to say this gradually, for the blow is heavy at best. Now you must hear me whether you are ready or not.'

The camera zoomed so close that Coquelin's visage filled the screen. That was a lousy trick, Heim thought. But, if he wasn't letting his own prejudices hoodwink him, this time it didn't work. Instead of underscoring every blemish – warts, moles, hairs, wrinkles – the close-up showed anger and unbreakable strength. Heim believed himself confirmed when the view moved back after a minute, to make Coquelin another man shuffling papers on a lectern.

66

'Mr. President, honorable delegates—' The translation could only suggest how the voice shifted, became the dry detached recital of an attorney making a technical point. 'The Federation was founded and still exists to end the tragic anarchy that prevailed among nations before, to bring them under a law that serves the good of all. Now law cannot endure without equal justice. The popularity of an argument must be irrelevant. Only the lawful cause may be admitted. In the name of France, I therefore advance the following points.

'1. The Constitution forbids each member nation to keep armed forces above the police level or to violate the territorial integrity of any other member nation in any way. To enforce this, the Peace Control Authority is vested with the sole military power. It may and must take such measures as are necessary to stop aggressive acts, including conspiracy to commit such acts. The individuals responsible must be arrested and brought to trial before the World Court.

'2. The naval branch of the Authority has been used beyond the Solar System, albeit only in relatively minor actions to suppress insurrection and riot or to protect the lives and property of humans on distant planets. By authorizing such action, and by negotiating agreements with various aliens, the Federation has *de facto* and *de jure* assumed the posture with respect to non-human societies that was traditional between governments on Earth prior to the Constitution. Hence Earth as a whole is a sovereign state with the lawful prerogative of self-defense.

'3. By attacking New Europe and subsequently occupying it, Alerion has committed an act of territorial aggression.

'4. If Alerion is not regarded as a sovereign state, negotiation of this dispute is legally impossible, and the Authority is required to take military measures against what can only be considered banditry.'

A roar went through the hall. Fazil banged his desk. Coquelin waited, sardonicism playing over his mouth. When order had been restored, the spokesman of France said:

'Evidently this assembly does consider Alerion to be sovereign like Earth. So, to proceed—

'5. If Alerion is indeed a legitimate state, then by the preamble to the Constitution it belongs to the family of nations.

Therefore it must be regarded as either (a) obliged to refrain from territorial aggression on pain of military sanctions, or (b) not so obliged, since it is not a member of the Federation.

'6. In case (a), Alerion is automatically subject to military sanctions by the Peace Control Authority. But in case (b), the Authority is also required, by the Constitution and by past precedent, to safeguard the interests of individual humans and of member states of the Federation. Note well, the *Authority* has that obligation. Not this honorable assembly, not the World Court, but the Peace Control Authority, whose action must under the circumstances be of a military nature.

'7. Accordingly, in either case an automatic state of war now exists between Alerion and the World Federation.'

Chaos broke loose.

Vadász had come in. He watched the scene for a time, as hundreds stood booing or cheering or screaming to be recognized, before he murmured: 'Is that not a weak point there?'

'No,' said Heim. 'Remember the Moslem League case. Also, I reread the Constitution, and it's quite clear. Of course, it helps that the thing was written before we'd met any non-humans comparable to us.' He turned to the mate. 'Radar reports?'

'Eh? Oh – oh, yes. A large craft about 10,000 kilometers starboard high, vector roughly like ours.'

'Damn! That'd be one of the Navy units, pulled in to guard Earth. Well, we'll have to see what happens.' Heim ignored the mob scene on the 3V, rested his eyes on the cold serenity of the Milky Way and thought that this, at least, would endure.

Somehow quiet was enforced. Coquelin waited until the silence had become deathly. He raised another typewritten sheet and resumed in the same parched tone:

'8. In the event of territorial aggression, member states of the Federation are required to give every appropriate assistance to the Peace Control Authority, in the name of the Federation.

'9. In the judgment of France, this imposes an inescapable duty to provide armed assistance to the colonists of New Europe. However, a member of the Federation is prohibited the manufacture or possession of nuclear weapons.

'10. There is no prohibition on individuals obtaining such weapons outside the Solar System for themselves, provided that they do not bring them back to the Solar System.

'11. Nor is there any prohibition on the unilateral authorization by a member state of the Federation of a *private* military expedition which so outfits itself. We grant that privateers were formerly required to be citizens of the country whose flag they flew, and that this might conflict with the national disarmament law. We grant also that eventually the issuance of letters of marque and reprisal was banned, by the Declaration of Paris in 1856. But while such treaties remain binding on their signatories, including France, they are not binding on the Federation as a whole, which is not a signatory and indeed has members such as the United States of America which never were signatories. And we have seen that the Federation is a sovereign state, possessing all rights and responsibilities not explicitly waived.

'12. Therefore the Federation has the unrestricted right to issue letters of marque and reprisal.

'13. Therefore, and in view of paragraphs 7, 8, and 9, France has the right and the duty to issue letters of marque and reprisal in the name of the Federation.

'France has done so.'

The 3V shrieked – more faintly each minute, as *Fox II* accelerated outward and outward. When she lost the Mars beam and reception ended, the racket in the Capitol had not yet subsided.

Penoyer said, 'Whew! What's next?'

'An interminable debate,' Heim said. 'Coquelin will fight for every comma. Meanwhile nothing can be done about jellyfishing to Alerion. Hopefully, the people with guts will see they aren't beaten at the outset, will rally round and – I don't know.'

'But us?'

'Maybe we can escape before someone realizes who that French privateer must be. Not that they can legally stop us without an Admiralty warrant; and you know how long that takes to get. But a nuclear shell is kind of final, and whoever fires it will have powerful friends in court.'

Vadász strummed his guitar and began to sing softly:

'*Morgenrot, Morgenrot*—' Heim wondered what that was, until he remembered the old, old Austrian cavalry song:

> *Morning red, morning red,*
> *Wilt thou shine upon me dead?*
> *Soon the trumpets will be blowing,*
> *Then must I to death be going,*
> *I and many trusty friends!*—

But it wasn't really sad, it had been chorused by troops of young merry men as they galloped with sunlight wild on banners and lances.

He laughed aloud. 'Hey! An idea. There were exactly thirteen points in Coquelin's speech. I wonder if he did that on purpose?'

None answered, except the plangent strings. He gave himself to thoughts . . . Lisa, Connie, Madelon, Jocelyn. . . . Earth and Moon lay far behind.

'PCA-SN *Neptune* to cruiser *Fox II*. Come in, *Fox II*.'

The voice rocketed them from their seats. 'Judas,' Penoyer whispered, 'that's a blastship.'

Heim checked the radar tapes. 'The one paralleling us. She's gone to an interception course. And if they use English on us, when we've got a French registry, they know—' He bit his lip and settled before the com relay console. '*Fox II* to *Neptune*,' he said. 'We read you. The master speaking. What's on your mind? Over.'

'This is Rear Admiral Ching-Kuo, commanding *Neptune*. Cease acceleration and stand by to be boarded. Over.'

Sickness fountained in Heim. 'What do you mean?' he blustered. 'We have clearance. Over.'

'You are suspected of illegal intentions. You are ordered to return to Earth orbit. Over.'

'Have you a warrant? Over.'

'I will show you my authorization when I board, Captain. Over.'

'That'll be too late, if you don't have any. Establish video contact and show me now. Otherwise I am not bound to obey. Over.'

'Captain,' said Ching-Kuo, 'I have my orders. If you do not follow instructions, I shall be forced to fire on you. Over.'

Heim's gaze flew among the stars. *No, no, no, not this! Another hour and we'd have been away!*

One hour!

A flaring went through him. 'You win, Admiral,' he said; it sounded like a stranger talking. 'Under protest, I yield. Give us time to compute a velocity-matching vector and we'll meet you. Over and out.'

He slammed down the switch and opened the intercom to the engine room. 'Captain to chief engineer,' he said. 'Are you there?'

'Indeed,' Uthg-a-K'thaq belched. 'All is satiswactory.'

'No. Somebody's uncorked the bottle on hell. There's a blast-ship which says if we don't stop and surrender, he'll shoot. Prepare for Mach drive.'

'Captain!' Penoyer yelled. 'This deep in the sun's field?'

'If the sync is perfect, we can do it,' Heim said. 'If not ... we're dead, no more. Uthg-a-K'thaq, do you believe we can?'

'*Gwurru!* What a thing to ask!'

'You overhauled those engines yourself,' Heim said. 'I trust you.'

Vadász's guitar shouted at his back.

For a moment the intercom bore only the throb of machines. Then: 'Cawtain, I am not God. Wut I think the chance is good for us. And I trust you.'

Heim opened the general intercom. 'Now hear this,' he said; music raged around the words. 'All hands stand by for Mach drive.'

Penoyer clenched his fists. 'Aye, aye, sir.'

The drone from aft rose until it was the noise of gales and great waters. Space twisted. Stars danced in the viewports.

Long ago, Ernst Mach of Austria ('*Morgenrot, Morgenrot*—') had held the key. Nothing exists in isolation. Inertia has no meaning without an inertial frame of reference: which must be the entire universe. Einstein showed inertial and gravitational mass are the same. But as for the phenomena themselves— Gravitation is describable by equations of a warped space. Inertia is, then, an inductive effect of the cosmic gravitational field on mass. If your gravitrons can bend space, not the small amount needed for lift and thrust, but through a closed curve, your ship has no resistance to accelerative force. Theoretically, you can go as fast as you like. There are no more boundaries.

Neptune fired. The missile lagged by a million kilometers. Her captain yammered for instrument readings. Perhaps, oh,

71

surely, surely, his prey had been torn apart by the forces generated with imperfect mesh of space curvatures here where the sun's power was still all-dominant. Nothing registered, no wreckage, no trace, except the howl of hydrogen atoms flung in bow wave and wake by a ship outpacing light. He dared not pursue.

Heim straightened. One by one, he eased his muscles. 'Well,' he said, 'we got away with it.' The words were poor for the victory within him. Vadász was doing better:

> *'Glory, glory, hallelujah!*
> *Glory, glory, hallelujah!*
> *Glory, glory, hallelujah!*
> *And we are outward bound!'*

Part Two

ARSENAL PORT

CHAPTER ONE

WHEN the Earth ship came, Gunnar Heim was bargaining with a devil-winged messenger from a nuclear smithy. The Aerie of Trebogir, for which Ro spoke, had weapons to sell; but there were conditions.

Non-human words hissed and whistled into the man's helmet pickup. Gregorios Koumanoudes translated into English. '—missile gets so large an initial velocity by drawing on the ship's own gravitrons for a launch impetus.'

Heim wished he could show horse-trader reluctance, as by thoughtfully scratching his head. But it would look silly under present circumstances. Damn this need to wear airsuits! Even on the lift platform where he stood, which kept his weight Earth normal, and even with the strength of a two-meter-tall body which he had gotten back into first-class condition on the voyage hither, the mass of equipment he must carry was tiring. Originally he had planned to stay inboard, put a 3V two-way outside *Connie Girl*, and thus meet with the Staurni; but Koumanoudes warned him against it. 'They'll respect you more, Captain, for coming out into their own environment,' the Greek had said. 'Irrational, sure, but they make a big thing of physical toughness. And they'll give a better deal to someone they respect.'

So – Heim scowled into harsh blue sunlight. 'I see the advantage,' he answered. 'However, with my own maneuvering handicapped, I'd be a sitting duck.'

Koumanoudes put his objection into the language that prevails between Kimreth heights and the Iron Sea. Ro spread his taloned hands, a startlingly humanlike gesture. 'The loss of maneuverability is negligible,' he said, 'as only a fractional second is needed for launch. Thereafter one immediately has full accelerative power available again. To be sure, the system must be synchronized with the engine complex, but it should not take long to make the necessary modifications on your ship.'

Unconsciously, Heim glanced skyward. Somewhere beyond that deep purple vault, those icily blue-tinged clouds, *Fox II* swung in orbit around Staurn; tenders flitted back and forth with cargoes of hell, men and notmen swarmed over the cruiser, working together to fit her for war. There was not much left to do. And every nerve in him throbbed to be away. Each day he spent here, Alerion grew stronger, the cause of men on New Europe more hopeless.

Still, one privateer, raiding in the Phoenix, was dreadfully alone. She needed any microscopic advantage he could find for her. Like this missile sling which Ro claimed they could make in the Aerie of Trebogir. It did sound promising. ...
'How long to install?' Heim asked.

Again four claw fingers, set around the entire palm of the hand, gestured. 'Some days. One cannot tell exactly without more knowledge than my kinfather's technologists possess about vessels of your particular class. May I suggest that the captain send his honored chief engineer to discuss such matters with our folk?'

'Um-m-m.' Heim considered. His gaze went past Ro, to Galveth, who waited impassively for something to be said that might concern the Lodge. But the blast gun remained idly cradled in the observer's arms. If Galveth had any expression, it was of sleepiness, his yellow eyes drooping. A human could never be sure, though, what went on in the narrow Staurni skulls.

It was even hard to tell individuals apart. A common alienness outweighed variable details. Ro and Galveth were each about three meters long; but half of that was in the thick, rudder-tipped tail, on whose double coil the legless torso sat. The keelbone jutted like a prow. The face was sharp-muzzled, with wolfishly fanged mouth and small round ears. Its mask appearance came less from the dark band across the eyes than from the nostrils being hidden under the chin. A gray growth, neither hair nor feathers but something in between, covered the entire hide. No clothes were worn except two pouched belts crossing from shoulder to waist. All was overshadowed by the immense chiropteran wings, seven meters in span.

When you looked closely, you saw differences, mainly that Galveth had grown lean and frosty-tinged while Ro was still

74

in the fierceness of youth. And Galveth wore the gold-ornamented harness reserved for Lodge members, Ro the red-and-black geometry of Trebogir's pattern.

Heim turned to Koumanoudes. 'What do you think?' he asked.

The stocky man shrugged. 'I'm no engineer.'

'But damnation, you and Wong have spent a couple of months here. You must have some notion who's honest and competent, who isn't.'

'Oh, that. Sure. Trebogir isn't one of the robber barons. He has a good name. You can deal with him.'

'Okay.' Heim reached a decision. 'Tell this messenger, then, that I am interested. I'll call C.E. down from *Fox* as soon as possible – right now he's got to help the contractor from the Hurst of Wenilwain install our fire-control computers – and we'll come to the Aerie and talk further about the proposal.'

'You can't be that blunt,' Koumanoudes said. 'Lodge members are, but they're different. A Nester is worse than an Arab or a Japanese for wanting flowery language.' He turned and began to form syllables.

Through the wind that rustled the low red-leaved forest surrounding the spaceport, through the beat of surf a kilometer distant, a sudden whine smote. It grew, became thunderous, the heavy air was split and a shadow fell across concrete field and lava-block buildings. Every head swung up.

A rounded cylinder was descending. The blue-white radiance was savage off its metal; spots danced before Heim's eyes when he turned them away. But he recognized the make. The heart jumped in his breast. 'A spaceship! Human built— What's going on?'

'I ... don't ... know.' Behind the dark faceplate, Koumanoudes' big-nosed countenance harshened. 'Nobody said a word. Galveth!' He rattled off a question.

The Lodge agent made a bland reply. 'He says he didn't think it mattered,' Koumanoudes translated.

'Blaze,' Heim said in anger, 'he knows about the Aleriona crisis! He must have at least some inkling of our trouble with our own government. The Lodge must've stopped that ship for inspection no later than yesterday. Why haven't we been warned?'

'I'm not sure how much the Staurni ever understood,' Koumanoudes said. 'To them it's ridiculous that we couldn't arm ourselves at home and take off whenever we wanted. Besides, those people can't have any real weapons along, or they wouldn't've been allowed to land.'

'They can have small arms,' Heim snapped. 'We do. Get rid of these bucks as fast as you can, Greg, and come inboard. I've got to alert the boys.'

He strode rapidly across the platform to the landing ramp and up to the airlock. There he must fume while pumps replaced the atmosphere of Staurn with something he could breathe, and while he himself was decompressed. The baffled rage that he had thought was left behind on Earth came back to possess him. So much could have happened in the couple of weeks that *Fox II* had needed to cross the hundred-odd light-years to this star, or in the three weeks that followed while she was being refitted. If the appeasement party had won out, if his privateering venture had been declared illegal—

Of course, he told himself, over and over, *that's not a Federation Navy ship. She's a small civilian ranger. But then, the Staurni don't let any warcraft but their own near this planet. If she's simply bringing an official order for me to come home— Well, all right, face the question: what then? Do I go on anyway – as a pirate?*

Sickly: *Wouldn't be much use. The hope was to create a situation that Earth could take advantage of. If Earth refuses the chance and disowns us, we can only be troublemakers to Alerion, until at last we're cornered and killed. I'll never see Lisa again.* It was as if once more he could feel a small body pressed against him in farewell. *They'll tell her, the whole rest of her life, her father was a criminal.*

But maybe, maybe even a pirate could accomplish something. There was Drake of the Golden Hind— *He sailed in another day, when men weren't afraid.*

The inner door opened. He moved on into his yacht, which was now an auxiliary for the starship, and opened his helmet.

Endre Vadász had the bridge. The minstrel's thin dark face was turned outward, staring through the viewport as the other vessel neared in a gravitron-distorted shimmer of light. When Heim's boots rang on the deck, he didn't look around, but said tonelessly, 'I have ordered the crew into battle gear, and brought your own rifle from your cabin.'

'Good man.' Heim took the weapon in the crook of an arm. There was assurance in that weight and solidity and beautiful deadly shape. It was a .30-caliber Browning cyclic, able to send forty rounds a minute through any atmosphere or none, the pride of his collection. Vadász, also in a collapsed airsuit with faceplate unlocked, had settled for a laser pistol.

'I am not certain,' the Hungarian remarked, 'what six men can do if they try to storm us. Yonder ship can easily hold five times as many.'

'We can stand 'em off till the boys arrive from *Fox*,' Heim said, 'and they total almost a hundred. Assuming the Lodge doesn't stop the fight.'

'Oh, that I doubt,' Vadász murmured with a slight smile. 'We aren't likely to damage their nice spaceport, and from everything I hear, they have no rules against bloodshed.' He pointed to several winged shapes, wheeling black against the clouds over the western end of Orling Island. 'They'll come enjoy the spectacle.'

Heim directed the radioman to get in touch with *Fox*. It would take a while. The beam must go through a ground station and a couple of relay satellites. Wong was in orbit to interpret between human and native workers, while Sparks's command of the language was slight. And the newcomer would be down in another minute.

I'm borrowing trouble, Heim tried to believe. *Yet why would any Terrestrial come here, except in connection with me?*

To trade? Yes, yes, an occasional merchant does call, from Earth or Naqsa or one of the other spacefaring worlds. That's why the weaponmakers of Staurn will accept my Federation credits. But surely not while the Aleriona trouble is so near explosion.

Beside him, Vadász was softly whistling. 'The Blue Danube,' now of all times? Well, maybe he wanted to remember, while he still could. . . .

The least quiver ran through ground and hull and Heim's bones as the stranger touched jacks to concrete. Her shadow fell engulfingly over *Connie Girl*. Through the intercom he heard a few oaths from his men, Sparks's mumble at the transmitter, the snore of a nuclear engine on Stand-by. A ventilator gusted air across his cheeks, which were sweating.

When Koumanoudes clumped in, Heim spun about with a jerkiness that revealed to him how tense he was. 'So?' the captain barked. 'Did you get any information?'

The Greek looked relieved. 'I think we can free-fall, sir. According to Galveth, they want to stay awhile, look around, and ask questions. A xenological expedition, in other words.'

'To this planet?' Heim scoffed.

'Well, after all, we are in Hydrus,' Vadász pointed out. 'The trouble is going on in the Phoenix. Quite some distance from here.'

'No further from The Eith than Alpha Eridani,' Heim said, 'where we had our biggest skirmish with the Aleriona. And that was many years ago. They're prowling through this whole sector. Besides, it takes time to organize an expedition. Why didn't we hear of it on Earth?'

'We were rather occupied,' Vadász said dryly. He went to the radiophone. 'Shall I try to call them?'

'What? ... Oh, yes. Of course.' Heim swore at himself for forgetting so simple an act.

The connection was made at once. 'MDS *Quest* of the U.S.A.,' said a mild young man. 'Captain Gutierrez is still busy, sir, but I can switch you to Dr. Bragdon. He's the head of the scientific team.'

The release was like a blow. Heim sagged in his suit. 'You're only here to make studies, then?'

'Yes, sir, for the University of Hawaii, under contract to the Federation Research Authority. One moment, please.'

The screen flickered to a view of a cabin, crowded with references both full-size and micro. The man in the foreground was also young, husky, with black hair and cragged profile. 'Victor Bragdon speaking,' he said, and then, his mouth falling open, 'Good heavens! Aren't you Gunnar Heim?'

The privateer captain didn't reply. His own astonishment was too much. The woman behind Bragdon leaned over the man's shoulder and met Heim's stare with wide hazel eyes. She was tall; an informal gray zipsuit clung to a figure strong and mature. Her face had strength too, rather than conventional good looks: straight nose, wide mouth, arching bones, framed by curly chestnut hair. But some years back it had troubled his sleep. When he saw the name Jocelyn Lawrie on the letterhead of a flyer from World Militants for Peace, an old hurt awakened, and he went on still more intensely with his preparations for war.

Surprise faded. Suspicion tightened his muscles. 'What are you doing here?' he rapped.

CHAPTER TWO

AFTERWARD he remembered with irony and sadness how careful he had been. Pleading an urgent requirement for his presence on *Fox II*, he raised his yacht within the hour. But Koumanoudes volunteered to stay behind, aboard the *Quest* on a 'courtesy call'. Heim knew the Greek had done a good job of preliminary arrangement-making on Staurn; how good he would be with his fellow humans was uncertain, but there was scant choice. It had to be him or Wong, the only ones who spoke the local language fluently and hence could use the spaceport's eavesdrop-proof maser line.

His report came after two watches. 'They're clean, skipper. I was toured around the whole ship and talked to everybody. There're five in the crew, plus captain, mate, and C.E. They're plain spacehands, who signed on for this cruise the same as they would for any other exploratory trip. You can't fake that. Anybody who's so good an actor works on 3V, not in the black.'

'They don't have to act,' Heim said. 'They only have to wear a poker face.'

'But these bucks didn't. They swarmed over me, asking every kind of question about us. On the whole, they thought we had a hell of a fine idea here. A couple of them wished they'd joined us.'

'Uh-huh. I'm not surprised. The common man often shows more common sense than the intellectual elite. But wait, now, do you include their officers in this?'

'The engineer, yes. Captain Gutierrez and the first officer ... well, they were stiff as meteorite plating. I don't know what they think. Probably they don't like us on principle, figure war should be left to the regular Navy. But I did make an excuse to see the articles of the expedition. It's bona fide, official papers and everything.'

'How about the scientific passengers?'

'A mixed bag. I think Bragdon and Mrs. Lawrie must be the only ones who've ever been out of the Solar System. There's another xenologist, a semanticist, a glossanalyst, a biologist, and half a dozen graduate students to help. I gather none have visited Staurn before.'

'Odd.'

'Charlie Wong and I hadn't either, boss, when you sent us off. They did the same as us, boned up on what information was available and learned the main language with RNA-electro cramming, en route. Anyhow, I can tell you there's nothing to fear from these academic types. I don't think any but Bragdon can handle a gun. They don't much care for us and what we stand for, so relationships were a tad strained even if nothing rude got said. But they're no threat.'

'They all feel this way?' Heim asked, with a curious little sinking in his spirit.

'No, funny thing, Bragdon and Mrs. Lawrie were both friendly. He remarked once he disagrees with your ideas but has a lot of respect for your guts. And she said she hopes you can come back soon.'

'I can,' Heim said softly. 'Oh, I can.'

An hour later, *Connie* accelerated planetward.

Seated on the bridge, Heim listened to the thrum of the yacht and his own pulse, underlying the flamenco that leaped from Vadász's guitar beside him. For a while neither man spoke, nor did their eyes leave the spectacle in the viewports.

Two and a fifth times the diameter of Earth, nine and a half times the mass, Staurn rolled immense against darkness. The seas shone royal blue, the continents, blurred by snow-colored cloud bands, were ocher and cinnabar. Along the horizon, atmosphere made a violent rim; over the whole, under the irradiation of a hot F5 sun, ran a fluorescence which near the poles became great banners of aurora, shaken aloft into space. Two moons were visible beyond, glacially luminous, and further yet there glittered strange constellations.

'When I see something like that,' Heim murmured at length, half to himself, 'I wonder.'

Vadász stopped playing and cocked a birdlike glance at him. 'What do you wonder?'

'Why the hell we waste time hating and killing, which we might use to— Argh, never mind.' Heim got out his pipe. 'It only takes one to make a quarrel.'

Vadász studied him. 'I've come to know you somewhat well, Gunnar,' he said. 'You are not given to the role of Hamlet. What is the real trouble?'

'Nothing!'

'Ah. Excuse me if I pry, but this whole enterprise depends on you. Is it the lady's unexpected arrival that is so disturbing?'

'A surprise, no more. We used to be friends.' Heim became busy loading his pipe. The Magyar's steady look forced him to explain further. 'My wife and I had quite a bit to do with the Lawries, years ago. They went off to Ourania in the Epsilon Indi System shortly before Connie died, to establish a machine-tool factory in the colony there. Things can't have worked out too well, because she came back last year, divorced. The conflict with Alerion was already serious, even if they hadn't yet attacked New Europe, and she became active in the peace movement. It had her shuttling around the world, so we only met again a few times, briefly, at large loud parties. I, uh, half doubted she'd speak to me now, after what I've done.'

'And are pleasantly amazed, eh? She is indeed attractive. You must find her especially so.'

'What do you mean?' Heim bridled.

'Oh ...' Vadász's grin was disarming. 'One does not wish to get too personal. However, Gunnar, busy though you were, I felt you were mistaken not to, um, prepare yourself for a long cruise in strictly male society.'

Heim grinned back. 'I'd trouble enough concocting stories to explain your absences. How could I tell Lisa her hero was out tomcatting?'

'Touché!' Vadász went tomato red and attacked his guitar with great vigor.

But he has a point, maybe, Heim thought. *I could have — well, Connie would've understood. The way she understood about Jocelyn. Lord knows there've been other women since— Maybe I was thinking too hard about Madelon on New Europe. Damned foolishness. Or— I don't know, I'm all confused.*

That was what he remembered, afterward.

—His finger was not quite steady when he pressed the button on her door. She opened it while the chime was still sounding. 'Gunnar,' she said, and took both his hands. 'I'm so glad you could come.'

'You were nice to invite me,' he said.

'Nonsense. When two old friends meet again, half-way between home and the Southern Cross, what else do they do but have a private gabfest? Come in, man.'

The door closed behind them. He looked around. Her cabin was large and comfortable, and she had made it her own. He

81

recognized some things from her lost San Francisco home – a Matisse and a Hiroshige reproduction, some worn volumes of Catullus, Yeats, Tagore, Pasternak, Mosunić-Lopez, the flute he had once loved to hear her play – and there were a few souvenirs of her years in the Epsilon Indi System, less from Ourania than from stark New Mars. His attention returned to her and stayed. She had on an electric blue dress and a Gean necklace of massive silver. The outfit was at once quiet and stunning. Or was that simply the contents?

Whoa, boy! he checked himself. Aloud: 'You haven't changed.'

'Liar. But thanks.' Her eyes dwelt on him. 'You have, anyway. Tired and bitter.'

'Why, no, I feel happier now than—' His protest was cut off. She let his hands go and went to a table where bottles and ice stood.

'Let's do something about it,' she said. 'As I recall, you're a Scotch drinker. And here's some sho-nuff Glenlivet.'

'Eh? You always preferred light wine.'

'Well, Vic – Dr. Bragdon, you know – he shares your taste, and very kindly gave us this from his locker.' She poured. For a moment the clear gurgle was the only sound in the universe.

What the devil right have I to feel jealous? 'I'm not sure what, uh, you're doing out here with him.'

'Officially I'm secretary to the expedition. I have such skills from my job before I married, and got the rust off them working for the peace movement. Then too, I've had experience on other planets, including planets where you need special equipment to live. I used to go to New Mars quite often, ostensibly with Edgar's mineral prospectors, actually to get away— No matter. That's past. When I heard about this expedition, I applied for a berth and, rather to my surprise, got it. I suppose that was partly because most qualified people were scared to come so near the big bad Aleriona, partly because Vic knew me and felt I could handle it.' She handed him a glass and raised her own. 'Welcome aboard, Gunnar. Here's to the old days.'

They clinked rims, wordless.

'When life was simple and splendid,' she added. Tossing off a sip of her Chablis, she toasted again, defiantly. 'And here's to the future. We'll make it the same.'

'Well, let's hope so.' His mouth creased upward. She'd always

been overly dramatic, but his own stolidity had found it a trai
more endearing than otherwise.

'Sit down.' She waved him to her lounger, but he took a
chair instead. Jocelyn chuckled and relaxed in the form-fitting
seat. 'Now,' she said, 'tell me about yourself.'

'Didn't you get a bellyful of me in the news?'

'There sure was plenty.' She clicked her tongue. 'The entir
Solar System in an uproar. Half the people wanted to hang you
and H-bomb France for commissioning you. The rest—' Her
humor waned. 'I hadn't known there was so much popular support for your side of the issue. Your departure crystallized it,
somehow.'

He gathered his nerve and said, 'Frankly, that's what I
hoped. One decisive gesture, to cut through that wretched
muddle. . . . Okay, you can throw me out.'

'No, Gunnar. Never.' She leaned over and patted his hand. 'I
think you're wrong, horribly wrong, but I never doubted you
mean well.'

'Same for you, of course. Wish I could say likewise for some
of your associates. And mine, I must admit. I don't like having
the approval of some pretty nasty fanatics.'

'Nor I. The Militants – I quit them when they started openly
applauding mob violence.'

'They tried to blackmail me through my daughter,' he said.

'Oh, Gunnar!' Her clasp tightened over his knuckles. 'And I
never came to see you while she was missing. There was this
work for the movement, way off on Venus, and by the time I
got back and heard, everything was finished and you were gone.
But . . . are you serious? Did Yore's people really—'

'I fixed that,' he said. ' 'Druther not say any more. We had to
keep it out of the news. I'm glad, Joss, you broke with them.'

'Not with what they meant in the beginning, though,' she
said. Tears glimmered suddenly in the long hazel eyes; he wondered on whose account. 'Another reason I wanted to get off
Earth. Everything was such a ghastly mess, no clear rights or
wrongs anyplace you searched.' She drew a breath before continuing, with swift earnestness:

'But can't you see what harm the French have done? It
looked as if the dispute with Alerion could be settled peace-
fully. Now the peacemakers have been tied in a legal knot, and
it's all they can do to prevent the extremists from taking over
control of Parliament. The Aleriona delegation announced they

weren't going to wait any longer. They went home. We'll have to send for them when our deadlock is broken.'

'Or come after them, if it breaks *my* way,' he said. 'What you can't see, you won't see, is that they've no intention of making any real peace. They want Earth out of space altogether.'

'Why?' she pleaded. 'It doesn't make sense!'

He frowned into his glass. 'That's something of a puzzle, I admit. It must make sense in their own terms; but they don't think like us. Look at the record, however, not their soft words but their hard deeds ever since we first encountered them. Including the proof that they deliberately attacked New Europe and are deliberately setting out to exterminate the French colonists there. Your faction denied the evidence; but be honest with yourself, Joss.'

'You be honest too, Gunnar— No, look at me. What can a single raider do but make the enmity worse? There aren't going to be any more privateers, you realize. France and her allies have been able to keep Parliament from illegalizing your expedition, so far. But the Admiralty has frozen all transfers of ships, and it'll take more of a legislative upheaval than France can engineer to get that authority out of its hands. You'll die out there, Gunnar, alone, for nothing.'

'I'm hoping the Navy will move,' he said. 'If, as you put it, I make enmity worse— Uh-uh, not a delusion of grandeur. Just a hope. But a man has to do what little he can.'

'So does a woman,' she sighed.

Abruptly, sweeping to her feet, taking his glass for a refill, smiling with an effort but not as a pretense: 'No more argument. Let's be only ourselves this evening. It's been such a long time.'

'Sure has. I wanted to see you, I mean really see you, when you came back to Earth, but we were both too busy, I guess. Somehow the chance never seemed to come.'

'Too busy, because too stupid,' she agreed. 'Real friends are so rare at best. And we were that once, weren't we?'

'Rawthuh,' he said, as anxious as she to walk what looked like a safe road. 'Remember our junket to Europe?'

'How could I forget?' She gave him back his glass and sat down again, but upright this time, so that her knee brushed his, 'That funny little old tavern in Amsterdam, where you kept bumping your head every time you stood up, till finally you borrowed a policeman's helmet to wear. And you and Edgar roared out something from the Edda, and— But you were both awfully sweet outside Sacre Coeur, when we necked and watched the sun rise over Paris.'

'You girls were a lot sweeter, believe me,' he said, not quite comfortably. A silence fell. 'I'm sorry it didn't last between you and him,' he ventured.

'We made a mistake, going outsystem,' she admitted. 'By the time we realized how much the environment had chewed our nerves, it was too late. He's got himself quite a good wife now.'

'Well, that's something.'

'What about you, Gunnar? It was so dreadful about poor Connie. But after five years, haven't you—?'

'After five years, nothing,' he said flatly. 'I don't know why.'

She withdrew herself a little and asked with much gentleness, 'I dare not flatter myself, but could I be to blame?'

He shook his head. His face burned. 'No. That was over with long ago. Let's discuss something else.'

'Sure. This is supposed to be a merry reunion. *A nuestra salud.*' The glasses clinked again.

She began to talk of things past, and presently he was chiming in, the trivia that are so large a part of friendship – do you remember, whatever became of, we did, once you said, we thought, do you remember, and then there was, we hoped, I never knew that, do you remember, do you remember? – and the time and the words and the emptied glasses passed, and finally somehow she was playing her flute for him, 'Au Clair de la Lune' and 'Gaudeamus Igitur', 'September' and 'Shenandoah', Pan-notes bright and cool through the whirl in him, while he had moved to the lounger and lay back watching the light burnish her hair and lose itself in the deep shadows below. But when she began 'The Skrydstrup Girl'

> *'Was it her that I ought to have loved, then,*
> *In a stone age's blossoming spring—'*

the flute sank to her lap and he saw her eyes shut and her mouth go unfirm.

'No,' she said. 'I'm sorry. Wasn't thinking. You taught it to me, Gunnar.'

He sat straight and laid a clumsily tender hand on her shoulder. 'Forget that business,' he said. 'I should've kept my big mouth shut. But there was no real harm done. It was no more than ... than one of those infatuations. Connie didn't hold it against you. She nursed me through the spell okay.'

'I wasn't so lucky,' she whispered.

Dumbfounded, he could only stammer: 'Joss, you never let on!'

'I didn't dare. But that was the real reason I talked Edgar into leaving Earth. I hoped— Gunnar, when I came back, why were we both such idiots?'

Then suddenly she laughed, low in her throat, came to him and said, 'We're not too late, are we? Even now?'

CHAPTER THREE

STAURN rotated once in about eighteen hours. Seven such days had passed when Uthg-a-K'thaq finished work on the naval computers and rode a tender down to Orling spaceport.

As his huge cetacean form wallowed into the yacht's chartroom, Endre Vadász, who had been waiting for him, backed up. *Phew!* the minstrel thought. *Decent and capable he is, but I always have to get reacclimated to that swamp stench. . . . How do I smell to him?*

'Hallo, C.E.,' he greeted. 'I hope you are not too tired to depart at once. We have spent too much time here already.'

'Quite,' replied the rumbling, burbling voice. 'I am inwatient as you wy now. Ewerything else can 'roceed without me and, I weliewe, reach com'letion simultaneously with this swecial missile tur-ret. That is, iw the Staurni system is as good as claimed.'

'Which is what you are supposed to decide.' Vadász nodded. Another irritating thing about Naqsans was their habit of solemnly repeating the obvious. In that respect they were almost as bad as humans. 'Well, I've seen to your planetside supplies. Get your personal kit together and meet us at the lift platform outside in half an hour.'

'Us-s-s? Who goes to this Nest?'

'You and the skipper, of course, to make decisions, and Gregorios Koumanoudes to interpret. Myself ... ah, officially this falls in the steward's department also, since the extra armament

86

will affect stowage. But in practice the steward's department is idle, bored, and in dire need of a jaunt. Then there are two from the *Quest*, Victor Bragdon and Jocelyn Lawrie.'

'Why come they with?'

'They're here for xenological research, you know. Accompanying us on a business trip to an important kin-father is a unique opportunity to observe laws and customs in action. So Bragdon offered to lend us one of his flyers, provided he and the woman could ride along. He wanted several of his people, actually, but Nesters limit the number of visitors at one time. Suspicious brutes. In any event, by using the flyer, we save this yacht for shuttle work and so expedite our own project.'

'I scent. No, you say "I see" in English.' Uthg-a-K'thaq's tone was indifferent. He turned and slap-slapped on webbed feet towards his cabin.

Vadász looked thoughtfully at his back until he had disappeared. *I wonder how much of our interhuman quarrels and tensions come through to him*, the Hungarian reflected. *Perhaps none. Surely he will think the business between Gunnar and Jocelyn is utter triviation, if he even notices.*

And he may well be right. Thus far, at least, it has only amounted to Gunnar's being often absent from our vessel. Which has done no harm at the present stage of things. The men gossip, but the tone I hear is simple good-natured envy. For myself, I am the last to begrudge a friend what scrap of happiness he can stumble upon. Therefore – why does it make me uneasy, this?

He threw off worry and pushed buttons on the radiophone extension. A middle-aged, scholarly-looking man glared from *Quest*'s saloon.

'Good day, Dr. Towne,' Vadász said cheerily. 'Would you please remind Captain Heim that we're leaving in half an hour?'

'Let him remind himself,' the glossanalyst snapped.

'Do you so strongly oppose our little enterprise over here that you will not even give a man an intercom call?' Vadász leered. 'Then kindly remind Mme. Lawrie.'

Towne reddened and cut the circuit. He must have some very archaic mores indeed. Vadász chuckled and strolled off to complete his own preparations, whistling to himself.

'*Malbrouck se va-t-en guerre—*'

—And aboard the *Quest*, Heim looked at a bulkhead clock, stretched, and said, 'We'd better start.'

Jocelyn laid a hand on his roan hair, another beneath his chin, and brought the heavy-boned homely face around until it was close to hers. 'Do we have to?' she asked.

The trouble in those eyes hurt him. He tried to laugh. 'What, cancel this trip and lose Vic his data? He'd never forgive us.'

'He'd be nearly as happy as I. Because it's far more important that ... that you come out of this lunacy of yours, Gunnar.'

'My dear,' he said, 'the only thing that's marred an otherwise delightful time has been your trying and trying to wheedle me into giving up the raider project. You can't. In the old Chinese advice, why don't you relax and enjoy it?' He brushed his lips across hers.

She didn't respond, but left the bed and walked across the cabin. 'If I were young again,' she said bitterly, 'I might have succeeded.'

'Huh? No, now, look—'

'I am looking.' She had stopped before a full-length optex beside her dresser. Slowly, she ran her hands down cheeks and breasts and flanks. 'Oh, for forty-three I'm quite well preserved. But the crow's feet are there, and the beginnings of the double chin, and without clothes I sag. You've been – good, kind – the last few days, Gunnar. But I noticed you never committed yourself to anything.'

He swung to his own feet, crossed the intervening distance in two strides, and towered over her; then didn't know what to do next. 'How could I?' he settled for saying. 'I've no idea what may happen on the cruise. No right to make promises or—'

'You could make them conditionally,' she told him. The moment's despair had left her, or been buried. Her expression was enigmatic, her tone impersonal. ' "If I come home alive," you might say, "I'll do such and such, if you're agreeable." '

He had no words. After some seconds she breathed out and turned from him. Her head drooped. 'Well, let's get dressed,' she said.

He put on the one-piece garment which doubled as underpadding for an airsuit, his motions automatic, his mind awash. *Okay, what do I want? How much of what I felt (do I still feel it?) was genuine and how much was just a grab at the past when lonesomeness had me off balance?*

I plain don't know.

His bewilderment didn't last long, because he was the least self-analytical of men. He shoved his questions aside for later examination and, with them, most of the associated emotions. Affection for Jocelyn remained in the forefront of his awareness, along with regret that she had been hurt and a puzzled wish to do something about it; but overriding all else was eagerness to be away. He'd cooled his heels long enough on this island. The flight to Trebogir's would be a small unleashing.

'C'mon,' he said with reborn merriment. His hand slapped the woman playfully. 'Should be quite a trip, you know.'

She turned about. Grief dwelt in her eyes and on her lips. 'Gunnar—' She must look down at her fingers, tensed against each other. 'You really don't think I'm ... a fool at best, a traitor at worst ... for not wanting a war ... do you?'

'*Hvad for pokker!*' he exclaimed, rocked back. 'When did I give you that idea?'

She swallowed and found no reply.

He took her by the forearms and shook her gently. 'You are a fool if you think I ever thought so,' he said. 'Joss, I don't want war any more than you. I believe a show of force now – one warning snap of teeth – may head off a fatal showdown later. That's all. Okay, you have a different opinion. I respect it, and I respect you. What've I done to make you suppose anything different? Please tell me.'

'Nothing.' She straightened. 'I'm being silly,' she said in a machine voice. 'We'd better go.'

They went silently downhall. At the locker outside Boathouse Three, Victor Bragdon was donning his airsuit. 'Hi, there,' he called. 'I'd begun to wonder what was keeping you. One of your men delivered your stuff last watch, Gunnar. Good thing, too. You'd never fit into anybody else's.'

Heim took the stiff fabric, zipped it shut around himself, and put on gloves and ankle-supporting boots with close attention to the fastenings. If the oxygen inside mingled with the hydrogen outside, he'd be a potential torch. Of course, in a flyer it was only a precaution to wear a full outfit; but he'd seen too often how little of the universe is designed for man to neglect any safety measure. Connecting the helmet to high-pressure air bottles and recycler tank, he hung the rig from his shoulders, but left the valves closed and the faceplate open. Now, the belt of food bars and medicines; canteen; waste unit; not the machine pistol, for you did not come armed into a Nest. ...

89

He saw that Jocelyn was having some trouble with her gear and went to help.

'It's so heavy,' she complained.

'Why, you wore much the same type on New Mars,' Heim said.

'Yes, but that was under half an Earth gravity.'

'Be glad we aren't under the full Staurnian pull, then,' Bragdon said genially. He bent to pick up a carrying case.

'What've you got there?' Heim asked.

'Extra camera equipment. A last-minute thought. Don't get alarmed, though. The field survival kit is aboard and double checked.' Bragdon was still grinning as he walked to the entry lock. His aquiline profile was rather carefully turned towards Jocelyn. Heim felt amused.

The boathouse seemed cavernous. The space auxiliary intended to rest here had been replaced by three atmospheric flyers built for work on subjovian planets; and one of them was out on a preliminary mapping flight. The humans wriggled through the lock of another bulky fuselage and strapped in, with Bragdon at the controls. He phonespoke to his dispatcher. The boathouse was evacuated, Staurn's air was valved in, the outer doors were opened. With a whirr of power, the vehicle departed.

It set down again immediately, to let in Vadász, Koumanoudes, and Uthg-a-K'thaq. The Naqsan looked still more ungainly in his own airsuit than he did nude, but it confined most of his odor. Bragdon made a last check of his instruments and lifted skyward.

'I'm excited as a boy,' he said. 'This'll be the first real look I've had at the planet.'

'Well, you should be able to play tourist,' Koumanoudes said. 'No bad weather's predicted. 'Course, we wouldn't be aloft anyway in a Staurnian storm. Fee-rocious.'

'Indeed? I thought wind velocities were low in a high-density atmosphere.'

'Staurn's isn't that dense. About three times Earth pressure at sea level, with gravity accounting for a good deal of it. Also, you've got water vapor, which rises to breed thunderstorms. And so damn much solar energy.'

'What?' Jocelyn cast a surprised glance aft, not too near the morning sun. At half again the distance of Sol from Earth, the disc had slightly less angular diameter; and, while it was nearly twice as brilliant, throwing a raw blue-tinged light across the world, its total illumination was likewise a little inferior to home. 'No, that can't be. Staurn gets only – what is it? – 20 per cent more irradiation than Earth.'

'You forget how much of that is ultraviolet,' Heim reminded her, 'with no free oxygen to make an ozone barrier.'

'A poor site for a nudist colony,' Vadász said. 'If the hydrogen, helium, and nitrogen don't choke you, or the methane and ammonia poison you, the UV will crisp you like a steak.'

'Brrr. When it's so beautiful, too.' Jocelyn pressed her nose against the port by her seat and stared downward.

They were high now, with Orling dropping behind at supersonic speed. The island reared Gibraltar-like from an indigo sea, beaches obsidian black, land turned a thousand subtle shades of red by its forest. There was a final glimpse of a radar, skeletal at the spaceport, then that scar was lost to view and one saw only a great peace brooding under westward cliffs of cumulus. On the edge of vision, kilometers away, a flock of Staurni winged in a V on an unknown errand.

As if to escape some thought, Jocelyn pointed at them and said, 'Pardon me if I'm dumb, but how can they fly? I mean, aren't hydrogen breathers supposed to have less active metabolisms than oxygen breathers? And is the air pressure enough to support them against nearly twice Terrestrial gravity?'

'They have bird-type bones,' Koumanoudes explained.

'As for the energy consideration,' Heim added, 'it's true hydrogen gives less energy per mole than oxygen, reacting with carbon compounds. But there are an awful lot of hydrogen molecules in a lungful, here. Besides, the enzyme systems are efficient. And – well, look. Staurnian plants photosynthesize water and methane to get free hydrogen and carbohydrates. Animals reverse the process. Only with that flood of ultraviolet on them, the plants build compounds more energy-rich than anything on Earth.'

'I see, I suppose.' She relapsed into her brown study.

The island fell below the wide horizon. They flew over wine darkness, streaked with foam, until the mainland hove into sight. There mountains climbed and climbed, red with wilderness at the foot, gray and ruggedly shadowed above, snow-peaked at the top. Sunlight glinted off a distant metallic speck. Heim tuned his and Jocelyn's viewport to full magnification.

The speck became a flyer, of gaunt unhuman design, patrolling above a cluster of fused-stone towers that clung to a precipice a kilometer over the surf. 'The Perch of Rademir,' he said. 'Better jog a little farther south, Vic. I'm told he's somewhat peeved at us, and he just might get an impulse to attack.'

Bragdon adjusted the autopilot. 'Why?'

'He wanted to sell us warheads, when Charlie Wong and I arrived to make arrangements,' Koumanoudes said. 'But the Roost of Kragan offered us a better price.'

Bragdon shook his head. 'I really don't understand this culture,' he said. 'Anarchy and atomic power. They can't go together.'

'What?' Vadász tautened in his seat. 'There is quite a literature on Staurn,' he said very slowly. 'Have you not even read it?'

'Oh, sure, sure,' Bragdon answered in haste. 'But it's a jumble. Nothing scientific. My own field work was mainly on Isis.'

'We aren't the best-prepared expedition that ever went out,' Jocelyn added. 'Quite hurriedly organized, in fact. But with all the trouble in this sector, the Research Authority decided it was urgent to get some solid information on the space-traveling societies hereabouts.'

'The Staurni aren't that, exactly,' Heim said. 'They have the capability, but use it only for planetary defense purposes. They'll trade with visitors, but aren't interested in looking for business themselves.'

'They must once— Say.' Bragdon turned in his seat to face the others. 'We've time to kill. Why don't you give us your version of the situation here? Even when I've read it before, it's helpful to have the material put in different words.'

Vadász narrowed his eyes and remained silent. Heim was chiefly conscious of Jocelyn's glove resting on his. He thought that somehow she was pleading with him. To keep away from the thing that divided them? He leaned back, easing the weight of his air equipment on to the rest bracket, and said:

'I'm no expert. But as I understand it, the Staurni are a rare thing, a strictly carnivorous intelligent race. Normally carnivores specialize in fighting ability rather than brains, you know. I once talked with a buck who'd visited here and poked around a little. He said he'd noticed fossil outcrops that suggested this continent was invaded long ago by a bigger, related species. Maybe the ancestral Staurni had to develop intelligence

92

to fight back. I dunno. However it happened, you've got a race with high-powered killer instincts and not gregarious. The basic social unit is, uh, a sort of family. A big family, with a system of companionate marriage so complicated that no human has ever figured it out, plus retainers with their own females and cubs; but still, a patriarchal household dominated by one big, tough male.'

The flyer rocked in a gust. Heim peered out. At their present speed, they were already crossing the spine of the mountains. In the west he saw foothills, tumbling off to the red and tawny plain of the Uneasy Lands.

'I shouldn't think that would make for advance beyond savagery,' Bragdon remarked.

'They managed it on Staurn, for a while. I don't know how. But then, does anybody know for sure what the evolutionary laws of human civilization are? Maybe being winged, more mobile than us, helped the Staurni. In time they got a planet-wide industrial culture, split into confederations. They invented the scientific method and rode the exponential curve of discovery on up to nuclear engines and gravitronics.'

'I think,' Uthg-a-K'thaq grunted, 'those nations were wuilt on conquest and slawery. Unnatural, and hence unstawle.'

Heim gave the trendriled face a surprised glance, shrugged, and went on: 'Could be. Now there is one stabilizing factor. A Staurni male is fiercer than a man during his reproductive years, but when he reaches middle age he undergoes a bigger endocrine change than we do. Without getting weak otherwise, he loses both sex drive and belligerence, and prefers to live quietly at home. I suppose under primitive conditions that was a survival mechanism, to give the females and cubs some protection around the Nest while the young males were out hunting. In civilization it's been a slightly mellowing influence. The oldsters are respected and listened to, somewhat, because of their experience.

'Nevertheless, the industrial society blew itself apart in a nuclear war. Knowledge wasn't lost, nor even most of the material equipment, but organization was. Everywhere the Staurni reverted to these baronial Nests. Between the productivity of its automated machines and the return of big game to hunt, each such community is damn near independent. Nobody's interested in any more elaborate social structures. Their present life suits them fine.'

93

'What about the Lodge?' Jocelyn asked.

'Oh, yes. There has to be some central group to arbitrate between Nests, defend the planet as a whole, and deal with outworlders. The Lodge grew up as a – I suppose quasi-religious organization, though I don't know a thing about the symbolism. Its leaders are old males. The more active jobs are done by what you might call novices or acolytes, younger sons and such, who sign on for the adventure and the concubines and the prospect of eventually becoming full initiates. It works pretty well.'

'It wouldn't with humans,' Bragdon said.

'Yeh,' Koumanoudes answered, 'but these people aren't human.'

'That's about everything I know,' Heim said. 'Nothing you haven't found in books and journals, I'm sure.'

He looked outside again. The prairie was sliding swiftly beneath; he could hear the whistle and feel the vibration of their passage. A herd of grazing beasts darkened the land and was gone. Eastward the last mountain-tops vanished. No one spoke for a considerable period. Heim was in fact startled to note how much time had gone by while they all sat contemplating the view or their own thoughts, before Bragdon ended the silence.

'One item I have not seen explained,' he said. 'Apparently each Nest maintains a nuclear arsenal and military production equipment. What *for*?'

'To fight,' Koumanoudes said. 'They get an argument the Lodge can't settle, like over territory, and hoo! They rip up the landscape. We'll probably see a few craters.'

'But . . . no. That sort of insanity smashed their civilization.'

'The last phase of their civilization, you mean,' Heim said. 'The present one isn't vulnerable. A Nest is mostly underground, and even the topside buildings are nearly blastproof. Radiation affects a Staurni a lot less than a human, he gets so much of it in the normal course of life; and they have medicines for an overdose here, same as us. And there are no incendiary effects, not in a hydrogen atmosphere. In fact, before atomic energy, the only way to smelt metals was to use a volcanic outlet – which there are plenty of on a big planet with a hot core.'

'So they have no restrictions,' Jocelyn murmured. 'Not even on selling the things offworld, for others to kill with.'

'We've been over that ground too mucking often,' Koumanoudes growled.

'Free-fall, Greg,' Heim warned. The woman's face was so unhappy.

Koumanoudes shifted in his seat, glared out, and grew suddenly rigid.

'Hey!' he barked.

'What's the matter?' Bragdon asked.

'Where do you think you're headed?'

'Why, to the Aerie of Trebogir.'

The Greek half rose. His forefinger stabbed at the bow viewports. Above the horizon, ghostly in its detachment, floated a white cone. The plain beneath rolled down toward a thread which wound blinding silver through a valley where cloud shadows ran.

'What the hell!' he exploded. 'That's the River Morh. Got to be. Only I know the map. Trebogir doesn't live anywhere in sight of a snowpeak. It must belong to Kimreth upland. We're a good five hundred kilometers north of where we should be!'

Sweat sprang forth on Bragdon's forehead. 'I did set a roundabout course, to get a better look at the countryside,' he admitted.

'And never told us?' Koumanoudes yanked at his harness. 'I should've noticed where the sun is. Get away from that pilot board. I'm taking over.'

Heim's eyes swung to Jocelyn. Her fists were clamped together and she breathed in deep uneven gulps.

Bragdon darted his hand into the carrying case by his seat. It lifted, and Heim stared down the barrel of a laser pistol.

'Sit back!' Bragdon ordered. 'I'll shoot the first one who unstraps himself.'

CHAPTER FOUR
_____

WHEN he cycled through the airlock, out of the flyer's interior gee-field, Staurn yanked at Heim so violently that he staggered. He tightened his leg muscles and drew himself erect. However well balanced, the load of gear on him was monstrous.

95

Jocelyn had gone ahead, to cover the prisoners as they emerged. She looked grotesquely different in her airsuit, and the dark faceplate was a mask over her features. He moved toward her.

'Stop!' In spite of the helmet pickups being adjusted to compensate for changed sound-transmission parameters, her voice was eerily different. He halted under the menace of her gun. It was a .45 automatic, throwing soft-nosed slugs at low velocity to rip open a man's protection.

He drew a long breath, and another. His own air was a calculated percentage composition at three atmospheres, both to balance outside pressure and to furnish extra oxygen for the straining cells. It made his words roar in the helmet: 'Joss, what is this farce?'

'You'll never know how sorry I am,' she said unevenly. 'If you'd listened to me, back on the ship—'

'Your whole idea, then, was to wreck my plan,' he flung at her.

'Yes. It had to be done. Can't you see, it had to! There's no chance of negotiating with Alerion when ... when you're waging war. Their delegates told Earth so officially, before they left.'

'And you believed them? Don't you know any more history than that?'

She didn't seem to hear. Words cataracted from her; through all the distortion, he could read how she appealed to him.

'Peace Control Intelligence guessed you'd come here for your weapons. They couldn't send an armed ship. The Staurni wouldn't have allowed it. In fact, France could block any official action. But unofficially— We threw this expedition together and took off after you. I learned about it because PCI found out I was an, an, an old friend of yours and interrogated me. I asked to come along. I thought, I hoped I could persuade you.'

'By any means convenient,' he bit off. 'There's a name for that.'

'I failed,' she said desolately. 'Vic decided this trip was his chance to act. We don't mean to hurt you. We'll take you back to Earth. Nothing more. You won't even be charged with anything.'

'I could charge kidnapping,' he said.

'If you want to,' she mumbled.

Hopelessness gutted him. 'What's the use? You'd get yourself a judge who'd put you on probation.'

Vadász appeared, then Koumanoudes, then Uthg-a-K'thaq. The Greek cursed in a steady stream.

Without a captain, without a chief engineer, Fox will have to go home, beaten before one blow is struck, Heim thought.

He looked around. They had landed on the west bank of the Morh. It ran wide and luminous through a sandy, boulder-strewn dale walled by low bluffs. The mountains of Kimreth reared opposite the sun, still many kilometers distant, not quite real in the blue-gray haze of intervening air, but a titan's rampart, dominated by the volcanic cone he had seen from afar. Underfoot the ground was covered by that springy mosslike red-yellow growth which was this world's equivalent of grass. Overhead the sky arched plum-dark, clouds scudding on a wind that boomed in his audio receptors. A flock of airborne devilfish shapes drifted into sight and out again.

How far have we come? What's going to happen?

Vadász moved to Heim's side, touched helmets, and muttered, 'Quickly, can we rush her? I do not think her aim will be good here.'

'Nor can we move fast,' Heim said. *Though ... would you really shoot me, Joss?*

His heart thuttered and sweat smelt sharp in his nostrils. But before he could nerve himself to try, Bragdon was out, and there was no question whether that laser pistol would be used.

'G'yaaru!' Uthg-a-K'thaq shouted. 'You hawe lewt the airlock owen!'

'I know,' Bragdon said. 'And I've set the pilot a certain way. Better lie down.' He eased himself to a sitting position.

The flyer whined and leaped forward. The glare off its metal blinded Heim. He saw what seemed a comet arc off the ground, to a hundred meters, loop about, and plunge. Instinct sent him flat on his belly.

Some distance away, the flyer crashed. The explosive mixture of hydrogen and oxygen went off. Blue flame spurted upward. Thunder coughed, again and again, and Heim heard shards scream above him. Then there was only a thick pillar of smoke and dust, while echoes tolled away and were lost in the wind.

He strained back to his feet. His head still rang. The other males did likewise. Jocelyn remained seated.

'Great ... jumping ... Judas,' Koumanoudes gasped. 'What have you done?'

'Don't be alarmed,' said Bragdon. 'We have other transportation coming.' He paused. 'I may as well explain. The object is to cripple your damned piracy by taking you back to Earth. I had various schemes in mind, but this chance suggested a simple method.

'One other flyer is out, with a couple of young men who know what's afoot and know approximately where I intended to do this. They can spot the wreckage from afar. We'll all go aboard and return to the *Quest*. Only we'll be on the floor, out of sight, and I'm sorry, but you'll be tied. Once back inside the ship, you'll be taken to a special cell we've got fixed. Jocelyn and I will stay concealed too. When you don't report in, your crew will get worried and go look for you. Naturally, Captain Gutierrez will lend every assistance. The wreck will be found – unfortunate crash, everybody killed. No one's likely to check so close that he'll see there are no human remains. But if anybody does, he'll conclude that we hiked off in a forlorn attempt to get help, and soon died. So, with much sorrow, two spoiled expeditions wend their separate ways home.'

'Can you rely on your crew?' Vadász asked, snake cold.

'They won't know the truth until *Quest* is again in space,' Bragdon said. 'Captain Gutierrez and First Officer Hermann do already. I don't expect the men will mutiny.'

'You filthy bastard—' Koumanoudes advanced a stiff-legged step.

'Halt,' Bragdon warned. 'I'm entirely prepared to shoot if I must. On the other hand, if you behave yourselves you'll be released unharmed on Earth.'

Heim hunched his shoulders. 'How will you prevent us from starting right out again?' he inquired.

'Have you forgotten? Your ship's now equipped for nuclear weapons. The moment she enters the Solar System, the Peace Control Authority is law-bound to seize her. And without their principal officers, where else can your men go?'

'Who are you working for, Bragdon?' Heim fleered. 'Alerion?'

'Mankind.' The answer was proud. 'In case you're interested, I'm not a xenologist, only a PCA officer on leave, and they'll cashier me for this. It's worth it, though. World Militants for Peace will see I get another job.'

'They engineered this, huh?' Koumanoudes snorted. 'Yeh. They've got members in government too.'

Heim spoke to Jocelyn. 'You never actually quit that gang, did you?'

'Please, please,' her whisper drifted down the wind.

'We may as well make ourselves comfortable,' Bragdon advised. 'This gravity will wear us out if we don't. The other vessel probably won't arrive for several hours, since we couldn't make exact timing or location arrangements, or risk radio.' He gestured with his gun. 'You sit before I do.'

Vadász was so near Heim that the captain alone heard the minstrel's indrawn hiss and noticed how he stiffened. 'Heigh-ho, Roger!' he murmured. 'Hook the first moon by.'

'What's that?' Bragdon challenged, for he saw his prisoners go taut.

'I would not translate in a lady's presence,' Vadász snarled.

It thrilled through Heim. *Spaceman's slang. 'Something's about to happen. Take your chance when you see it.'* The blackness and coldness departed him. His pulse slammed with preparation to fight.

'Are you skizzy, though?' Vadász continued. 'We can't stay here.'

'What d'you mean?' Bragdon demanded.

'Next to a river like this. Flash floods. We will get tumbled around, our suits torn open, we are dead unless we get on higher ground.'

'You lie!'

'No, no. Look at those mountains. Think. A dense atmosphere under strong gravity has a high density gradient, therefore a high temperature gradient. This is autumn. It gets cold enough at night, above snowline, to freeze ammonia. But the stuff liquefies again about noon, and pours down into the riverbeds. The gravity pulls it so fast that it goes fifty kilometers or better before it evaporates. Isn't that true, Gregorios? You were the one who told me.'

'Sure,' Koumanoudes said. 'That's what the name Morh means. Floodwater.'

'If this is some trick—' Bragdon began.

It sure as blaze is, Heim's thought leaped. *There's no such phenomenon. But the yarn sounds plausible to a newcomer – I hope – how I hope!*

'I swear I'll shoot on any suspicion,' Bragdon said.

99

Heim started to walk away from him. 'Do, if you want,' he retorted. 'That's an easier way to die than in an ammonia flood. You can't stop me trying to get on top of those bluffs.'

His back was tense against the firebeam. But only Jocelyn's cry reached him: 'Vic, no, don't! What's the harm?'

'I . . . guess none, except that it's a difficult climb,' Bragdon conceded. 'Okay. You people go first. Jocelyn will cover me while I follow. If you feel like running away, once you're over the crest, I don't mind too much. You can't get far before the flyer comes, and we'll catch you then. Or if you find some hiding place, Staurn will kill you for me.'

Step by heavy step, Heim wound among the scattered rocks until he reached the nearest bank. It was bare gritty earth, mingled with stones, not high or steep but a daunting obstacle when this weight bore on him. He commenced trudging upward. The slope gave way under his boots, slid past in a hiss and a rattle, he lost his footing and went to hands and knees.

Fumbling erect, he proceeded cautiously. Before long he was half drowned in sweat, his heart raced and the air burned his throat. Through blurred eyes he saw Vadász and Koumanoudes toiling behind. Uthg-a-K'thaq made it with less trouble, down on his stomach, pushing with wide feet and scrabbling with powerful swimmer's arms; but still the Naqsan's breath was noisy across the wind.

Somehow they got to the top. Heim and his engineer gave the others a hand. They crouched on the brink and wheezed.

There was a stone under Heim's glove. His fingers closed.

As strength returned, he saw Bragdon half-way up. The Peaceman was taking his time, frequent lengthy rests, during which he stood gun in hand and glared at the privateers. Jocelyn waited below. Now and then sand or pebbles skittered around her, dislodged by Bragdon, but she didn't try to dodge. Her suited form looked black in the lightning-blue sun-dazzle; her pistol reflected it moltenly.

Vadász knelt between Heim and Koumanoudes. He squeezed their hands. No other signal or explanation was needed.

Heim threw his stone. An instant later, their own missiles whizzed from his men. Accelerated at nineteen hundred centimeters per second per second, the rocks flew as if catapulted.

He didn't know whose hit Bragdon. He saw the man lurch and fall. Then he and his folk were on their way down again.

100

Leap – slide – run – skip – keep your feet in the little avalanche you make – charge in your weight like a knight at full gallop!

Jocelyn had not been struck. He saw her stumble back, slow and awkward, and bounded past the collision of Bragdon and Koumanoudes. Dust boiled from his bootsoles. Twice he nearly fell. It could have snapped his neck at the speed he now had. Somehow he recovered balance and raged on ahead.

Down to the valley floor! He must tumble or run, faster than man had ever run before. His body was a machine gone wild, he fought to steer it and slow it but the momentum was overwhelming. Each footfall slammed through muscle and bone to rattle his teeth. The blood brawled in his ears.

Jocelyn had shot once while he plunged. The slug whanged wide. He saw the gun slew around to take closer aim. No chance for fear or hope. He had nothing but velocity. Yet it was too great for common sense to perceive. In her panic and her anguish she hesitated before shooting anew. The time was a fractional second. A man attacking her on Earth would have taken the bullet point blank. Heim crashed by before she could squeeze trigger. His fist shot out. He did not snatch the gun. His blow tore it from her grasp and spun it meters away.

On flat terrain he braked himself: to a normal run, a jog, a halt. He wheeled. Jocelyn had been knocked down by his mere brush against her. She was still struggling to regain her feet. Through his own deep gasps, he heard her weep. He plodded to retrieve the pistol.

When he had it, he looked for the others. Uthg-a-K'taq slumped on his feet in the rubble under the bluff. Two men stood half crouched nearby. One held the laser. A third sprawled unmoving between them, suit rent and blackened.

Heim steadied one shaking hand with the other and took aim. 'Endre!' he called, hoarse and in horror.

'We have him,' rang back the voice of the armed man. It sank till the wind nearly overrode it. 'But Gregorios is done.'

Slowly, Heim dragged his way thither. He could not see through the Greek's sooted faceplate. In a dull fashion he was glad of that. The laser beam had slashed open fabric and body, after which gases mixed and exploded. Blood was streaked round about, garish scarlet.

A gruesome keening lifted from the Naqsan. '*Gwurru shka ektrush,* is this war? We do not thus at home. *Rahata, rahata.*'

'Bragdon must have recovered himself and shot as Gregorios jumped him,' Vadász said drearily. 'The impact jarred his gun loose. I got it and came back here, where they both had rolled. C.E. held him pinned meanwhile.'

Heim stared long at the Peaceman. Finally, mechanically, he asked, 'Any serious injuries?'

'No,' Bragdon replied in the same monotone. 'At least, no bones broken. I've a headache.' He stumbled off, lowered himself to the ground, and lay there with an arm across his faceplate.

'I thought we could get away with this,' Vadász said, eyes fixed on the dead man.

'We did,' Heim answered. 'Wars have casualties.' He clapped the minstrel's shoulder and walked towards Jocelyn. Sweat, runneling down his body, squelched in his boots. He felt a tightness in chest and gullet as if he were about to cry, but he wasn't able.

'You all right, Joss?' he asked.

She backed away. 'I won't hurt you,' he said.

'But I shot at you!' Her voice was as a frightened child's.

'That's in the game.' He laid his arms around her and drew the helmet against his breast. She sobbed for minutes. He waited it out from a vague sense of duty. Not that he hated her; there was a strange ashy vacuum where she had been in him. His emotions were engaged with the man who had died, his thoughts with what must be done.

At last he could leave her, seated and silent. He went on to the wrecked flyer. Fragments and cargo were scattered from hell to breakfast. He found an unharmed entrenching tool and several machetes and carried them back.

'Start digging, Bragdon,' he said.

'What?' The man jerked where he lay.

'We're not going to leave Greg Koumanoudes unburied. It'll have to be a shallow grave, but— Get busy. Somebody will spell you when you're tired.'

Bragdon rose, centimeter by centimeter. 'What have you done?' he cried. 'I didn't kill that man. You did, with your insane attempt to – to what? Do you think you can stand off our flyer?'

'No,' Heim said. 'I don't plan to be here when it arrives.'

'But – but – but—'

'You left your motor running.' Heim gave him the tool and

continued on to Vadász. Uthg-a-K'thaq bestirred himself and came to help, scooping dirt with his hands.

'Did you think of anything beyond getting control?' Heim asked the Magyar.

'No,' said Vadász. 'A dim idea of – I knew not what, except that my forefathers never quit without a fight.'

'Sit down and let's look at the poopsheets.' Every suit had a pocket loaded with charts and other local information. There wasn't much about Staurn. Heim unfolded the map of this region. It fluttered and crackled in the wind. He spread it across his knees. 'Greg would have known what these symbols mean. But look—' His finger traced the outlines. 'Those mountains are the Kimreth boundary and this is the River Morh; we know that. Now, see, Mount Lochan is marked as the highest in the northern sierra. In fact, no other peak stands that much bigger than its neighbors. So yonder old volcano has to be Lochan. Then we're about *here*.'

'Yes.' A certain life returned to Vadász's speech. 'And here is the Hurst of Wenilwain on Lochan's northern slope. About a hundred airline kilometers hence, would you not say? I doubt we can survive that big a walk. But if we can get moderately near, someone flying on patrol or on a hunt ought to spy us.'

'And Wenilwain knows us. Uh-huh.' Heim shook his head. 'It's a long chance to take, I admit. What are these areas marked between us and him? The Walking Forest; the Slaughter Machines; Thundersmoke.'

'Let me try—' Vadász riffled through the pitifully thin handbook. 'No entry. But then, this is a stat of the map annotated by Gregorios and Charles, on the basis of what they learned while dealing with the natives. They must have planned to pass the information on when they got home. It's a common practice.'

'I know. And Greg's dead. Well, we'll find out.'

'What of those?' Vadász pointed at Bragdon painfully digging, Jocelyn huddled by herself.

'They have to come along, I'm afraid. For one thing, it'll puzzle and delay their friends, not to find anybody here, and so give us time to find cover. For another thing, we'll need every hand we can get, especially when we hit the foothills.'

'Wait!' Vadász slapped the ground. His voice bleakened. 'Gunnar, we cannot do it. We have air recyclers, but nothing for water except a day's worth in these canteens. That isn't even allowing for what we will need to reconstitute powdered food. And you know that ten kilometers a day, afoot, will be fantastic progress.'

Heim actually noticed himself smiling, lopsidedly. 'Haven't you ever met that trick? We won't be far from native water at any time; notice these streams on the map. So we fill our canteens, put the laser pistol at wide beam and low intensity, and boil out the ammonia.'

'Spending the capacitor charges,' Vadász objected. 'That leaves only your slugthrower for defense.'

'Shucks, Endre, local tigers are no problem. We're as unsavory to them as they'd be to us. Our biggest enemy is the gravity drag; our second biggest the short food and medicine supply; our third, maybe, bad weather if we hit any.'

'M-m-m ... as you say. I would still like to know precisely what the Slaughter Machines are. But – yes, of course, we will try.' The minstrel got up almost bouncily. 'In fact, you have made me feel so much better that I think I can take my turn at digging.'

They had not much time to spare, enough barely to scrape a little earth over the fallen man and hear Vadász sing the Paternoster. Then they departed.

CHAPTER FIVE

FOUR Staurnian days? Five? Heim wasn't sure. The nightmare had gone on too long.

At first they made good time. The ground rolled quite gently upward, decked with sparse forest that hid them from aerial searchers without hindering their feet. They were all in trim physical shape. And their survival gear, awkward though it seemed, was a miracle of lightness and compactness.

Yet between it and the gravity, each was carrying a burden equal to more than his own Earth weight. 'Good time' meant an average of hardly over one kilometer per hour.

Then the land canted and they were on the slopes of Kimreth's foothills. Worse, their bodies were beginning to show cumulative effects of stress. This was nothing so simple as exhaustion. Without a sealtent, they could never take off their airsuits. The recyclers handled volatile by-products of metabolism; but slowly, slowly, the fractional percent that escaped chemical treatment built up. Stench and itch were endurable, somewhat, for a while. Too much aldehyde, ketone, organic acid, would not be.

And high gravity has a more subtle, more deadly effect than overworking the heart. It throws the delicate body-fluid balance – evolved through a billion years on *one* smaller planet – out of kilter. Plasma seeps through cell walls. Blood pools in the extremities, ankles swell while the brain starves. On Staurn this does not happen fast. But it happens.

Without the drugs in their medikits, gravanol, kinesthan, assorted stimulants and analgesics, the travelers would not have traveled three days. When the drugs gave out (and they were getting low) there would be perhaps one day in which to go on, before a man lay down to die.

Is it worth it? gibbered through the querning in Heim's skull. *Why didn't we go back home? I can't remember now.* His thought fluttered away again. Every remnant of attention must go to the Sisyphus task of picking up one foot, advancing it, putting it down, picking up the other foot, advancing it. ... Meanwhile a death-heavy weight dragged at his right side. *Oh, yes, Jocelyn,* he recalled from a remote past. *The rest of us have to take turns helping her along.*

She stumbled. Both of them came near falling. 'Gotta rest,' her air-warped voice wavered.

'You rested ... till ten minutes ago. ... Come!' He jerked brutally on the improvised harness which joined them.

They reeled on for another five hundred seconds. 'Time,' Vadász called at the end. They lowered themselves down on their backs and breathed.

Eventually Heim rose to his knees. His vision had cleared and his head throbbed a bit less. He could even know, in a detached way, that the scenery was magnificent.

Eastward the hills up which he was laboring swooped in long curves and dales towards the illimitable hazy plain. The gentled light of an evening sun turned their colors – tawny and orange, with red splashes to mark stands of forest – into a smoldering richness. Not far away a brook twisted bright among boulders, until it foamed over in a series of cataracts whose noise was like bells through the still air. A swarm of insectoidal creatures, emerald bodies and rainbow wings, hovered above the pools it made.

Westward the mountains loomed dark and wild against the sun, which was near their ridge. Yet it tinged Lochan's snow-cone, a shape as pure as Fuji's, with unearthly greens and blues under a violet heaven. The crags threw their shadows far down the sides, dusking whatever was ahead on Heim's route. But he saw that, a kilometer hence, a wood grew. His field glasses showed it apparently thick with underbrush. But it was too far to go around – he couldn't see the northern or southern end – while it was probably not very wide.

Vadász had also been looking in that direction. 'I think best we call this a day,' he said.

'It's early yet,' Heim objected.

'But the sun will soon go below that high horizon. And we are exhausted, and tomorrow we shall have to cut our way through yonder stuff. A good rest is a good investment for us, Gunnar.'

Hell, we've been sleeping nine hours out of the eighteen! Heim glanced at the others. Their suits had become as familiar to him as the seldom seen faces. Jocelyn was already unconscious. Uthg-a-K'thaq seemed to flow bonelessly across the place where he lay. Vadász and Bragdon sat tailor style, but their backs were bent. And every nerve in Heim carried waves of weariness.

'All right,' he said.

He hadn't much appetite, but forced himself to mix a little powder with water and squeeze the mess through his chowlock. When that was done, he stretched himself as well as his back-pack allowed. Some time had passed before he realized that he wasn't sleepy. Exhausted, yes; aching and throbbing; but not sleepy. He didn't know whether to blame overtiredness or the itch in undepilated face and unwashed skin. *Lord, Lord, what I'd give for a bath, clean sheets to lie between, clean air to breathe!* He braked that thought. There was danger enough without adding an extra psychological hazard.

Pushing himself to a seated position, he watched the light die on Mount Lochan. The sky darkened toward night, a few stars trembled, the little crescent of the outer moon stood steely near the zenith.

'You too?'

Heim shifted so he could see through his faceplate who had

joined him. Bragdon. Reflexively, his hand dropped to his pistol.

Bragdon laughed without humour. 'Relax. You've committed us too thoroughly.' After a moment: 'Damn you.'

'Who made this mess in the first place?' Heim growled.

'You did, back in the Solar System. . . . I've heard that Jews believe death itself to be an act of expiation. Maybe when we die here on Staurn, you'll make some amends for him we had to bury.'

'I didn't shoot him,' Heim said between his teeth.

'You brought about the situation.'

'Dog your hatch before I take a poke at you.'

'Oh, I don't hold myself guiltless. I should have managed things better. The whole human race is blood guilty.'

'I've heard that notion before, and I don't go along with it. The human race is nothing but a species. Individuals are responsible for what they personally do.'

'Like setting out to fight private wars? I tell you, Heim, that man would be alive today if you'd stayed home.'

Heim squinted through the murk. He could not see Bragdon's face, nor interpret nuances in the transformed voice. But — 'Look here,' he said, 'I could accuse you of murder in the course of making your own little foreign policy. My expedition is legal. It may even be somewhat more popular than otherwise. I'm sorry about Greg. He was my friend. More, he was under my command. But he knew the risks and accepted them freely. There are worse ways to die than in battle for something that matters. You do protest too much.'

Bragdon started backward. 'Don't say any more!'

Heim hammered pitilessly. 'Why aren't you asleep? Could it be that Greg came back in your dreams? Have you been thinking that your noisy breed may be powered less by love than by hate? Would you like to chop off the finger that pulled trigger on a man who was trying to do his best for Earth? Can you afford to call anyone a murderer?'

'Go to hell!' Bragdon screamed. 'Go to hell! Go to hell!' He crawled off on all fours. Some meters distant, he collapsed and shuddered.

Maybe I was too rough on him, Heim thought. *He's sincere. . . . Fout on that. Sincerity is the most overrated virtue in the catalogue.* He eased himself back to the turf. Presently he slept.

Sunrise woke him, level across the Uneasy Lands and tinging

107

Mount Lochan with fire. He felt more stiff and hollow-headed each dawn, but it helped to move about, fix a cold breakfast and boil a fresh supply of water. Bragdon was totally silent; no one else said many words. But as they started the long slog toward the forest – a whole kilometer uphill – Vadász began to sing.

> 'Trois jeunes tambours, s'en revenaient de guerre.
> Trois jeunes tambours, s'en revenaient de guerre,
> Et ri, et ran, ra-pa-ta-plan,
> S'en revenaient de guerre.—'

When he had finished, he went on to 'Rimini', 'Marching through Georgia', 'The British Grenadiers', and 'From Syrtis to Cydonia'. Heim and Jocelyn panted with him in the choruses and perhaps Uthg-a-K'thaq, or even Bragdon, got some help too from the tramping rhythms and the brave images of home. They reached the woods sooner, in better shape, than expected.

'Thanks, Endre,' Heim said.

'My job, you know,' Vadász answered.

Resting before they went among the trees, Heim studied the growth more closely. At a distance, by dawnlight, he had seen that it wound across the hills along a fault line, and was as sharply bordered as if artificial. Since the northwestern edge was well above him on a steep rise, he had also made out a curious, churned sweep of soil on that side, which passed around the slopes beyond his purview. Now he was too near to see anything but the barrier itself.

'Not brushy after all,' he observed in surprise. 'Only one kind of plant. What do you think of that?'

'We are none xenowotanists,' the engineer grunted.

The trees were about four meters tall; nothing grows high on Staurn. And they were no thicker than a man's arm. But numberless flexible branches grew along the stems, from top to bottom, each in turn split into many shoots. In places the entanglement of limbs was so dense as to be nearly solid. Only the upper twigs bore leaves; but those were matted together into a red roof beneath which the inner forest looked night-black.

'This'll be machete work,' Heim said. 'We shouldn't have to move a lot slower than usual, though. One man cuts – that doesn't look too hard – while the others rest. I'll begin.' He unlimbered his blade.

Whick! Whick! The wood was soft, the branches fell right

and left as fast as he could wield his tool. In an hour the males ran through a cycle of turns, Jocelyn being excused, and were far into the forest. *With the sun still only a couple of hours up,* Heim exulted.

'Take over, Gunnar,' Vadász rattled. 'The sweat is gurgling around my mouth.'

Heim rose and advanced along the narrow trail. It was hot and still in here. A thick purple twilight soaked through the leaves, making vision difficult where one stood and impossible a few meters off. Withes rustled against him, springily resisting his passage. He felt a vibration go back through the machete and his wrist, into his body, as he chopped.

Huh! Odd. Like the whole interlocked wilderness shivering.

The trees stirred and soughed. Yet there was no breath of wind.

Jocelyn shrieked.

Heim spun on his heel. A branch was coiling down past her, along her airsuit. Something struck his back. He lifted his machete – tried to – a dozen tendrils clutched him by the arm. He tore free.

An earthquake rumble went through the gloom. Heim lost balance under a thrust. He fell to one knee. Pain shot through the point of impact. The tree before his eyes swayed down. Its many-fingered lower branches touched the soil and burrowed. Leaves drew clear of each other with a crackling like fire. He glimpsed sky, then he was blinded by their descent about his head.

He shouted and slashed. A small space opened around him. The tree was pulling loose its roots. Groaning, shuddering, limbs clawed into the earth, it writhed forward.

The entire forest was on the march. The pace wasn't quick, no faster than a man could walk on Staurn, but it was resistless. Heim scrambled up and was instantly thrown against a tangle of whipping branches. Through airsuit and helmet he felt those buffets. He reeled away. A trunk, hitching itself along, smote him in the stomach. He retched and dropped his machete. Almost at once it began to be covered, as limbs pulled from the ground and descended for the next grab along their way. Heim threw what remained of his strength against them. They resisted with demoniac tenacity. He never knew how he managed to part them long enough to retrieve the blade.

Above the crashing and enormous rustle he heard Jocelyn

scream again, not in startlement but in mortal terror. He knelt to get under the leaves and peered wildly about. Through swaying, lurching trunks, snake-dancing branches, clawing twigs, murk, and incandescent sunlight spears, he saw her. She had fallen. Two trees had her pinned. They could break bones or rip her suit when they crawled across her body.

His blade flew in his hand. A battle cry burst from his mouth. He beat his way to her like a warrior hewing through enemy lines. The stems had grown rigid, as if they had muscles now tightened. His blows rebounded. A sticky fluid spurted from wounds he made. 'Gunnar, help!' she cried in sightlessness. He cleared brush from her until he could stoop and pull her free.

'You okay?' He must shout to be heard in the racket. She lay against him and sobbed. Another tree bent down upon them. He yanked her to her feet.

'To me!' he bellowed. 'Over here!'

Uthg-a-K'thaq wriggled to join him. The Naqsan's great form parted a way for Bragdon. Vadász wove lithely through the chaos.

'Joss in the middle,' Heim ordered. 'The rest of us, back to back around her. We can't outrun this mess, can't stay here either. We'd exhaust ourselves just keeping our feet. Forward!'

His blade caught a sunbeam and burned in its arc.

The rest was chop, wrestle, duck, and dodge, through the moving horror. Heim's awareness had gone coldly lucid; he watched what happened, saw a pattern, found a technique. But the strength to keep on, directly across that tide, came from a deeper source. It was more than the simple fear of death. Something in him revolted against his bones being tumbled forever among these marching trolls.

Bragdon gave way first. 'I can't ... lift ... this ... any more,' he groaned, and sank to the earth. Wooden fingers closed about one leg.

Uthg-a-K'thaq released him. 'Get in the middle, then,' the Naqsan said. 'Hel' him, you Lawrie.'

Later in eternity, Vadász's machete sank. 'I am sorry.' The minstrel could barely be heard. 'Go on.'

'No!' Heim said. 'We'll all get out, or none.'

'Let me try,' Jocelyn said. She gave Vadász into the care of Bragdon, who had recovered a little, and took his knife herself. Her blows were weak, but they found she could use the tool as a crowbar to lever a path for herself.

And ... sunlight, open sky, turf under Lochan's holy peak. They went a few meters farther before they toppled.

Heim woke a couple of hours afterward. For a while he blinked at heaven and found curious shapes in the clouds, as if again he were a boy on Gea. When memory came back, he sat upright with a choked oath.

The trees were still moving past. He thought, though, they had slowed down. Northwestward, opposite to their direction, he saw their trail of crumbled earth. The most distant part that he could spy was overlaid with pale yellow, the first new growth.

Uthg-a-K'thaq was the only other one awake. The Naqsan flopped down beside him. 'Well, skiwwer, now we know what the Walking Worest is.'

'I'd like to know how it works,' Heim said.

Rest had temporarily cleared his mind. An answer grew. 'I'm only guessing, of course,' he said after a minute, 'but it could be something like this. The ultraviolet sunlight makes plant chemistry hellish energetic. That particular species there needs something, some mineral maybe. Where faulting exposes a vein of it, a woods appears.'

'Not likely mineral,' Uthg-a-K'thaq corrected. 'You cannot hawe liwe dewendent on sheer geological ac-cident.'

'Geology operates faster on a big planet than a terrestrial one, C.E.,' Heim argued. 'Still, I'll agree it makes poor ecology. Let me think. . . . Okay, let's say you get bacteria laying down organic stuff of a particular kind, wherever conditions are right. Such deposits would be fairly common, exposed fairly often. Those trees could broadcast spores that can lie dormant for centuries, waiting for a chance to sprout. All right, then, they consume the deposit at a tremendous rate. Once mature, such a forest has to keep moving because the soil gets exhausted where it stands. Reproduction is too slow; the trees themselves have to move. Evidently sunlight starts them on their way, because you remember they didn't begin till mid-morning and now in the afternoon they're coming to a halt.'

'What hawwens when they hawe eaten out the whole wein?'

'They die. Their remains go back to the soil. Eventually everything gets reprocessed into the material they need, and the spores they've left wake to life.' Heim grimaced. 'Why am I trying to play scientist? Defense mechanism? I've *got* to believe that thing is natural.'

111

'We came through it aliwe,' Uthg-a-K'thaq said calmly. 'Is that not suwwicient?'

Heim didn't reply. His gaze drifted west, whither he had yet to go. Did he see a vague plume of mist on the lower steeps of Lochan? It was too distant for him to be sure. But – Thundersmoke? *Whatever that is. No need to worry about it now. First we've got to get past the Slaughter Machines.*

CHAPTER SIX

Two more days – twenty kilometers? They could not have done that much were they not crossing a flat space, a plateau on the lap of Lochan.

It was dreary country, treeless, rock-strewn, sparsely covered with low yellowish scrub. Many streams ran down toward the Morh, their tinkle the only sound except for an endless whittering wind; but the banks held no more life than the dusty stretches beyond. Alone the ranges that hemmed in the world on three sides, and the splendid upward leap of the snowcone ahead, redeemed this landscape.

The first evening they camped in sight of a crater. Its vitrified walls gleamed reddish black, like clotted blood, in the last sunlight. Vadász pointed and remarked, 'I thought this region is barren because runoff from above leached the soil. Now I find otherwise.'

'How so?' Heim asked, incurious in his fatigue.

'Why, yonder is plain to see as bombwork. There must have been an industrial center here once, that was destroyed in the war.'

'And you'd let the same happen to Earth!' Bragdon's accusation was the first word he had spoken in more than a day.

Heim sighed. 'How often must I explain?' he said, more to Jocelyn than to the Peaceman. 'Earth has space defenses. She can't be attacked – unless we drift on from crisis to crisis till matters get so bad that both sides have to build fleets big enough to take the losses in breaking through. All I want is to head off that day by settling with Alerion now. Unfortunately, Alerion isn't interested in a reasonable settlement. We've got to prove to them that they haven't any alternative.'

'Womwardment does not account wor the inwertility here,' said Uthg-a-K'thaq. 'The war was three or wour Earth centuries ago. Radioactiwity disawweared long since. Something else has kewt nature 'rom recowering.'

'Oh, to hell with it,' Jocelyn moaned. 'Let me sleep.'

Heim lay down too. He thought with a dull unease that they should set a watch – but no, everyone was exhausted. . . . Unconsciousness took him.

The next day they saw two metallic shapes at a distance. There was no question of detouring for a closer look, and in any event they had something else to occupy what small part of their minds could be spared from the ever more painful onward march. The end of the plateau was coming into sight. Between the edge and the mountain's next upward slope was an escarpment. Right and left stretched those obsidian cliffs, sheer, polished, not high but unscalable in this gravity without equipment the party didn't have. To go around them – at whatever unseen point they stopped – would take days; and the survival drugs could not last for such a journey.

Only in the center of view was the line broken. A bank of vapor roiled from the foot of the scarp for several kilometers up the mountainside above. Like an immense curtain it hid the terrain; plumes blew off the top, blizzard color against the deep sky, and a roaring grew louder as the walkers neared.

'That has to be Thundersmoke,' Vadász said. 'But what is it?'

'A region ow – I hawe not the English,' Uthg-a-K'thaq answered. 'Tsheyyaka. The ground weneath is hot, and water woils out.'

'Geysers and hot springs,' Heim said. He whistled. 'But I've never seen or heard of anything their size. They make Yellowstone or Dwarf's Forge look like a teakettle. Can we get through?'

'We must.' Uthg-a-K'thaq bent his head so that all three eyes could peer through his faceplate. Evolved for the mists of his own planet, they could see a ways into the infrared. 'Yes-s-s. The cliwws are crum'led. Makes an incline, though wery rugged and with water rushing ewerywhere.'

'Still, thank God, a high gravity means a low angle of repose. And once into those meadows beyond, we should have a chance of meeting hunters or patrollers from the Hurst.' Heim straightened a little. 'We'll pull through.'

A while later he saw a third gleam of steel among the bushes.

This one was so near the line of march that he altered course to pass by. They didn't know exactly where they could best start into Thundersmoke anyway.

The object grew as he plodded. During rest periods he found he could not keep his gaze off. The shape was no uglier than much else he had seen, but in some indescribable fashion it made his spine crawl. When at last he dragged himself alongside and stopped for a look, he wanted to get away again, fast.

'An ancient machine.' Vadász spoke almost too softly to be heard through the grumble and hiss from ahead. 'Abandoned when the bomb struck.'

Corrosion was slow in this atmosphere. Paint had worn off the iron, which in turn was eroded but still shiny in places. The form was boxlike, some two meters square and five long, slanting on top toward a central turret. The ruins of a solar-power accumulator system could be identified, together with a radar sweep and, Heim thought, other detector instruments. Several ports in body and turret were shut, with no obvious means of opening them. He parted the brush around the base and saw that this had been a hovercraft, riding an air cushion and propelled by net backward thrust in any direction.

'A vehicle,' he said. 'After the war it just sat, I guess. Nobody can have moved back to the Lochan region for a long time. Those other things we glimpsed must be similar.'

Jocelyn clutched at his hand. He was reminded of his daughter when she was small and got frightened. 'Let's go, Gunnar,' she begged. 'This is too much like dead bones.'

'I wonder,' he remarked, carefully matter-of-fact, 'why the metal wasn't salvaged. Even with atomic energy, I should think the natives on a fireless planet would value scrap iron.'

'Taboo?' Vadász suggested. 'These wrecks may well have dreadful associations.'

'Maybe. Though my impression is that the Staurni look back on their war with a lot less horror than we remember our Exchange – and Earth got off very lightly.' Heim shifted the burden of air system and supply pack on his shoulders. 'Okay, we'll push on. The sun's low, and I don't fancy camping among ghosts.'

'Can you give us a song, Endre?' Jocelyn asked. 'I could use one.'

'I shall try.' The minstrel's voice was flattened as well as distorted in tranmission, but he croaked:

'*While goin' the road to sweet Athy, harroo, harroo!—*'

Engaged in helping the woman along, Heim paid no attention to the words at first. Suddenly he realized that Vadász was not singing 'When Johnny Comes Marching Home' at all, but the cruel old Irish original.

> '*—Where are the legs on which ye run*
> *When first ye went to carry a gun?*
> *Indeed your dancing days are done.*
> *Och, Johnny, I hardly knew ye.*

> '*With their guns and drums and drums and guns the*
> *enemy nearly slew ye.*
> *Och, Johnny, me dear, ye look so queer, Johnny, I*
> *hardly knew ye!*'

Heim glanced at Bragdon. One could almost read the thought in that helmet: How can these devils admit to themselves what war really means? The gloved hands clamped into fists: I know! I had to bury it.

> '*—Ye haven't an arm and ye haven't a leg,*
> *Ye're an eyeless, noseless, chickenless egg.*
> *Ye'll have to be put in a bowl to beg.*
> *Och, Johnny, I hardly knew ye.*

> '*With their guns and drums and drums and guns—*'

It was not good to hear in this slain land. But maybe Endre had no choice. Whatever haunted the machine receding too slowly into distance, had touched him likewise.

Everyone was unspokenly glad of the exhaustion which tumbled them into sleep that night. Yet Heim rested ill. Dreams troubled him, and several times he started awake ... what noise? A change in the geysers? No, something metallic, a creak, a rattle, a buzz, far off but limping closer; imagination, nothing else. He sank back into the feverish dark.

Dawn was wet with mists blown from Thundersmoke, a bare three or four kilometers away. White vapors coiled along the ground and hazed the countryside so that vision faded shortly into grayness. Overhead the sky was a bowl of amethyst and

Lochan's cap too bright to look at. Heim closed his chowlock on a mouthful of concentrate – the rest was a lump in his stomach – and stared blearily around. 'Where's Joss?'

'She went yonder,' Vadász said. 'Um-m ... she ought to be back now, eh?'

'I'll go find her.' Heim settled the weight on his body and lumbered into the fog.

She hunched not far off. 'What's the matter?' he called through the gush and burble of water.

Her form scarcely moved. 'I can't,' she said thinly.

'What can't you?'

'Go any further. I can't. Pain, every joint, every cell. You go on. Get help. I'll wait.'

He crouched, balancing on hands as well as feet. 'You've got to march,' he said. 'We can't leave you alone.'

'What can hurt me worse? What does it matter?'

Remorse smote him. He laid an arm across her and said without steadiness, 'Joss, I was wrong to make you come. I should have left you behind for your friends— But too late now. I don't ask you to forgive me—'

'No need, Gunnar.' She leaned against him.

'—but I do tell you you've got to make the trek. Three or four more days.' *Can't be any longer, because that's when we run out of supplies.* 'Then you can rest as much as you want.'

'Rest forever,' she breathed. Moisture ran down her faceplate like tears, but she spoke almost caressingly. 'I used to dread dying. Now it's sweet.'

Alarm cut through his own weariness. 'There's another reason you can't stay here by yourself. You'd let go all holds. This is the wrong time of month for you, huh? Okay.' He took the waste unit she had not refolded and slung it on his own back. His gloves groped at her pack.

'Gunnar!' She started. 'You can't carry my load too!'

'Not your air rig, worse luck. The rest is only a few kilos.' The fresh weight gnawed at him. He climbed to his feet again and reached down for her hands. 'C'mon. Allez oop.'

The breeze shifted and from the north came the sound of his dreams. Clank, bang, groan, close enough to override the thunders. 'What's that?' she shrilled.

'I dunno. Let's not find out.' His own heart missed a beat, but he was grimly pleased to see how she scrambled erect and walked.

116

At camp, Vadász and Uthg-a-K'thaq stared vainly for the source of the new noise. Bragdon was already stumping off, lost in an apathy which must stem from more than tiredness. The others followed him without speculating aloud.

The sun swung higher and began to burn off the fog. Steam still shrouded the natural cut in the cliffs, though the Naqsan said he could make out details of the nearer part. The humans saw scores of boulders, some big as houses, and thousands of lesser rocks that littered the final kilometer before the climb began. Among them washed hot, smoking streams, which turned the ground into mud tinted yellow by sulfur. Where pools had formed the hues were red and green, microscopic organisms perhaps. . . .

The pursuing clatter had strengthened. Vadász tried to sing, but no one listened and he soon quit. They tottered on, breathing hard, pausing less often to rest than had been their wont.

The moment came without announcement. Heim cast a glance behind and stopped dead. '*Fanden i helvede!*' he choked. His companions slewed around to see.

Between the lifting of fog and its own nearness, the thing had become visible a kilometer or so to their rear. It was another machine like the one they had found. But a twisted, weather-eaten detector frame still rose above the turret, and the body moved . . . slowly, crippledly, loose parts vibrating aloud, air blower spitting and jerking, the whole frame ashudder, it moved in their wake.

Jocelyn suppressed a cry. Bragdon actually jumped backward a step. Panic edged his tone: 'What's that?'

Heim beat down his own quick fear. 'An abandoned vehicle,' he said. 'Some kind of automaton. Not quite worn out. Scarcely any moving parts, you know.'

'But it's following us!' Jocelyn quavered.

'Probably set to patrol an area, home on any life it detects, and—' A crazy hope fluttered through Heim's brain, unshared by his guts. 'Maybe we're being offered a ride.'

'*Suq?*' asked Uthg-a-K'thaq in astonishment. After a moment, thoughtfully: 'Yes-s-s, is wossiwle. Or at least, grant a radio that wunctions, we could call.'

'No.' Vadász's helmet rolled with headshaking. 'I do not trust the looks.'

Heim ran a tongue which had gone wooden over his lips. 'It's moving quicker than we can, I think,' he said. 'We'll have to

117

settle with it one way or another.' Decision came. 'Wait here. I'll go back and see.'

Vadász and Jocelyn caught his arms simultaneously. He shook them off. 'Damnation, I'm still the captain,' he rapped. 'Let me be. That's an order.'

He started off. The hurt in his muscles dwindled. Instead there came an odd, tingling numbness. His mind felt unnaturally clear, he saw each twig and leaf on the haggard bushes around, felt how his feet struck soil and the impact that traveled through his shins to knees, smelled his own foulness, heard the geysers boom at his back. Earth seemed infinitely remote, a memory of another existence or a dream he had once had, unreal; yes, despite its vividness this world was unreal too, as hollow as himself. *I'm afraid,* he thought across an unbridgeable abyss. *That machine frightens me worse than anything ever did before.*

He walked on. There was nothing else to do. The detector lattice swiveled stiffly about, focused invisible unfelt energies on him. The robot changed direction to intercept. Several armor plates crashed loose. Blackness gaped behind them. The whole body was leprous with metal decay.

How long has it wandered this upland? For what?

The turret rotated. A port tried to open, got half-way, and stuck. The machine grated inside. Another port at the front of the body slid back. A muzzle poked forth. The slug-thrower spoke.

Heim saw dirt fly where the bullets hit, a hundred meters short. He whipped about and ran. The thing growled. Swaying on an unstable air cushion, it chased him. The gun raved a minute longer before stopping.

The Slaughter Machines! beat through Heim's skull, in time with his gasps for wind and the jar of footfalls. *Robots to guard whatever there was where that crater is now. Guard it by killing anything that moved. But a missile got through, and the robots alone were left, and hunted and killed till they wore out, and a few are still prowling these barrens, and today one of them has found us.*

He reached the others, stumbled, and rolled in a heap. For a minute he lay half stunned. Vadász and Uthg-a-K'thaq helped him rise. Jocelyn hung on to his hand and wept. 'I thought you were dead. I thought you were dead.'

'He would be,' said Vadász, 'but explosives have deteriorated. . . . Watch out!'

Another port had opened, another tube thrust clear. Across the distance, through a red blur in his vision, Heim saw coils, a laser projector, and lasers don't age. He grabbed Jocelyn to pull her behind him. A beam sickled, brighter than the sun. It struck well to the left. Bushes became charcoal and smoke. The beam traced a madman's course, boiled a rivulet, shot skyward, winked out.

'The aiming mechanism,' Uthg-a-K'thaq said. For once his own voice was shaken. 'Has worn to uselessness.'

'Not if the thing gets close,' Bragdon whimpered. 'Or it can slugger us, or crush us, or— Run!'

The terror had gone from Heim. He felt a cold uplifting: no pleasure of combat, for he knew how thin their chance was, but total aliveness. The matter grew crystalline in his mind, and he said: 'Don't. You'll wear yourself out in no time. This is a walking race. If we can get to Thundersmoke, or even to those boulders, ahead of the bullets, we may be able to hide. No, don't shed your packs. We won't be allowed to retrieve them. Walk.'

They struck out. 'Shall I sing for you?' Vadász asked.

'No need,' Heim said.

'I thought not. Good. I do need the breath.'

Heim took the rear. The engine coughed and banged behind. Again and again he could not control himself, he must stop and turn about for a look. Always death was closer. Old, old, crumbling, crazed, half blind and half palsied, the thing which had never been alive and would not die shivered along just a little faster than a man could stride on Staurn. The noise from it was an endless metal agony. Once he saw an armor plate drop off, once the air drive went awry and almost toppled the ponderous bulk; but it came on, came on. And the rocks of refuge ahead grew nearer with nightmare slowness.

Jocelyn began to stagger. Heim moved to give her support. As if the change in configuration had tripped some relay in a rotted computer, the slug-thrower spat anew. Several of the bullets buzzed past them.

Bragdon joined Heim on the woman's other side. 'Let me help,' he panted. She leaned on them both. 'We . . . won't make it,' Bragdon said.

'We might,' Heim snapped, for he dreaded a return of that negation he had seen in Jocelyn this dawn.

'We could . . . maybe . . . if we moved steady. You could. Not me. Not her. Got to rest.' Bragdon left the remainder unsaid: *The pursuer needs no rest.*

'Get into that water, among those rocks,' Vadász said. 'Lie low. Then maybe that *pokolgép* cannot see us.'

Heim followed his gesture. Somewhat to the left, a scatter of stones lay in a muddy pool. None were bigger than a man, but— A light artillery shell passed overhead. The cannon crack rang back off the unattainable cliffs. The shell struck, splintered a boulder, but did not explode.

'Let's try,' he agreed.

They splashed through muck and crouched belly-down in shallow red water. Heim was careful to hold his automatic free, Vadász his laser. Pistols seemed pathetic against the monster's size and armament; but a man took care of his weapons. Mist blown from Thundersmoke pattered upon them. Heim wiped his faceplate and stared between two rocks.

The machine had halted. It snarled to itself, jerked guns right and left, swept detectors through a hemisphere. 'Good Lord,' Vadász whispered, 'I think indeed it has lost us.'

'The water cools oww our in'rared radiation,' Uthg-a-K'thaq replied as hushedly. 'We are maywe under its radar weams, and maywe the owtical circuits are wad. Or the memory system has gone to wieces.'

'If only— No.' Heim's pistol sank in his fist.

'What did you think?' Jocelyn asked, frantic.

'How to disable what's left of the detector lattice. Could be done by a laser beam – see that exposed power cable? Only you'd never get close enough before you were spotted and killed.'

The short pulse-stopping hope, that the machine might give up and go away, crashed. It started grinding about a spiral, a search curve. Heim plotted that path and muttered: 'Should be here inside half an hour. However, first it'll move away. Which gains us some slight meterage. Be ready to start when I give you the word.'

'We'll never make it, I tell you,' Bragdon protested.

'Not so loud, you crudhead. We don't know that the thing hasn't still got ears.'

As if in response, the robot stopped. It rested a moment on the whirr from its air blowers; the lattice horns wove around, tilted, came to a halt. . . . It continued along the spiral.

'You see?' Vadász said with disgust. 'Keep trying, Bragdon. You may yet destroy us.'

The Peaceman made a strangled noise. 'Don't,' Jocelyn begged. 'Please.'

Uthg-a-K'thaq stirred. 'A thought,' he belched. 'I do in truth weliewe we cannot outrun the enemy to shelt-er. But can Slaughter Machines count?'

Vadász's breath hissed inward. 'What's this?'

'We hawe lit-tle to lose,' the Naqsan said. 'Let us run, excewt for one who waits here and keews the laser. Can he get unnoticed in cutting range ow the wistol weam—'

'He could be killed too easily,' Heim said. But hope shuddered anew in him. *Why not? Better go down fighting, whatever happens. And I might even save her.*

'Okay,' he said slowly. 'Give me the gun and I'll bushwhack our friend.'

'No, skipper,' Vadász said. 'I am no hero, but—'

'Orders,' Heim said.

'Gunnar—' broke from Jocelyn.

Uthg-a-K'thaq plucked the laser out of Vadász's grasp. 'No time wor human games,' he snorted. 'We were not here without him, and he is the least usewul. So.' He thrust the weapon at Bragdon. 'Or dare you not?'

'Gimme!' Heim snatched for it.

Bragdon drew away. 'That thing out there,' he said in a remote voice. 'What comes of war. Think about that, Heim.'

Vadász wallowed through the water and silt, after him. Heim saw the robot stop again to listen. 'Get out of here!' Bragdon yelled. 'I'll let it see me if you don't!'

The machine plowed through the bushes, over streams and stones, directly towards them.

No chance to argue. Bragdon must go ahead and be a damn fool. Heim got to his feet with a sucking splash. 'Follow me – everyone!' Jocelyn slithered from the pool with him. They started off together.

Thundersmoke brawled before them. The engine chugged hoarse behind. A gun chattered. Mist swirled in their view, settled on their faceplates, blinded them. Staurn hauled them downward, laid rocks to trip them, brewed mud to glue their boots. Heim's heart smashed at his ribs as if it were also a cannon. He didn't know how much he leaned on Jocelyn or she on him. There was no awareness of anything but noise, weight, and vast drowning waters.

Vadász shouted.

Heim lurched against a boulder, got his back to it, and lifted his automatic. But the hunter machine was not about to pounce.

Near the thing was, most horribly near. Bragdon's tiny form crept from ambush. Up to that iron body the man went, braced himself on widespread legs, aimed his pistol and fired.

The laser sword hewed. Metal framework glowed white where struck. Trigger held fast, Bragdon probed for the power cable.

Something like a bull's bellow rose out of the robot. It swung clumsily around. Bragdon stood where he was, dwarfed under its bulk, steadily firing. Ports opened in the armor, where they were able. Guns came out. A few still worked. Heim hauled Jocelyn to the ground and laid himself above her. A wild beam hit the boulder where he had made his stand. Rock flowed from the wound.

The guns could not reach as low as Bragdon. The machine clanked forward. Bragdon severed the detector powerline. 'Run Victor!' Vadász howled. 'Get out of the way!' Bragdon turned and tripped. The robot passed over him.

And on, firing, firing, a sleet of bullets, shells, energy beams, poison gases, destruction's last orgasm; senseless, witless, futureless, the Slaughter Machine rocked south because it chanced to be headed that way.

Heim rose and hurried toward Bragdon. *Maybe he's all right. An air cushion distributes weight over a large area.* Bragdon did not stir. Heim came near and stopped.

Dimly, through the clamor of geysers and departing engine, he heard Jocelyn call, 'I'm coming, Gunnar!'

'No,' he cried back. 'Don't.'

There were sharp blades in the bottom of the iron shell. They must move up and down, clearing the ground by a few centimeters. He did not want her to see what lay before his eyes.

CHAPTER SEVEN

DRUMROLL in the earth: vapor puffed from a sulfurous cone. Then the spout came, climbing until a pillar for giants stood white and crowned. Another died; but there were more, everywhere among the tumbled black stones, as far as Heim could see through a whirl of fog. There was no distance. He groped in chaos. Water chuckled around his boots, over and over again he slipped on wetness. The damp was interior too, sweat soddened his skin. Strange, he thought in what detachment he could muster from the weariness with which he trembled, strange that his lungs should be a dry fire.

Jocelyn's gasps reached him, where she crawled at his side. Half his strength was spent to help her along. Otherwise he heard nothing but the titanic forces that churned about them. Uthg-a-K'thaq's broad shape was visible ahead, leading the way. Vadász toiled in the rear. Light waned as the sun sank behind the mountain, to end the day after they piled a cairn over their newest dead.

We've got to keep going, chanted idiotically in Heim. *Got to keep going. Got to keep going.* And underneath: *Why?*

For the sake of the battle he intended to fight? That had become meaningless. The only battle was here, now, against a planet. For Lisa, then? A better cause, that she should not be fatherless. But she could well survive him. Grief dies young in the young. To discharge his own responsibility to those he commanded? Better still; it touched a deep-lying nerve. Yet he was no longer in command, when his engineer saw more clearly and moved more surely than any human could.

Reasons blew away like geyser smoke. Death lured him with promises of sleep.

Animal instinct raised his hackles. He cursed the tempter and went on.

A mudpot bubbled on a level stretch. The farther bank was a precarious hill of boulders. Water rushed among them, struck the mud below, and exploded in steam. Uthg-a-K'thaq beckoned the others to wait, flopped down on his belly, and hitched himself forward. Mineral crusts were treacherous, and whoever fell into one of those kettles might be cooked alive before the rest heaved him out against gravity.

Jocelyn used the pause to lie flat. Maybe she slept, or fainted; small difference any more. Heim and Vadász remained standing. It would have been too much effort to rise again.

On the edge of visibility, among the clouds around the hilltop, Uthg-a-K'thaq waved. Heim and Vadász wrestled Jocelyn back to her legs. The captain led the way, stooped so he could make out the leader's track through gray soft precipitate powders.

123

When he came to the rise, hands and feet alike must push him over the high-stacked stones. Often a lesser chunk got loose and bounced hollowly down to the mudpot. Safest would have been to go one at a time, his dimmed consciousness realized now. The least slip could—

'*Gunnar!*'

He scrambled around, and almost went down in the same minor avalanche where Jocelyn rolled.

Somehow he was up, bounding through the hot fog as he had plunged to attack centuries ago. Stones turned under his soles, water spurted where he struck. Nothing existed but his need to stop her before she went into the cauldron below.

Her limbs flailed, her fingers clawed, dislodging more rocks that tumbled across her. He reached bottom. His boots sank in ooze. There was not too much heat on this fringe of the pot. But had there been, he would not have noticed. Those boulders which had spun downward faster than the woman and sunk immediately gave footing. He knelt and braced himself.

The mass poured at him, around him. He laid hold on Jocelyn's air cycler and became a wall.

When the landslip was done, he pulled his smeared self clear and fell beside her. Vadász saw they would go no further than the verge of the mudsink, ended his own haste, and picked a cautious way to join them. Presently Uthg-a-K'thaq arrived too.

Heim roused some minutes later. The first he noticed was the Naqsan's voice, weirdly akin to the voice of the kettle: 'Wery much harm wor us. Lac-king him, can we long liwe?'

'Joss,' he mumbled, and fought to rise. Vadász helped him. He leaned on the Magyar a while until strength returned.

'*Hála Istennek,*' gusted from the helmet beside his. 'You are not hurt?'

'I'm okay,' Heim said. His entire being seemed one bruise, and blood welled from abrasions. 'Her?'

'Broken leg at the minimum.' Vadász's fingers touched the unnatural angle between left hip and thigh of the motionless figure. 'I don't know what else. She is unconscious.'

'Her suit is intact,' Uthg-a-K'thaq said. *First silly remark I've heard from him,* trickled through Heim. *If the fabric had torn, we wouldn't worry about bones.*

He shoved Vadász aside and bent over her. When the faceplate had been wiped clean, he could make out her features in

124

the dimming light. Eyes were closed, lips half parted, skin color-less and sweat-beaded. He was dismayed at how sunken her cheeks were. Laying an audio pickup against her speaker, he was barely able to detect breath, rapid and shallow.

He poised on his knees. To stave off the future, he asked, 'Did anyone see what happened?'

'A stone moved when she put her weight on,' Vadász said, 'She started to roll and half the hillside went with her. Some recent quake must have unstabilized it. I will never know how you got down here so fast, not falling.'

'Who cares?' Heim gritted. 'She's in shock. I don't know if that's due to anything more than the leg fracture, she being so weakened to begin with. Could be worse injuries, like spinal. We don't dare move her.'

'What then can we do?' the engineer asked. Heim realized that command had passed back to him.

'You two go on,' he said. 'I'll stay with her.'

'No!' Vadász exclaimed involuntarily.

Uthg-a-K'thaq spoke in some remnant of his pedantic way. 'You can giwe her no aid, woth sealed in airsuits. We others may well need an ex-tra wair ow hands. A diwwicult wassage is wewore us.'

'As battered as I am, I'd hinder you more than help,' Heim said. 'Besides, she can't be left alone. Suppose there's another rockslip, or this mudpot boils higher?'

'Cawtain, she is done already. Unconscious, she cannot take her grawanol. Without that, in shock, heart wailure comes quickly. Kindest to owen her helmet now.'

Rage and loss flew out of Heim: 'Be quiet, you cold-blooded bastard! You goaded Bragdon to die, on purpose. One's enough!'

'*Gwurru*,' the Naqsan sobbed, and retreated from him.

The venom dissipated, leaving emptiness. 'I'm sorry, C.E.,' Heim said dully. 'Can't expect you to think like a Terrestrial. You mean well. I suppose men's instincts are less practical than yours.' Laughter shook chains in his throat. 'Speaking about practicality, though, you've got something like an hour of light. Don't waste it. March.'

Vadász considered him long before asking, 'If she dies, what will you do?'

'Bury her and wait. I can stretch out the water in these can-teens if I sit quiet, but you'll need the laser for your own drink.'

'And you will then have nothing to, to fall back on. No, this is foolishness.'

'I'll keep the automatic, if that makes you happier. Now get going. I'll hoist a beer with you yet.'

Vadász surrendered. 'If not on ship,' he said, 'then in Valhalla. Farewell.'

Their hands clasped, pair by pair. Minstrel and engineer began to climb. A geyser spat not far off, steam blew down the wind, the two shapes were lost to sight.

Heim settled himself.

A chance for sleep, he thought. But that desire was gone. He checked Jocelyn's breathing – no change – and stretched out beside her, glove upon her glove.

Resting thus, he grew clearer-headed. With neither excitement nor despair he weighed the likelihood of survival. It wasn't great. Zero for Joss, of course, barring miracles. For the other three, about fifty-fifty. The walkers should emerge from Thundersmoke tomorrow evening, more or less. Then they had perhaps two days (allowing those tough bodies one day without chemical crutches) in which to cross the high meadows towards Wenilwain's castle. It was still distant, but the folk of the Hurst ranged widely. Doubtless they even crossed above Slaughter Land now and then, on their way to the plains and the sea. (*Hm, yes, that's why they leave the robots alone. A free defense. Carnivore souls for sure.*) Given a break, the travelers might have been spied days ago.

Well, the break was not given. So Joss must die in this wet hell, under a sun whose light would not reach Earth for a century: Earth of the green woods where she had walked, the halls where she danced, the garden where she played her flute for him until he frightened her with babbled impossibilities. As that sun smoldered to extinction behind the fogs, Gunnar Heim pondered the riddle of his guilt toward her.

He had forced her here. But he did so because if she stayed behind she would betray his hopes for his planet. (*Are you certain of that, buck? In fact, are you certain your way is the right one?*) The choice would never have arisen except for the plot she had joined in. Yet that was evoked by his own earlier conspirings.

He gave up. There was no answer, and he was not one to agonize in unclarity. This much he knew: if the time aboard the *Quest* had not matched those dreams he buried long ago

126

for Connie's sake, it had still been more dear than he deserved, and when Joss died a light would forever go out in him.

Blup-blup, said the mudpot beneath. A hot spring seethed louder. A geyser roared in thickening dusk, echoes resounded from unseen walls and water rilled among the shadow shapes of boulders. Heavy as his own flesh pressed against unyielding painful jumble, night flowed across the world.

Gloom lightened when the nearer moon rose, close to full, a shield bigger than Luna seen from Earth, iron bright and mottled with a strange heraldry. Heim dozed a while, woke, and saw it well above him. A thin glow surrounded the disc, diffusion in the upper mists. But most of the sky was open and he could make out stars. The lower fog rolled ashen through Thundersmoke gulch.

His drowsy eyes tried to identify individual suns. Could that bright one near Lochan's ghostlike peak be Achernar? If so, curious to look from here upon his emblem of victory. *I wonder if Cynbe could be watching it too. Wherever he is.*

Better check on Joss. He commenced pulling his stiffened frame off the rocks.

What's that?

WHAT'S THAT?

The sight was a lightning bolt. For a second he could not believe. A long V trailed across the moon—

Staurni, in flight home to the Hurst!

Heim soared erect. 'Hey! Hallo-o-o! You up there, come down, help, help, help!'

The bawling filled his helmet, shivered his eardrums, tore his larynx; and was lost within meters of noise-troubled air. He flapped his arms, knew starkly that the blurring vapors made him invisible from so high above, saw the winged ones pass the disc and vanish into darkness. A beast yell broke from him, he cursed every god in the cosmos, drew his automatic and fired again and again at heaven.

That little bark was also nothing. And not even a glint from the muzzle. Heim lifted the useless thing, which could only kill Joss, to hurl it into the mud.

His hand sank. The metal moonlight seemed to pierce his skull, he was instantly cold, utterly aware, tracing the road he must follow as if on a battle map.

No time to lose. Those wings beat fast. He squatted, unbuckled his air system, hauled its packboard around in front of

127

him. The valve on the hose into his suit closed readily, but the coupling beyond resisted. And he had no pliers. He threw all his bear strength into his hands. The screw threads turned. The apparatus came free.

Now he was alone with whatever air his suit contained; the recycler depended on pressure from the reserve bottles. He cracked their valves. Terrestrial atmosphere, compressed more than Staurn's own, streamed forth.

The reaction must be kindled, and he had no laser. Heedless of ricochet or shrapnel, he laid the automatic's mouth against the cock and pulled trigger. The bang and the belling came together. Alloy shattered, the bullet screamed free, the air tanks became a lamp.

Its flame was wan blue under the moon. Heim held the pack-board steady with one hand and fanned with the other. 'Please,' he called, 'please, look this way, she'll die if you don't.' A far-off part of him observed that he wept.

The fire flickered out. He bent near the pressure gauge, trying to read it in the unpitying moonlight. Zero. Finished.

No, wait, that was zero net. There were still three atmospheres absolute. And hydrogen diffused inward faster than oxygen did outward. Explosive mixture? He scrambled to put the bottles behind a large rock. Leaning across, he shot straight into them and threw himself down.

Flame blossomed anew, one fury and the crash toning away, whine of flying fragments, a grating among lesser stones as they sought new rest, nothingness. Heim got carefully up.

An infinite calm descended upon him. He had done what he could. Now it was only to wait, and live or die as the chance befell. He returned to Jocelyn, listened to her breath, and lay down beside her.

I ought to be in suspense, he thought vaguely. *I'm not. Could my air be poisoned already? . . . No, I should last an hour or so if I don't move. I'm just . . . fulfilled, somehow.* His eyes went to the moon, his thoughts to Connie. He had no belief in survival after death, but it was as if she had drawn close to him.

'Hi, there,' he whispered.

And— 'Hai-i-i-i!' winded down the reaches of heaven, the air sang, and bat wings eclipsed the moon. Weapons flashed clear, the flock whirled around in their search for an enemy, fangs glittered, and devil shapes came to earth.

Only they didn't act like devils, once they saw. A warrior

128

bayed into the midget transceiver he carried. A vehicle from the Hurst descended within minutes. Her mother could not have raised Jocelyn more tenderly onto a stretcher and into the machine. Wolf-gray Wenilwain himself connected an oxygen bottle to Heim's suit. The flyer lifted and lanced eastward for Orling.

'But ... listen ... *jangir ketleth*—' Heim desisted. His few pidgin phrases couldn't explain about Endre and C.E. No matter, really. He'd soon be at the yacht; Wong could interpret via radio; the last survivors would be found no later than sunrise. Heim fell asleep smiling.

CHAPTER EIGHT

HER cabin was quiet. Someone had hung a new picture on the bulkhead where she could see it: a beach, probably on Tahiti. Waves came over a sapphire ocean to foam against white sands; in the foreground, palm trees nodded at Earth's mild winds.

She laid down her book as the tall man entered. Color mounted in her face. 'Gunnar,' she said very low. 'You shouldn't be up.'

'Our medic wants me on my back till we leave,' he said, 'but the hell with him. At least, I had to come see you before you go. How're you feeling?'

'All right. Still weak, of course, but Dr. Silva says I'm making a good recovery.'

'I know. I asked him. Enzyme therapy is a wonder, eh?' Heim searched for a phrase. Nothing sufficed. 'I'm glad.'

'Sit down, you idiot!'

He pulled the lounger close to her bed and lowered himself. Even in a flyer, the trip had left him lightheaded. Several days yet must pass before his vigor was restored. The gun at his hip caught on the adjuster console. He pulled it free with a muttered oath.

Amusement touched her lips. 'You needn't have brought that. Nobody's going to kidnap you.'

'Well, hopefully not. Call it insurance.'

Her smile faded. 'Are you that angry?'

'No. Two good men died, the rest of us went through a nasty time. I'm sorry it happened, but you can't take an episode in a war to heart.'

Her look reminded him of a trapped small animal. 'You could press charges of murder.'

'Good Lord!' he exclaimed. 'What kind of swine do you take me for? We went out together on a field trip. Our engine failed, we made a crash landing where one man was killed, and hiked after help. If your people will stick by that story, mine will.'

A thin hand stole toward him. He took it and did not let go. Her hazel eyes caught him in turn. Silence grew.

When he could hold out no more, and still lacked meaningful words, he said, 'You're hauling mass at dawn, right?'

'Yes. The scientists – those who thought this was a genuine trip – they want to stay. But Captain Gutierrez overruled them. We've lost our purpose.' Quickly: 'How long will you remain?'

'About another Earth week, till the new missile units are fitted. To be sure, we'll lose time getting out of the planetary system. The Lodge has to escort us, and won't let us arm our warheads till we're beyond defensive limits. But still, I figure we'll be on the move inside of ten days.'

Again muteness, while they looked at each other, and away, and back. 'What do you plan on doing at home?' he tried.

'Wait for you,' she said. 'Pray for you.'

'But – no, look, your, uh, your political work—'

'That's no longer relevant. I haven't changed my mind – or have I? It's hard to tell.' Her free hand rubbed her forehead confusedly. The motion stirred her hair, awakening light in the chestnut tresses. 'I don't think I was wrong in principle,' she said after a bit. 'Maybe I was in practice. But it doesn't matter any more. You see, you've changed the universe. Earth is committed.'

'Nonsense!' His face smoldered. 'One ship?'

'With you her captain, Gunnar.'

'Thanks, but . . . but you flatter me and— Wait, Joss, you do have a job. Sentiment at home might swing too far in the other direction. The last thing any sane person wants is a jehad. You keep telling 'em the enemy is not too evil to live. Remind 'em there'll be peace negotiations eventually, and the more reasonable we are then, the more likely the peace is to last. Okay?'

He saw that she braced herself. 'You're right, and I'll do my poor best,' she said. 'But talking politics is only an evasion.'

'What do you mean?' he stalled.

Her mouth quirked afresh. 'Why, Gunnar, I do believe you're scared.'

'No, no, nothing of the sort. You need rest. I'd better go.'

'Sit,' she commanded. Her fingers closed about his palm. The touch was light, but it would have been easier to break free of a ship grapple.

Red and white chased each other across her countenance. 'I have to explain,' she said with astounding steadiness. 'About what happened earlier.'

His skin prickled.

'Yes, I hoped to persuade you not to fight,' she said. 'But I learned more was involved. Infinitely more.'

'Uh, uh – the past, sure—'

'When you come back,' she asked, 'what are *you* going to do?'

'Live quietly.'

'Ha! I'd like to make book on that. For a while, though, you will be home on Earth.' Her tone dropped. 'Oh, God, you must.' She raised her head. 'I'll be there too.'

He must summon so much will to speak that none was left for holding his eyes off the deck. 'Joss,' he said, word by word, 'you remember too many things. So do I. There was that chance once, which we did better to pass up. Then we met again, both free, both lonesome, and I admit I also thought the chance might have come again. Only it hadn't. Time switched the dice on us.'

'No, that isn't true. Sure, at first I believed otherwise. Our casual meetings after I returned from Ourania, and the political barrier between us – damn all politics! I thought you were simply attractive, and half that must be because of a friendship we'd never revive. I dreamed a little on the way here, but they seemed like just ordinary woman-type daydreams. How could you hurt me?' She paused. 'It turned out you could.'

'I'm trying not to,' he said desperately. 'You're too good for soothing with lies.'

She let his hand go. Her own fell open upon the blanket. 'So you don't care.'

'I do, I do. But can't you see, I didn't break with Connie the way you did with Edgar. When she, well, helped me about you, we pulled still closer together. Then she died. It cut me off at the roots. I guess without thinking about it I've looked ever since for a root that strong. I'm a coward, afraid to settle for anything less, because afterwards someone else might happen by who— It wouldn't be fair to you.'

She rallied. 'You've outgrown believing in permanent infatuation, haven't you? We understand what really matters between two people. If you're trying to warn me you might be restless— I wouldn't be jealous at your wandering a little. As long as you always came back.'

'I don't want to wander. Physically isn't important. I wouldn't want to mentally. That one time was bad enough. And when I heard about New Europe, I remembered a girl there. I was young and stupid, skittish about being tied down, which is especially bad for a Navy man. So I left when my leave was up without committing myself. Next time I arrived, she'd moved; I dithered whether to track her down, finally didn't, and soon after got posted too far away to visit that planet. Now—'

'I see. You want to make sure about her.'

'I have to.'

'But that was twenty years or more ago, wasn't it?'

He nodded. 'I've got to find out what happened to her, see her safe if she's still alive. Beyond that, yes, I'm doubtless being foolish.'

She smiled then. 'Go ahead. I'm not too worried.'

He rose. 'I must leave now. Neither of us is in any shape for emotional scenes.'

'Yes. I'll wait, darling.'

'Better not. Not seriously, anyhow. Hell alone knows what'll happen to me. I might not return at all.'

'Gunnar!' she cried, as if he had struck her. 'Never say that!'

He jollied her as best he could, and kissed her farewell, and departed. While his pilot flitted him the short way back to the yacht, he looked out. A flock of Staurni hunters was taking off. Sunlight flared across their weapons. The turmoil in him changed toward eagerness – to be away, to sail his ship again – as he watched those dragon shapes mount into the sky.

Part Three

ADMIRALTY

CHAPTER ONE

STRICTLY speaking, the Phoenix is a constellation in the skies of the Solar System, about half-way between ecliptic plane and south celestial pole. It is a mistake to apply the name to that region of space, some hundred and fifty light-years in the same direction from Earth, where the suns of Alerion and New Europe are found. But because a human colony makes a number of neighboring systems interesting – as places to visit, mine, trade, explore, fight, be *related* to – a name is required for such a vaguely defined territory. Once bestowed, however carelessly, it remains.

And perhaps this one was not altogether a misnomer. The Phoenix of myth is reborn in fire. Nuclear energies bore Lamontagne the long way to Aurore. When he saw that that sun had a world where men could settle, he raised the tricolor like a flame in its heavens. Hope burned high in the folk who moved to New Europe, labored, begot, and bequeathed. Then the warcraft of Alerion came, with hellfire aboard.

A ship raised from the planet. Forces pulsed in her gravitrons, meshed with the intervowen fields of the cosmos, drove her out at ever-mounting speed. As Aurore fell behind, space grew less distorted by the star's mass. She would soon reach a point where the metric approximated a straight line so nearly that it was safe to draw the forces entirely around her, cut off that induction effect known as inertia, and outpace light.

A million kilometers away, *Fox II* observed her: saw by visible light and infrared, felt with a ghostly quickly-brushing whisker of radar, heard faint ripples of her drive in space, snuffed the neutrinos from her engines, and came to carnivore alertness.

'Damn!' said Gunnar Heim. 'We should have spotted that beast hours ago. They must have installed extra screening.'

First Officer David Penoyer studied the data-analysis tapes.

'Seems to be a moderate-sized transport ship. Same class as the *Ellehoi* we took last month, I'd guess. If so, we've got more legs than she does.'

Heim gave a restless shove with one foot. His huge body made a free-fall curve through the air to a viewport. Stars crowded it beyond counting; the Milky Way rivered in silver around an endless clear black; nebulae and remote galaxies glimmered across more distance than man will ever comprehend. He had no time for awe; he stared outward with eyes gone wintry blue as a giant sun and said: 'She'll be outside the Mach limit long before we can come anywhere near matching velocities. I know it's theoretically possible for a ship to lay alongside another going FTL, but it's never been done and I'm not about to try. If nothing else, there'd be too much interstellar gas turbulence.'

'Well, but – Captain, we don't have to make a prize of her. I mean, if we simply accelerate, we'll catch her inside the limit. Then she's either got to turn on the Machs and probably get ripped apart, or face our barrage.'

Heim's blocky features bent into a grimace. 'And she might take the chance rather than surrender. I'd hate to spoil our record. Four months of commerce raiding, eighteen Aleriona ships captured, and we haven't had to kill anybody yet.' He ran a hand through his roan hair. 'If only— Wait!' He swung about and pushed the intercom controls. 'Captain to chief engineer. Listen, you can make a gravitron do everything but wash dishes. Could we safely make a very short FTL run from here?'

Penoyer shaped a soundless whistle.

'The matter is one ow 'recise adjustment, skiwwer,' rumbled Uthg-a-K'thaq's voice. 'We succeeded in it when we lewt the Solar Sys-tem. Wut now, awter cruising so long without an owerhaul—'

'I know.' Heim's faded blue tunic wrinkled with his shrug. They didn't have uniforms on *Fox*. 'All right, I suppose we do simply have to destroy them. War isn't a game of tiddlywinks,' he added, largely to himself.

'A moment, 'lease.' The intercom brought clicking noises. C.E. must be using his Naqsan equivalent of a slide rule, Heim thought. 'Yes-s-s. I hawe recalculated the sawety margin. It suwwices.'

'Whoops!' Heim's yell rang between the bulkheads. 'Hear

134

that, Dave?' He pounded Penoyer on the back.

The blond man catapulted across the bridge, choked, and sputtered, 'Yes, sir, very good.'

'Not just that we won't have to blot out lives,' Heim exulted. 'But the money. All that lovely, lovely prize money.'

And a prize crew to take her back to Earth, the business part of him recalled. *We're damn near down to a skeleton complement. A few more captures and we'll have to call a halt.*

Fiercely: *So we don't sell the last one, but send word by it. Whoever wants to sign on again can meet us at Staurn, where we'll be refilling our magazines. With the kind of bank account I must have now, I can refit for a dozen more cruises. We won't stop till we're blown out of space – or the Federation gets off its duff and makes some honest war.*

He gave himself entirely to the work of preparation. When battle stations were piped, a cheer shivered the length of the ship. Those were good boys, he thought with renewed warmth. They'd drawn reluctant lots to choose who must bring the seized Aleriona vessels home, and even so fights had broken out over the privilege of daily risking death in the Auroran System. Of course, the ones who stayed got a proportionately larger share of booty. But they had signed on his privateer for much more than that.

'Engines to full output!' If the enemy were on the *qui vive,* they would immediately observe on their instruments that another vessel orbited here. Radar alone was useless at such distances, for what was registered might as well be a meteorite: until it awoke.

'Internal field to standard!' Earth weight came back.

'Turning vectors: roll three points, pitch four and half points, yaw twelve points!' Stars wheeled across the ports.

'Acceleration maximum!' There was no sense of pressure in the compensating gee-field that webbed through the hull. But the engines growled.

'Stand by for Mach drive! On the mark, five, four, three, two, one, zero!'

Starlight wavered, as if seen through a sheet of running water, and steadied again. In that brief passage, the fantastic acceleration of inertialessness did not build up a speed so great that aberration or Doppler effect counted. But the remote disc of Aurore shrank yet farther.

135

'Cut Mach drive!' An electronic signal had sent the command before Heim's automatic words were well begun.

Computers chattered beneath Penoyer's hands. *Fox* had returned to normal well ahead of the Aleriona ship. The latter was still traveling at more than the privateer's kinetic velocity, but it would now be no trick to match vectors inside the Mach limit.

'Number Four Turret, give her one across the bows!' The missile streaked forth. Atomic fire dazzled momentarily among the constellations.

'Sparks, connect me on the universal band,' Heim ordered. He realized he was sweating. The outflank maneuver would not have been possible save for Uthg-a-K'thaq's non-human sensitivity in the tuning of a gravitronic manifold, and the engineer could have been mistaken. But beneath the released terror, joy sang in the captain. *We've got them! One more blow struck!*

A siren wailed. The ship trembled. Automatons reacted; great clangings and thumps resounded through her plates.

'My God!' Penoyer's cry came thin. 'They're armed!'

The viewports darkened, that eyes not be burned out by the intolerable brightnesses which blossomed around. Riven fragments of atoms sleeted through vacuum, were whirled away by the ship's hydromagnetic field, spat X-rays into her material shielding and vanished starward. The meteorite detectors shouted of shrapnel thrown at kilometers per second by low-yield warheads.

Time was lacking in which to be afraid. 'Parry her stuff,' Heim commanded his gunners. 'Laser Turret Three, see if you can cripple her Mach rings.'

Beyond so elementary a decision, he was helpless. Nor could his highly skilled men do a great deal more than transmit it to their robots. The death machines were too fast, too violent for human senses. Radar beams locked on, computers clicked, missiles homed on missiles and destroyed them before they could strike. A blinding beam of energy probed from the Aleriona craft. There was no stopping it; but before it inflicted more than minimal damage, *Fox*'s own heavy laser smote. Armor plate vaporized, the ray burned through, the enemy weapon went dark. The Terrestrial fire-lance drew a seared line across the Aleriona hull as it probed for the exterior fittings of the interstellar drive. That was no easy target, with the relative position of the two vessels shifting so rapidly. But the computers solved the problem in milliseconds. The other ship crammed on acceleration, trying to shake loose. For a moment the laser pierced only emptiness. Then, remorselessly, it found its mark again and gnawed away.

'Fire Control to bridge. His Mach's disabled, sir.'

'Good. He can't go FTL on us now, whatever happens,' Heim said. 'Bridge to radio room. Keep trying to make contact. Bridge to engine room. Prepare for velocity-matching maneuvers.'

The fight died away. It had not been long. The disproportion between a hastily armed merchantman and a cruiser equipped like a regular Navy unit was too great. Not ludicrous – a single missile that exploded near enough would have killed the human crew by radiation if nothing else – but nonetheless too great. *Fox* had warded off every threat with an overwhelmingly larger concentration of immensely more powerful weapons. A dark peace descended in space. The stars came back in the viewports.

'Whee-ew,' Penoyer said faintly. 'Jolly near got us by surprise alone, didn't he?'

'He obviously hoped to,' Heim nodded. 'I suppose after today we'd better expect every unescorted transport to be able to fight back.' Those that were convoyed he left alone. They weren't many, with Alerion's strength stretched thin in the Marches and with quite a few warships searching the deeps for him. His prey were the carriers of the cargo which New Europe's occupiers must have to make their conquest impregnable.

However closely he had skirted obliteration, he felt no delayed panic. If asked about that, he would have said he was blessed with a phlegmatic temperament. But the truth was that upwelling triumph left no room for other feelings. He must force himself to speak coolly: 'I'm not worried. Pleased, in fact. We showed up better in combat than I had a right to expect with such a higgledy-piggledy crew.'

'Oh, I don't know, sir. You've drilled us aplenty.' Penoyer fumbled for a cigaret. 'Those explosions may have been noticed. Somebody bigger might come out investigating.'

'Uh-huh. We won't stay to admire the local scenery.'

'But what about this capture? She can't make the Solar System.'

'We'll park her in a cometary orbit, not likely to be detected, and repair at leisure— Hoy, there's an answer to our call.'

The conscreen smoldered with the simulated light of a red dwarf sun. An Aleriona looked out. He was of rank, Heim saw from the fineness of the muliebrile visage, the luster of golden hair and silvery fur. Even in this moment of rage and grief, his language was music that would have haunted a Beethoven.

Heim shook his head. 'Sorry, I don't know the High Speech. *Parlez-vous français?*'

'Not truth,' sang the other captain. 'In the star meadows fare we here aboard, needless of New Europe's tongue. To you the rover yield we *Meroeth*.'

It was a relief finding one who had some English. So far there'd been two with Spanish, one each with French and Chinese. Otherwise sign language worked, when you had a gun in your hand. 'You know what we are, then?' Heim said.

'All know now of that which is named for the swift animal with sharp teeth. Ill may you prosper,' crooned the Aleriona.

'Thanks. Now look. We'll send a boarding party. Your crew will be brigged, but we don't plan to mistreat anybody who doesn't force us to. In fact, if you have any casualties— None? Good. You'll be taken to Earth in your ship and interned for the duration of the war.'

Within himself, Heim wondered about that. Earth was far, Sol itself lost to naked vision. He had no way to get their news. A prize crew could not return and rendezvous with a ship fighting alone against an empire, dependent for survival on unpredictable motion through immensity. He supposed Parliament had had to concede France's claim that the World Federation was indeed at war with Alerion and his own expedition lawful. Otherwise Earth ships would be out here – Earth officials, at least, aboard Aleriona ships which invited his approach – to order him home.

But there was no word, no help, nothing in the six months since he had left except his own solitary battle. The last Aleriona prisoner he talked to had said the two fleets were still merely glaring at each other in the Marches, and he believed it. *Are they deadlocked yet about whether to fight or negotiate? Will they never see that there can't be negotiation with an enemy who's sworn to whip us out of space, till we prove we can beat*

138

him? Merciful God, New Europe's been gripped for almost a year!

Sorrow touched the lonely face in the screen. 'Could we have gotten well-wrought engines of war, might we have slain you.' Hands slim, four-fingered, and double-jointed caressed one of the flowering vines that bedecked the bridge, as if seeking consolation. 'Evilly built are your machines, men-creatures.'

Oh, ho! so this Q-boat was outfitted right on New Europe. Did somebody there get the idea? 'Cease acceleration and stand by to be boarded,' Heim said.

He cut the circuit and issued orders. Treachery was still possible. *Fox* must maintain her distance and send boats. He would have liked to go himself, but his duty was here, and every man was eager to make the trip. Like small boys playing pirate ... well, they had taken some fabulous treasures.

Not that *Meroeth* was likely to hold much of interest. Alerion wanted New Europe as a strong point – above all, wanted simply to deny it to humans and thus deny the entire Phoenix – rather than a colony. The cargoes that went from The Eith to Aurore were industrial or military, and thus valuable. No important resources were sent back; at the end of so long a line of communications, the garrison of New Europe must devote everything they could to the task of producing and putting into orbit those defenses which would make the planet all but invulnerable.

Still, the ships didn't always return empty. Some of the plunder Heim had taken puzzled him. Was it going to Alerion for the sake of curiosity, or in a hope of eventual sale to Earth, or—? Whatever the reason, his boys had not argued with luck when they grabbed a holdful of champagne!

Vectors were matched. The boats went forth. Heim settled himself in the main control chair and watched them, tiny bright splinters, until they were swallowed by the shadow of the great shark-nosed cylinder he guarded. His thoughts ran free: Earth, prideful cities and gentle skies; Lisa, who might have grown beyond knowing; Jocelyn, who had never quite left him – and then New Europe, people driven from their homes to the wilderness, a certain idiot dream about Madelon—

The screen buzzed. He switched it on. Blumberg's round face looked out at him from a shell of combat armor. The helmet was open. Heim didn't know if the ember light within that ship could account alone for the man's redness.

'Boarding party reporting, sir.' Blumberg was near stammering in his haste.

Unease tensed Heim's belly muscles. 'What's wrong?' he demanded.

'Nothing ... situation in hand ... but sir! They've got humans aboard!'

CHAPTER TWO

A short inertialess flight took *Fox* so far outsystem that the probability of being detected was quite literally infinitesimal. Heim left the automatics in charge and decreed a celebration.

The mess seethed with men. Only twenty-five privateers remained, and a dozen New Europeans, in a room that had once held a hundred; but they filled it, shouting, singing, clashing their glasses, until the bulkheads trembled. In one corner, benign and imperturbable, Uthg-a-K'thaq snaked bottle after bottle of champagne from the cooler he had rigged, sent the corks loose with a pistol crack, and poured for all. Suitably padded, gunner Matsuo Hayashi and a lean young colonist set out to discover whether karate or Apache technique worked best. Dice rattled across the deck, IOUs for loot against promises of suitably glowing introductions to girls on the planet, come victory. A trio of college-bred Ashanti stamped out a war dance while their audience made tom-toms of pots and pans. Endre Vadász leaped onto the table, his slim body poised while his fingers flew across the guitar strings. More and more of the French began to sing with him:

> '*C'est une fleur, fleur de prairie,*
> *C'est une belle Rose de Provence.*
> *Sa chevelure ressemble à la nuit*
> *Et ses beaux yeux semblent à la mysotin.—*'

At first Heim was laughing too loudly at Jean Irribarne's last joke to hear. Then the music grew, and it took him. He remembered a certain night in Bonne Chance. Suddenly he was there again. Roofs peaked around the garden, black under the stars, but the yellow light from their windows joined the light of Diane rising full. A small wind rustled the shrubs, to mingle scents of rose and lily with unnamed pungencies from native blooms. Her hand was trusting in his. Gravel scrunched beneath their feet as they walked toward the summer-house. And somewhere someone was playing a tape, the song drifted down the warm air, earthy and loving.

> *'Quand du village elle se promène,*
> *C'est un plaisir de la voir marcher;*
> *Sa jolie taille ronde et gracieuse*
> *Comme une vague souple et mystérieuse.'*

His eyes stung. He shook his head harshly.

Irribarne gave him a close look. The New European was medium tall, which put him well below Heim, spare of build, dark-haired, long-headed, and clean-featured. He still wore the garments in which he had been captured, green tunic and trousers, soft boots, beret tucked in scaly leather belt, the uniform of a planetary constabulary turned *maquisard*. Lieutenant's bars gleamed on his shoulders.

'Pourquoi cette tristesse soudaine?' he asked.

'Eh?' Heim blinked. Between the racket in here, the rustiness of his French, and the fact that New Europe was well on the way to evolving its own dialect, he didn't understand.

'You show at once the trouble,' Irribarne said. Enough English speakers visited his planet, in the lost days, that town dwellers usually had some command of their language.

'Oh ... nothing. A memory. I spent several grand leaves on New Europe, when I was a Navy man. But that was – Judas, last time was twenty-one years ago.'

'And so you think of aliens that slither through streets made empty of men. How they move softly, like hunting panthers!' Irribarne scowled into his glass, lifted it, and drained it in a convulsive gesture. 'Or perhaps you remember a girl, and wonder if she is dead or else hiding in the forests. *Hein?*'

'Let's get refills,' said Heim brusquely.

Irribarne laid a hand on his arm. *'Un moment, s'il vous plaît.* The population of the whole planet is only five hundred thousand. The city people, that you would meet, they are much less. Perhaps I know.'

'Madelon Dubois?'

'From Bonne Chance in origin? Her father a doctor? But yes! She married my own brother Pierre. They live, what last I heard.'

Darkness passed before Heim's eyes. He leaned against the bulkhead, snapped after air, struggled back to self-control but could not slow his heart. '*Gud ske lov*,' he breathed. It was as close to a prayer as he had come since childhood.

Irribarne considered him through shrewd, squinted brown eyes. 'Ah, this matters to you. Come, shall we not speak alone?'

'All right. Thanks.' Heim led the way. Irribarne was hard put to keep up. Behind them, arms around each other's shoulders, the men were roaring forth:

> '*Chevaliers de la table ronde,*
> *Goûtons voir si le vin est bon—*'

while Vadász's chords belled through all.

Heim's cabin seemed the more quiet after he shut the door. Irribarne sat down and glanced curiously about the neat, compact room, Shakespeare, Bjørnson, and Kipling in book editions with worn bindings, micro reels of less literary stature, a model of a warship, pictures of a woman and a girl. '*Votre famille?*' he asked.

'Yes. My wife's dead, though. Daughter's with her grandfather on Earth.' Heim offered one of his few remaining cigars and began to stuff a pipe for himself. His fingers were not absolutely steady and he did not look at the other man. 'How is your own family?'

'Well, thank you. Of course, that was a pair of weeks ago, when my force was captured.' Irribarne got his cigar going and leaned back with a luxurious sigh. Heim stayed on his feet.

'How'd that happen, anyway? We've had no real chance to talk.'

'Bad luck, I hope. It is a uranium mine on the Côte Notre Dame. Not much uranium on Europe Neuve, you know, she is less dense than Earth. So to blow it up would be a good *frappement* – strike at Alerion. We took a sport submarine we found in Port Augustin, where the mountains come down to the Golfe des Dragons, and started. We knew the one thing those damned dryworlders do not have is submarine-detection equipment. But the mine was better guarded than we expected. When we surfaced to go ashore at night, a shell hit. Chemical

142

explosive only, or I would not sit here. Their troopers waited
and got, you say, the drop. There was talk about shooting us
for an example, or what is worse to squeeze information from
us. But the new high commander heard and forbid. I think he
has come to have charge of hunting you, my friend, so this also
we must thank you for. We were going to Alerion. They spoke
about prisoner exchange.'

'I see.'

'But you make stalls. It is news of Madelon you wish, no?'

'Hell, I hate to get personal— Okay. We were in love, when
I had a long sick leave on New Europe. Very innocent
affair, I assure you. So damned innocent in fact, that I shied
away a bit and— Anyhow, next time I came back she'd
moved.'

'Indeed so. To Château St. Jacques. I thought always
Pierre got her ... on the rebound? Now and then she has
laughed about the big *Norvégien* when she was a girl. Such
laughter, half happy, half sad, one always makes of young
memories.' Irribarne's gaze grew stiff. 'Pierre is a good husband.
They have four children.'

Heim flushed. 'Don't misunderstand me,' he said around his
pipe. 'I couldn't have married better than I did either. It was
just – she was in trouble, and I hoped I could help. Old friendship, nothing else.'

He didn't believe he was lying. A few thoughts had crossed
his mind, but they were not unduly painful to bury. That Madelon had lived gladly, that she still lived, was enough.

'You have that from us all,' Irribarne said heartily. 'Now
tell me more before we return to the festival. I hear you are a
private raider commissioned by France. But why has the Navy
been so slow? When do they come?'

God help me, Heim thought. *I wanted to spare them till
tomorrow.*

'I don't know,' he said.

'*Nom d'un chien!*' Irribarne sat bolt upright. 'What is it that
you say?'

Slowly, Heim dragged the tale from himself: how it came
about that the Deepspace Fleet lay chained and muzzled while
Parliament wrangled, and quite possibly nothing except *Fox*'s
buccaneering prevented a resumption of those talks which to
Alerion were only a more effective kind of war.

'*Mais ... mais ... mais ... vous – cette astronef—*'

Irribarne checked his stutter, caught breath, and said carefully, 'This ship has ranged in the Auroran System. Have you, yourself, taken no proof we live?'

'I tried,' Heim said. Back and forth he paced, smoke fuming, heels banging, big useless hands clasped behind his back till the nails stood white. 'The prisoners who went home with my prizes, they could have been interrogated. Not easily; Aleriona don't respond like humans; but somebody could've ripped the truth from them! I guess nobody did.

'I also made a pass by New Europe. Not hard to do, if you're quick. Most of their defense satellites still aren't equipped, and we detected no warships too close to outrun. So I got photographs, nice clear ones, showing plainly that only Coeur d'Yvonne was destroyed, that there never had been a firestorm across Garance. Sent them back to Earth. I suppose they convinced some people, but evidently not the right ones. Don't forget, by now a lot of political careers are bound up with the peace issue. And even a man who might confess he was wrong and resign, if it involved just himself, will hesitate to drag his party down with him.

'Oh, I'm sure sentiment has moved in our favor. It'd already begun to do so when I left. Not long after, at Staurn for munitions, I met some late-comers from Earth. They told me the will to fight was becoming quite respectable. But that was four months ago!'

He shifted his pipe, stopped his feet, and went on more evenly: 'I can guess what the next line of argument has been for the appeasement faction. "Yes, yes," they say, "maybe the New Europeans still are alive. So isn't the most important thing to rescue them? We won't do that by war. Alerion can wipe them out any time she chooses. We have to trade their planet for their lives." That's probably being said in Parliament tonight.'

Irribarne's chin sank on his breast. '*Un demi million d'hommes,*' he mumbled. Abruptly: 'But they will die all the same. Can one not see that? We have only a few more weeks?'

'What?' Heim bellowed. His heart jolted him. 'Is the enemy fixing to burn you out?'

That could be done quite easily, he knew in horror. *A thousand or so megatons exploded at satellite height on a clear day will set a good part of a continent afire. Madelon!*

'No, no,' the colonist said. 'They need for themselves the resources of the planet, in fortifying the system. A continental firestorm or a radioactive poisoning, that would make large trouble for them too. But the vitamin C.'

Piece by piece, the story came out. Never doubting Earth would hurry to their aid, the seaboard folk of Pays d'Espoir fled inland, to the mountains and forests of the Haute Garance. That nearly unmapped wilderness was as rich in game and edible vegetation as North America before the white man. With a high technology and no population pressure, the people were wealthy; hardly a one did not own hunting, fishing, and camping gear, as well as a flyer capable of going anywhere. Given a little camouflage and caution, fifty thousand scattered lodges and summer cottages were much too many for the Aleriona to find. On the rare occasions when they did find one, the inhabitants could resort to tent or cave or lean-to.

Portable chargers, equally able to use sunlight, wind, or running water, were also standard outdoor equipment, which kept up power cells. Ordinary miniature transceivers maintained a communications net. It did the enemy scant good to monitor. He had come with people that knew French, but his own ossified culture had not allowed for provincial dialect, *Louchébème,* or Basque. The boldest men organized raids on him, the rest stayed hidden.

With little axial tilt, New Europe enjoys a mild and rainy winter in the temperate zone, even at fairly high altitudes. It seemed that the humans could hold out indefinitely.

But they were not, after all, on Earth. Life had arisen and evolved separately here, through two or three billion years. Similar conditions led to similar chemistry. Most of what a man needed he could get from native organisms. But similarity is not identity. Some things were lacking on New Europe, notably vitamin C. The escapers had packed along a supply of pills. Now the store was very low. Alerion held the farmlands where Terrestrial plants grew, the towns where the biochemical factories stood.

Scurvy is a slow killer, working its way through gums, muscles, digestion, blood, bones. Most often the victim dies of something else which he no longer has the strength to resist. But one way or another, he dies.

'And they know it,' Irribarne grated. 'Those devils, they know our human weakness. They need only wait.' He lifted one fist. 'Has Earth forgotten?'

'No,' Heim said. 'It'd be bound to occur to somebody. But Earth's so confused. . . .'

'Let us go there,' Irribarne said. 'I myself, all my men, we are witnesses. Can we not shame them till they move?'

'I don't know,' Heim said in wretchedness. 'We can try, of course. But – maybe I'm being paranoid – but I can still imagine the arguments. "Nothing except negotiation can save you. Alerion will not negotiate unless we make prompt concessions."

'I know damn well that once inside the Solar System, *Fox* won't be allowed to leave again. The law, you see, only units under the Peace Authority can have nuclear weapons, or even weapon launchers, there. And we do. Our possession is legal now, on a technicality, but it won't be when we enter Federation space.'

'Can you not dismantle your armament?'

'That'd take weeks. It's been integrated with the ship. And – what difference? I tell you, your appearance on Earth might cost us the war. And *that* would set Alerion up to prepare the next aggression.' Heim thought of Madelon. 'Or so I believe. Could be wrong, I suppose.'

'No, you are right,' Irribarne said dully.

'It might be the only way out. Surrender.'

'There must be another! I will not be so fanatic that women and children surely die. But a risk of death, against the chance to keep our homes, yes, that is something we all accepted when we went into the *maquis*.'

Heim sat down, knocked out his pipe, and turned it over and over in his hands while he stared at the model of his first command. Inexplicably his emotions began to shift. He felt less heavy, there was a stirring in him, he groped through blackness toward some vague, strengthening glimmer.

'Look,' he said, 'let's try to reason this through. *Fox* is keeping the war alive by refusing to quit. As long as we're out here fighting, the people at home who think like us can argue that Alerion is being whittled down at no cost to the taxpayer. And, *ja*, they can beat the propaganda drums, make big fat heroes of us, stir the old tribal emotions. They haven't the political pull to make the Authority order the Navy to move; but they have enough to keep us from being recalled. I deduce this from the simple facts that the Navy has not moved and we have not been recalled.

'Obviously that's an unstable situation. It's only kept going

146

this long, I'm sure, because France tied Parliament in legal knots as to whether or not there really was a war on. The deadlock will be resolved one way or another pretty soon. We want to tilt the balance our way.

'Okay, one approach is for you people to let it be known you are alive – let it be known beyond any possible doubt – and also make it plain you are not going to surrender. You'll die before you give in. The way to do that is . . . let me think, let me think . . . yes. We've got *Meroeth*. With some repairs, she can make the passage; or else we can make another capture. We stay here, though, ourselves. What we send is – not a handful of men – a hundred women and children.' Heim's palm cracked against his knee. 'There's an emotional appeal for you!'

Irribarne's eyes widened until they were rimmed with white. '*Comment?* You are crazy? You cannot land on Europe Neuve.'

'The space defenses aren't ready yet.'

'But . . . no, they do have some detector satellites, and warcraft in orbit, and—'

'Oh, it's chancy,' Heim agreed. He had no real sense of that. Every doubt was smothered in upsurging excitement. 'We'll leave *Fox* in space, with most of your men aboard. If we fail, she can snatch another prize and send your men back in that. But I think I have a way to get *Meroeth* down, and up again, and stay in touch meanwhile. We'll need some computer work to make sure, but I think it might pan out. If not, well, you can show me how to be a guerrilla.'

'Ah.' Irribarne drew deeply on his cigar. 'May I ask if this idea would seem so attractive, did it not offer a way to see Madelon?'

Heim gaped at him.

'Pardon,' Irribarne blurted. 'That was not badly meant. Old friendship, as you said. I like a loyal man.' He extended his hand.

Heim took it and rose. 'Come on,' he said rather wildly. 'We can't do anything till tomorrow. Let's get back to the party.'

CHAPTER THREE

ELSEWHERE *Fox* plunged dark, every engine stilled, nothing but the minimum of life-support equipment in operation, toward the far side of the moon Diane. It was not garrisoned, and a diameter of 1275 kilometers makes a broad shield. Even so, the tender that went from her carried brave men. They might have been spotted by some prowling Aleriona warcraft, especially in the moments when they crammed on deceleration to make a landing. Once down on that rough, airless surface, they moved their boat into an extinct fumarole for concealment, donned space gear, and struck out afoot. Their trip around to the planet-facing hemisphere was a miniature epic; let it only be said that they completed their errand and got back. Rendezvous with the ship was much too risky to attempt. They settled in the boat and waited.

Not long after, a giant meteorite or dwarf asteroid struck New Europe, burning a hole across the night sky and crashing in the Océan du Destin a few hundred kilometers east of the Garance coast. A minor tidal wave shocked through the Baie des Pêcheurs, banged watercraft against their docks at Bonne Chance, raced up the Bouches du Carsac, and was still observable – a rumbling foam-crested front, sleekly black under the stars – as far inland as the confluence of the River Bordes. Atmospherics howled in every Aleriona detector.

They faded; alerted flyers returned to berth; the night stillness resumed.

For all but the men aboard *Meroeth*.

When the fifty thousand tons to which she was grappled hit the outermost fringes of atmosphere, she let go and dropped behind. But she could not retreat far. Too many kilometers per second of velocity must be shed in too few kilometers of distance, before ablation devoured her. That meant a burst of drive forces, a blast of energies from a powerplant strained to its ultimate. The enemy's orbital detection system was still inadequate; but it existed in part, and there were also instruments on the ground. Nothing could hide this advent – except the running, growing storm in the immediate neighborhood of a meteorite.

Radar would not pierce the ions which roiled at the stone's face and streamed back aft. Optical and infrared pickups were blinded. Neutrino or gravitronic detectors aimed and tuned with precision might have registered something which was not of local origin. But who would look for a ship in the midst of so much fury? Air impact alone, at that speed, would break her hull into a thousand flinders, which friction would then turn into shooting stars.

Unless she followed exactly behind the meteorite, using its mass for a bumper and heat shield, its flaming tail for a cloak.

No autopilot was ever built for that task. Gunnar Heim must do it. If he veered from his narrow slot of partial vacuum, he would die too quickly to know he was dead. For gauge he had only the incandescence outside, instrument readings, and whatever intuition was bestowed by experience. For guide he had a computation of where he ought to be, at what velocity, at every given moment, unreeling on tape before his eyes. He merged himself with the ship; his hands made a blur on the console; he did not notice the waves of heat, the buffetings and bellowings of turbulence, save as a thunderstorm deep in his body.

His cosmos shrank to a firestreak, his reason for being to the need of holding this clumsy mass nose-on to the descent pattern. Once, an age ago, he had brought his space yacht down on a seemingly disastrous path to Ascension Island. But that had been a matter of skillfully piloting a slender and responsive vessel. Tonight he was a robot, executing orders written for it by whirling electrons.

No: he was more. The feedback of data through senses, judgment, will, made the whole operation possible. But none of that took place on a conscious level. There wasn't time!

That was as well. Live flesh could not have met those demands for more than a few seconds. The meteorite, slowed only a little by the air wall through which it plunged, outraced the spaceship and hit the sea – still with such force that water had no chance to splash but actually shattered. *Meroeth* was as yet several kilometers aloft, her own speed reduced to something that metal could tolerate. The pattern tape said CUT and Heim slammed down a switch. The engine roar whirred into silence.

He checked his instruments. 'All's well,' he said. His voice

149

sounded strange in his ears, only slowly did he come back to himself, as if he had run away from his soul and it must now catch up. 'We're under the Bonne Chance horizon, headed southwest on just about the trajectory we were trying for.'

'Whoo-oo-oo,' said Vadász in a weak tone. His hair was plastered lank to the thin high-cheeked face; his garments were drenched.

'Bridge to engine room,' Heim said. 'Report.'

'All in order, sir,' came the voice of Diego Gonzales, who was third engineer on *Fox*. 'Or as much as could be expected. The strain gauges do show some warping in a couple of the starboard bow plates. Not too bad, though. Shall I turn on the coolers?'

'Well, do you like this furnace?' grumbled Jean Irribarne. Heat radiated from every bulkhead.

'Go ahead,' Heim decided. 'If anyone's close enough to detect the anomaly, we've had it anyway.' He kept eyes on the console before him, but jerked a thumb at Vadász. 'Radar registering?'

'No,' said the Magyar. 'We appear to be quite private.'

Those were the only men aboard. No more were needed for a successful landing; and in case of failure, Heim did not want to lose lives essential to *Fox*.

Gonzales, for instance, was a good helper in his department, but Uthg-a-K'thaq and O'Hara could manage without him. Vadász had been a fairly competent steward, and as a minstrel had a lot to do with keeping morale high. Nevertheless, he was expendable. One colonist sufficed to guide *Meroeth*, and Irribarne had pulled rank to win that dangerous honor. The rest must bring their story to Earth, did the present scheme miscarry. As for Heim himself—

'You can't!' Penoyer had protested.

'Can't I just?' Heim grinned.

'But you're the skipper!'

'You can handle that job every bit as well as I, Dave.'

Penoyer shook his head. 'No. More and more, I've come to realize it. Not only that this whole expedition was your idea and your doing. Not even the way you've led us, as a tactician, I mean, though that's been like nothing since Lord Nelson. But damn it, Gunnar – sir – we won't hang together without you!'

'I'm far too modest to have any false modesty,' Heim drawled. 'What you say may well have been true in the begin-

150

ning. We're a motley gang, recruited from all over Earth and every man a rambunctious individualist. Then there was the anti-Naqsan prejudice. I had to get tough about that a few times, you remember. Now, though, after so long a cruise, so much done together – we're a crew. A God damn *ship*. C.E.'s proved himself so well and so often that we haven't a man left who won't punch you in the nose if you say a nasty word about Naqsans. And as for tactics, Dave, half the stunts we've pulled were your suggestion. You'll manage fine.'

'Well ... but ... but why you, sir, to go down? Any of us with a master pilot's certificate can do it, and say wizard to the chance. You going bloody well doesn't make sense.'

'I say it does,' Heim answered. 'End of discussion.' When he used that tone, nobody talked further. Inwardly, however, he hadn't felt the least stern.

Madelon—

No, no, ridiculous. Maybe it's true that you never really fall out of love with anyone; but new loves do come, and while Connie lived he had rarely thought about New Europe. For that matter, his reunion with Jocelyn Lawrie on Staurn had driven most else out of his mind. For a while.

No doubt he'd only been so keyed up about Madelon because of ... he wasn't sure what. A silly scramble after his lost youth, probably. She was middle-aged now, placidly married, according to her brother-in-law she had put on weight. He wanted to see her again, of course, and chuckle affectionately over old follies. But all he need do was instruct *Meroeth*'s pilot to make sure the Irribarnes were among the evacuees.

Insuwwicient, as C.E. would burble, he thought. *Common sense had very limited uses. This goes beyond. Too many unforeseen things could happen. I want to be in the nucleus, personally.*

A new sound filled the hull, the keening of sundered air, deepening toward a hollow boom, as *Meroeth* dropped below sonic speed. Heim looked out the forward viewport. The ocean reached vast beneath, phosphor-tinged waves from horizon to horizon. A shadow loomed in the distance, which Vadász told him from the radar must be an island. So, the Iles des Rêves already, at the end of the Notre Dame peninsula. He wanted to get the archipelago between him and whatever guardian instruments were at the uranium mine farther north, before he switched the gravitrons back on. It would take some doing. This hulk wasn't meant for aerodynamic maneuvers. He applied the least bit of lift to get her nose up.

Immensely preferable would have been to land in the Océan des Orages and come eastward over Pays d'Espoir, crossing unpopulated Terre Sauvage to reach the central mountains of the continent. But while meteorites are plentiful, his had had too many requirements to meet. It must be large, yet not too large to nudge into the right orbit in a reasonable time; the point at which *Fox* grappled and towed must be fairly near the planet but not dangerously near; the path after release must look natural; it must terminate in one of those seas at night. You couldn't scout the Auroran System forever, but must settle for the first half-way acceptable chunk of rock that happened along. Meanwhile *Meroeth* could be reconverted: lights, temperature, air systems adjusted for human comfort, Mach units repaired, the interior stripped of plants and less understandable Aleriona symbols, the controls ripped out and a new set put in of the kind to which Terrestrials were accustomed. The bridge had a plundered look.

Onward the ship fell, slower and lower until the ocean seemed to rise and lick at her. Vadász probed the sky with his instruments, awkwardly – he had gotten hasty training – and intently. His lips were half parted, as if to give the word 'Fire!' to Irribarne in the single manned gun turret. But he found only night, unhurried winds, and strange constellations.

It would not have been possible to travel this far, undetected, across a civilization. But New Europe has 72 per cent of Earth's surface area; it is an entire world. Coeur d'Yvonne had been almost the only outpost on another continent than Pays d'Espoir, and that city was annihilated. The Aleriona occupied Garance, where the mines and machines were: a mere fringe of immensity. Otherwise they must rely on scattered detector stations, roving flyers, and the still incomplete satellite system. His arrival being unknown to them, the odds favored Heim.

Nonetheless ... careful, careful.

When the archipelago was behind him and his ship almost plowing water, he turned the engines on again. Like a flying whale, *Meroeth* swung about and lumbered westward. An island passed near. He made out surf on a beach overshadowed by trees, and imagined he could hear its wash and the soughing leaves, could even smell the warm odors of a semitropical forest. The sight was dim, only half real – indeed an island of

152

dream. *Men's dreams,* he thought angrily. *No one else's.*

Crossing the Golfe des Dragons, he felt naked in so much openness and increased speed. Northwestward now the ship ran. Diane hove into view, nearly full. The moon was smaller than Luna seen from Earth – twenty-two minutes angular diameter – and less bright, but still a blue-marked tawny cornucopia that scattered metal shards across the sea.

Then the mainland rose, hills and woods and distant snowpeaks. Heim reached for altitude. 'Better get on the radio, Jean,' he said. 'We don't want them to run and hide when they see us, not to mention attack. What's the name of that place again where we're headed?'

'Lac aux Nuages,' Irribarne said.

Heim studied a map. 'Yes, I see it here. Big upland lake. Isn't it too conspicuous to make a safe headquarters?'

'There is ample concealment, precisely because it is large and misty and has so many islands,' Irribarne answered. 'Besides, if there is a raid one can always retreat into the wilderness around about.' The intercom bore the sound of his footsteps leaving the gun turret for the radio room, and presently a harsh clatter of Basque.

The land beneath grew ever more rugged. Rivers ran from the snows, leaped down cliffs, foamed into steep valleys, and were lost to sight among the groves. A bird flock rose in alarm when the ship passed over; there must be a million pairs of wings, blotting out half the sky. Vadász whistled in awe. '*Isten irgalmazzon!* I wondered how long the people could stay hidden, even alive, in the bush. But three times their number could do it.'

'Yeh,' Heim grunted. 'Except for one thing.'

The lake appeared, a wide wan sheet among darkling trees, remotely encircled by mountains whose glaciers gleamed beneath the moon. Irribarne relayed instruction. Heim found the indicated spot, just off the north shore, and lowered ship. The concealing waters closed over him. He heard girders groan a little, felt an indescribable soft resistance go through the frame to himself, eased off power, and let the hull settle in ooze. When he cut the interior gee-field, he discovered the deck was canted.

His heart thuttered, but he could only find flat words: 'Let's get ashore.' Even in seven tenths of Terrestrial gravity, it was a somewhat comical effort to reach the emergency escape

153

lock without falling. When the four men were crowded inside, clothes bundled on their necks, he dogged the inner door and cranked open the outer one. Water poured icily through. He kicked to the surface and swam as fast as possible toward land. Moonlight glimmered on the guns of the men who stood there waiting for him.

CHAPTER FOUR

THE tent was big. The trees that surrounded it were taller yet. At the top of red-brown trunks, they fountained in branches whose leaves overarched and hid the pavilion under cool sun-flecked shadows. Their foliage was that greenish gold hue the native 'grasses' shared, to give the Garance country its name. Wind rustled them. Through the open flap, Heim could look down archways of forest to the lake. It glittered unrestfully, outward past the edge of vision. Here and there lay a wooded island, otherwise the only land seen in that direction was the white-crowned sierra. Blue with distance, the peaks jagged into a deep blue sky.

Aurore was not long up. The eastern mountains were still in shadow, the western ones still faintly flushed. They would remain so for a while; New Europe takes more than seventy-five hours to complete a rotation. The sun did not look much different from Earth's: about the same apparent size, a little less bright, its color more orange than yellow. Heim had found Vadász in the dews at dawn, watching the light play in the mists that streamed over the lake, altogether speechless.

That time was ended. So too was the hour when Colonel Robert de Vigny, once constabulary commandant, now beret-crowned king of the *maquis*, returned to headquarters. (He had not been directing a raid, but finding some technicians and arranging for their transportation to the Ravignac lodge, where a major hydroelectric generator needed repairs. Of such unglamorous detail work is survival made.) Ended even was the first gladness of reunion, with Irribarne who had been lost, with Vadász after a year and Heim after a generation. 'Bon, passons aux affaires sérieuses,' he said, and sat down behind his desk.

Vadász found a chair, slumped low, and stared at his boots. Heim kept his feet, met the green gaze, but found no words. 'You tell him, Jean,' he mumbled at length. 'My French is shot to hell.'

De Vigny stiffened himself, like a man expecting a blow. He was grizzled and not tall, but his back was rifle straight and the face might have belonged to a Trajan. '*Continuez*,' he said without tone. The Basque snapped to attention. '*Repos*,' de Vigny invited, but Irribarne seemed unable to stand at ease while the news jerked out of him.

At the end, the colonel remained expressionless. One hand drummed a little on the desktop. 'So,' he said most quietly, in French. 'Earth has abandoned us.'

'Not all Earth!' Vadász exclaimed.

'No, true, you are here.' The mask dissolved; one could see muscles tighten along jaws and mouth, calipers deepen on either side of the gray toothbrush mustache, a pulse at the base of the throat. 'And, I gather, at considerable risk. What is your plan, Captain Heim?'

Now the privateer found words more easily. He stayed with English, though, which de Vigny could follow. 'As I explained to Lieutenant Irribarne, Earth needs to be convinced of two things. First, that you people survive; second, that you won't go along with any appeasement that costs you your homes. Well, the men of yours who're now in space, on my ship, might be a clinching proof of the first point. But men have always bragged about how hard they'll fight, so any such claims they may make could be discounted.'

'And rightly so,' de Vigny remarked. 'One has often in history heard nations declare they will fight to the last man, but none have ever done it. And there has never been any question of fighting to the last woman and child. If Earth does not soon come to help, I shall most certainly try to save us by making whatever bargain I can with Alerion.'

'I'm coming to that,' Heim said. 'If we can send some of your women and children, it'll make the whole thing more real to the average Earth-dweller. They'd be a powerful help to the faction there which does want victory. Three ways: plain old emotional appeal; living proof that standing up to Alerion doesn't necessarily mean total disaster; and, well, a woman who says her people don't want to surrender is more convincing than a man. The balance of opinion at home seems to be pretty delicate. They might be enough by themselves to tip it.'

'They *might*. You deal in hypotheses, Monsieur Captain. I must deal with the reality that we shall soon be getting sick.'

'If they also carried word you aren't about to – what then?'

'*Hein?*' De Vigny balled his fist. 'What do you propose?'

'That we get you your vitamins. Look, aren't the Aleriona having a lot of trouble operating your machines? And aren't you causing still more with your raids?'

'Yes. But this is hardly significant.'

'It is when they're in a tearing hurry to complete the space fortifications and I've thrown them way behind schedule. I think if you offered to leave them alone, and maybe even send them some technicians, they'd swap. Give you the pills you need. Of course, you'd have to make sure those really were vitamin C capsules, but that shouldn't be too hard to arrange.'

'What?' Irribane cried. 'Bargain with the enemy?'

'It is not uncommon in war.' De Vigny stroked his chin. 'Indeed, those are the terms I was planning to make, if I could, when we are desperate. They will understand we are buying time in the hope of deliverance. But if they do not know that deliverance may, after all, be expected— Yes. Why should they not take an easy way of getting us off their necks? They will assume we can be dealt with later. . . . To be sure, they may demand unconditional surrender, insist we come down to the lowlands where we can be penned up.'

'If they do,' Heim said, 'I think we might manage to grab warehouse stocks or even manufacturing facilities. A joint operation between your forces and my ship. Or if that doesn't look feasible—' He swallowed bitterness. 'We can throw in an offer that I go home.'

'Name of a name,' de Vigny breathed. 'That would surely fetch them. But let us make the less costly proposal first, not admitting we have any communication with you, and hold this bargaining counter in reserve.'

'Oh, sure. Besides, we have to get the transport with the evacuees safely away, which needs surprise.'

De Vigny considered him. 'You are most strangely concerned about a hundred or two of women and children. I attach less importance to them. Our continued existence here, as free men, is more apt to make Earth move. However . . . two hundred saved are still two hundred, so have your way.

156

But how do you propose to get such a lumbering, overloaded craft beyond the Mach limit?'

'*Fox* will make a covering raid when I send word.'

'What? She is that close, undetected? How the devil? And how can a maser beam find her when Aleriona radar can't?'

'My engineer is off explaining the setup to your technical staff. Let us stick to the tactical side for now. The diversion should be ample. One well-armed ship, striking by surprise, can raise all kinds of hell. Once *Meroeth*'s in space, *Fox* will escort her to the limit. According to all our information – from instruments, radio monitor, captured documents, and so forth; we've got a man who can puzzle out the language if you give him time – most of the enemy strength here is chasing through the Auroran System and beyond, looking for me. So we ought to be out of danger well before they can bring more power to bear against us than *Fox* can handle.'

The colonel frowned. 'You juggle too many unknowns for my taste.'

'Or mine,' Heim said dryly. But one way to clear away some of 'em is obvious. Let me go along with your delegation to the Aleriona. They won't know I'm not just another colonist. But I know them pretty well. I ought to, after so many years sparring with them. I also have a professional Navy eye, which they won't be expecting. Endre should come too. He's got a poet's grasp of nonhuman psychologies. Between us, we can not only help you make a better deal, but carry back a lot of useful information to base our specific plans on.'

'M-m-m ... well—' De Vigny pondered a moment. Then crisply: 'So be it. Time is short, and we do not really have much to lose. This, then, is the schedule as I understand it. We begin at once to arrange evacuation. During the next few days, the people chosen can flit in by ones and twos. We must also load supplies, and must not be observed doing it. But my men can run a cargo tube from the forest to one of your locks below water, without exposing it to the sky.

'Meanwhile I establish radio contact with the Aleriona and ask for a parley. They will doubtless agree, especially since their new chief of naval operations seems, from Lieutenant Irribarne's account, to be a rather decent fellow. I daresay they will receive our representatives already tomorrow.

'If we can reach an agreement, cessation of guerrilla operations and perhaps the supplying of some engineers in exchange

157

for vitamins – good. Whether that works out or not, the delegation returns here.

'Then your ship attacks to get this transport safely away.

'After that, if we are provided with the capsules, you continue your warfare in space as long as possible. If not, and if we cannot steal them, I call the enemy again and offer an end to your activities, provided he supplies us. This he is virtually sure to accept.

'At large cost or small, we shall have gained time, during which we hope Earth will come to help. Am I right?'

Heim nodded and got out his pipe. 'That's the idea,' he said.

De Vigny's nostrils dilated. 'Tobacco? One had almost forgotten.'

Heim chuckled and threw the pouch on the desk. De Vigny picked up a little bell rang it. An aide-de-camp materialized in the tent entrance, saluting. 'Find me a pipe,' de Vigny said. 'And, if the captain does not object, you may find one for yourself too.'

'At once, my colonel!' The aide dematerialized.

'Well.' De Vigny unbent a trifle. 'Thanks are a poor thing, monsieur. What can New Europe *do* for you?'

Heim grew conscious of Vadász's half jocose, half sympathetic regard, blushed, and said roughly, 'I have an old friend on this planet, who's now Jean Irribarne's sister-in-law. See to it that she and her family are among the evacuees.'

'Pierre will not go when other men stay,' the Basque said gently.

'But they shall most certainly come here if you wish,' de Vigny said. He rang for another aide. 'Lieutenant, why do you not go with Major Legrand to my own flyer? It has a set which can call to anywhere in the Haute Garance. If you will tell the operator where they are, your kin—' When that was done, he said to Heim and Vadász, 'I shall be most busy today, it is plain. But let us relax until after lunch. We have many stories to trade.'

And so they did.

When at last de Vigny must dismiss them, Heim and Vadász were somewhat at loose ends. There was little to see. Though quite a few men were camped around the lake, the shelters were scattered and hidden, the activity unobtrusive. Now and then a flyer came by, as often as not weaving between tree trunks under the concealing foliage. Small radars sat in camouflage, watching for the unlikely appearance of an Aleriona vessel. The engineers could not install their loading tube to the ship before night, unless one of the frequent fogs rose to cover their work. Men sat about yarning, gambling, doing minor chores. All were eager to talk with the Earthlings, but the Earthlings soon wearied of repeating themselves. Toward noon a degree of physical tiredness set in as well. They had been up for a good eighteen hours.

Vadász yawned. 'Let us go back to our tent,' he suggested. 'This planet has such an inconvenient rotation. You must sleep away a third of the daylight and be awake two thirds of the night.'

'Oh, well,' Heim said. 'It wouldn't be colonizable otherwise.'

'What? How?'

'You don't know? Well, look, it has only half Earth's mass, and gets something over 85 percent of the irradiation. The air would've bled away along ago, most of it, except that air loss is due in large part to magnetic interaction with charged particles from the sun. Even a G5 star like Aurore spits out quite a bit of stuff. But slow spin means a weak magnetic field.'

'Another thanks due to Providence,' the Hungarian said thoughtfully.

'Huh!' Heim snorted. 'Then we've got to blame Providence for Venus keeping too much atmosphere. It's a simple matter of physics. The smaller a planet is, and the closer to its sun, the less difference of angular momentum between the inner and outer sections of the dust cloud that goes to form it. Therefore, the less rotation.'

Vadász clapped his shoulder. 'I do not envy you your philosophy, my friend. God is *good*. But we are in mortal danger of becoming serious. Let us, I say, return to the tent, where I have a flask of brandy, and—'

They were not far from it then, were crossing a meadow where flame-colored blossoms nodded in the golden grass. Jean Irribarne stepped from under the trees. 'Ah,' he hailed, '*vous voilà.* I have looked for you.'

'What about?' Heim asked.

The lieutenant beamed. 'Your friends are here.' He turned and called, ' 'Allo-o-o!'

They came out into the open, six of them. The blood left Heim's heart and flooded back. He stood in a sunlit darkness that whirled.

159

She approached him timidly. Camp clothes, faded and shapeless, had today been exchanged for a dress brought along to the woods and somehow preserved. It fluttered light and white around her long-legged slenderness. Aurore had bleached the primly braided brown hair until it was paler than her skin; but still it shone, and one lock blew free above the heart-shaped face. Her eyes were violet.

'Madelon,' he croaked.

'Gunnar.' The handsome woman took both his hands. '*C'est si bon te voir encore. Bienvenu.*'

'*À nej*—' The breath rasped into him. He pulled back his shoulders. 'I was surprised,' he said limpingly. 'Your daughter looks so much like you.'

'Pardon?' The woman struggled with long unused English.

Her husband, an older and heavier version of Jean, interpreted while he shook Heim's hand. Madelon laughed. '*Oui, oui, tout le monde le dit. Quand j'étais jeune, peut-être. Danielle, je voudrais que tu fasses la connaissance de mon vieil ami Gunnar Heim.*'

'*Je suis très honorée, monsieur.*' She could scarcely be heard above the wind as it tossed the leaves and made light and shadow dance behind her. The fingers were small and cool in Heim's, quickly withdrawn.

In some vague fashion he met teen-age Jacques, Cécile, and Yves. Madelon talked a lot, without much but friendly banalities coming through the translations of the Irribarne brothers. All the while Danielle stood quiet. But at parting, with promises of a real get-together after sleep, she smiled at him.

Heim and Vadász watched them leave, before going on themselves. When the forest had closed upon her, the minstrel whistled. 'Is that indeed the image of your one-time sweetheart, yonder girl?' he asked.

'More or less,' Heim said, hardly aware that he talked to anyone else. 'There must be differences, I suppose. Memory plays tricks.'

'Still, one can see what you meant by – Forgive me, Gunnar, but may I advise that you be careful? There are so many years to stumble across.'

'Good Lord!' Heim exploded angrily. 'What do you take me for? I was startled, nothing else.'

'Well, if you are certain ... You see, I would not wish to—'

'Shut up. Let's find that brandy.' Heim led the way with tremendous strides.

CHAPTER FIVE

DAY crept toward evening. But life kept its own pace, which can be a fast one in time of war. At sunset Heim found himself on a ness jutting into the lake, alone with Danielle.

He was not sure how. There had been the reunion and a meal as festive as could be managed, in the lean-to erected near the Irribarne flyer. Champagne, which he had taken care to stow aboard *Meroeth,* flowed freely. Stiffness dissolved in it. Presently they sprawled on the grass, Vadász's guitar rang and most voices joined his. But Heim and Madelon kept somewhat apart, struggling to talk, and her oldest daughter sat quietly by.

They could not speak much of what had once been. Heim did not regret that, and doubted Madelon did. Meeting again like this, they saw how widely their ways had parted; now only a look, a smile, a bit of laughter could cross the distance between. She was an utterly good person, he thought, but she was not Connie or even Jocelyn. And, for that matter, he was not Pierre.

So they contented themselves with trading years. Hers had been mild until the Aleriona came. Pierre, the engineer, built dikes and power stations while she built their lives. Thus Heim found himself relating the most. It came natural to make the story colorful.

His eyes kept drifting toward Danielle.

Finally – this was where the real confusion began as to what had happened – the party showed signs of breaking up. He wasn't sleepy himself, though the wine bubbled in his head, and his body demanded exercise. He said something about taking a stroll. Had he invited the girl along, or had she asked to come, or had Madelon, chuckling low in the way he remembered, sent them off together with a remark about his needing a guide? Everybody had spoken, but between his bad French and hammering pulse he wasn't sure who had said what. He did recall that the mother had given them a little

161

push toward the deeper forest, one hand to each.

Song followed them a while ('*Auprès de ma blonde, qu'il fait bon, fait bon, fait bon—*), but by the time they reached the lakeshore they heard simply a lap-lap of wavelets, rustle of leaves, flute of a bird. Aurore was going down behind the western peaks, which stood black against a cloud bank all fire and gold. The same long light made a molten bridge on the water, from the sun toward him and her. But eastward fog was rolling, slow as the sunset, a topaz wall that at the top broke into banners of dandelion yellow in a sky still clear with day. The breeze cooled his skin.

He saw her clasp arms together. '*Avez-vous froid, mademoiselle?*' he asked, much afraid they would have to go back. She smiled even before he took off his cloak, probably at what he was doing to her language. He threw it over her shoulders. When his hands brushed along her neck, he felt his sinews go taut and withdrew in a hurry.

'Thank you.' She had a voice too light for English or Norwegian, which turned French into a song. 'But will you not be cold?'

'No. I am fine.' (Damn! Did *fin* have the meaning he wanted?) 'I am—' He scratched around for words. 'Too old and ... *poilu?* ... too old and hairy to feel the weather.'

'You are not old, Monsieur Captain,' she said gravely.

'Ha!' He crammed fists into pockets. 'What age have you? Nineteen? I have a daughter that which she – I have a daughter a few years less.'

'Well—' She laid a finger along her jaw. He thought wildly what a delicate line that bone made, over the small chin to a gentle mouth; and, yes, her nose tipped gaily upward, with some freckles dusted across the bridge. 'I know you are my mother's age. But you do not look it, and what you have done is more than any young man could.'

'Thanks. Thanks. So. Nothing.'

'Mother was so excited when she heard,' Danielle said. 'I think Father got a little jealous. But now he likes you.'

'Your father is a good man.' It was infuriating to be confined to this first-grade vocabulary.

'May I ask you something, monsieur?'

'Ask me anybody.' The one rebellious lock of hair had gotten free again.

'I have heard that we who go to Earth do so to appeal for

162

help. Do you really think we will matter that much?'

'Well, uh, well, we had a necessity to come here. That is to say, we have now made establish communication from your people to mine in space. So we can also take people like you away.'

A crease of puzzlement flitted between her brows. 'But they have spoken of how difficult it was to get so big a ship down without being seen. Could you not better have taken a little one?'

'You are very clever, mademoiselle, but—' Before he could construct a cover-up, she touched his arm (how lightly!) and said:

'You came as you did, risking your life, for Mother's sake. Is that not so?'

'Uh, uh, well, naturally I thought over her. We are old friends.'

She smiled. 'Old sweethearts, I have heard. Not all the knights are dead, Captain. I sat with you today, instead of joining in the music, because you were so beautiful to watch.'

His heart sprang until he realized she had been using the second person plural. He hoped the sunset light covered the hue his face must have. 'Mademoiselle,' he said, 'your mother and I are friends. Only friends.'

'Oh, but of course. I understand. Still, it was so good of you, everything you have done for us.' The evening star kindled above her head. 'And now you will take us to Earth. I have dreamed about such a trip since I was a baby.'

There was an obvious opening to say that she was more likely to make Earth sit up and beg than vice versa, but he could only hulk over her, trying to find a graceful way of putting it. She sighed and looked past him.

'Your men too, they are knights,' she said. 'They have not even your reason to fight for New Europe. Except perhaps Monsieur Vadász?'

'No, Endre has no one here,' Heim said. 'He is a troubadour.'

'He sings so wonderfully,' Danielle murmured. 'I was listening all the time. He is a Hungarian?'

'By birth. Now he has no home.' *Endre, you're a right buck, but this is getting to be too much about you.* 'I have – have— When you to arrive on Earth, you and your family use my home. I come when I can and take you in my ship.'

She clapped her hands. 'Oh, wonderful!' she caroled. 'Your

daughter and I, we shall become such good friends. And afterward, a voyage on a warship— What songs of victory we will sing, homeward bound!'

'Well – um— We return to camp now? Soon is dark.' Under the circumstances, one had better be as elaborately gentlemanly as possible.

Danielle drew the cloak tight around her. 'Yes, if you wish.' He wasn't sure whether that showed reluctance or not. But as she started walking immediately, he made no comment, and they spoke little en route.

The party was indeed tapering off. Heim's and Danielle's return touched off a round of good-nights. When she gave him back his cloak, he dared squeeze her hand. Vadász kissed it, with a flourish.

On their way back through leafy blue twilight, the minstrel said, 'Ah, you are the lucky one still.'

'What do you mean?' Heim snapped.

'Taking the fair maiden off that way. What else?'

'For God's sake!' Heim growled. 'We just wanted to stretch our legs. I don't have to rob cradles yet.'

'Are you quite honest, Gunnar? ... No, wait, please don't tie me in a knot. At least, not in a granny knot. It is only that Mlle. Irribarne is attractive. Do you mind if I see her?'

'What the blaze have I got to say about that?' Heim retorted out of his anger. 'But listen, she's the daughter of a friend of mine, and these colonial French have a medieval notion of what's proper. Follow me?'

'Indeed. No more need be said.' Vadász whistled merrily the rest of the way. Once in his sleeping bag, he drowsed off at once. Heim had a good deal more trouble doing so.

Perhaps for that reason, he woke late and found himself alone in the tent. Probably Diego was helping de Vigny's sappers and Endre had wandered off – wherever. It was not practical for guerrillas to keep a regular mess and the campstove, under a single dimlight, showed that breakfast had been prepared. Heim fixed his own, coffee, wildfowl, and a defrosted chunk of the old and truly French bread which is not for tender gums. Afterward he washed, depilated the stubble on his face, shrugged into some clothes, and went outside.

No word for me, evidently. If any comes, it'll keep. I feel restless. How about a swim? He grabbed a towel and started off.

Diane was up. Such light as came through the leaves made the forest a shifting bewilderment of black and white, where his flash-beam bobbed lonely. The air had warmed and cleared. He heard summery noises, whistles, chirps, croaks, flutters, none of them quite like home. When he emerged on the shore, the lake was a somehow bright sable, each little wave tipped with moonfire. The snowpeaks stood hoar beneath a universe of stars. He remembered the time on Staurn when he had tried to pick out Achernar; tonight he could do so with surety, for it burned great in this sky. His triumph, just about when Danielle was being born— *'Vous n'êtes pas vieux, Monsieur le Capitaine.'*

He stripped, left the beam on to mark the spot, and waded out. The water was cold, but he needed less will power than usual to take the plunge when it was waist deep. For a time he threshed about, warming himself, then struck out with long quiet strokes. Moonlight rippled in his wake. The fluid slid over his skin like a girl's fingers.

Things are looking up, he thought with a growing gladness. *We really do have a good chance to rescue this planet. And if part of the price is that I stop raiding – why, I'll be on Earth too.*

Did it sing within him, or had a bird called from the ness ahead?

No. Birds don't chord on twelve strings. Heim grinned and swam forward as softly as he was able. Endre's adrenal glands would benefit from a clammy hand laid on him from behind and a shouted 'Boo!'

The song strengthened in his ears:

> *'Röslein, Röslein, Röslein rot,*
> *Röslein auf der Heiden.'*

As it ended, Heim saw Vadász seated on a log silhouetted against the sky. He was not alone.

Her voice came clear through the night. *'Oh, c'est beau. Je n'aurais jamais cru que les allemands pouvaient avoir une telle sensibilité.'*

Vadász laughed. *'Vous savez Goethe vécut il y a longtemps. Mais pourquoi rappeler de vieilles haines pendant une si belle nuit?'*

She shivered. *'L'haine n'est pas morte. Elle nous entoure.'*

He drew his cloak around them both. *'Oubliez tout cela, made-*

165

moiselle. L'affaire est en bonne mains. Nous sommes venus ici pour admirer, parler, et chanter, n'est-ce pas?'

'*Oui.*' Hesitantly: '*Mais mes parents—*'

'*Pff! Il n'est pas tard. La nuit, le jour, c'est la même chose pour les Neo-Européens. Vous n'avez pas confiance en moi? Je suis aussi innocent qu'une grenouille perclue de rhumatismes. Vous avez entendu mes coassements.*'

Danielle giggled. '*Coassez encore, je vou en prie.*'

'*Le souhait d'une si charmante demoiselle est un ordre. Ah s . . quelque chose à la Magyar? Un chant d'amour.*'

The strings toned very softly, made themselves a part of night and woods and water. Vadász's words twined among them. Danielle sighed and leaned a bit closer.

Heim swam away.

No, he told himself, and again: *No. Endre isn't being a bastard. He* asked *me.*

The grip on his throat did not loosen. He ended his quietness and churned the water with steamboat violence. *He's young. I could have been her father. But I junked the chance.*

I thought it had come back.

No. I'm being ridiculous. Oh, Connie, Connie!

Ved Gud – His brain went in rage to the tongue of his childhood. *By God, if he does anything—! I'm not too old to break a man's neck.*

What the hell business is it of mine?

He stormed ashore and abraded himself dry. Clothes on, he stumbled through the woods. There was a bottle in the tent, not quite empty.

A man waited for him. He recognized one of de Vigny's aides. 'Well?'

The officer sketched a salute. 'I 'ave a message for you, monsieur. The colonel 'as contact the enemy. They receive a delegation in Bonne Chance after day 'as break.'

'Okay. Good night—'

'But, monseiur—'

'I know. We have to confer. Well, I'll come when I can. We've plenty of time. It's going to be a long night.' Heim brushed past the aide and closed his tent flap.

CHAPTER SIX

BELOW, the Carsac Valley rolled broad and rich. Farmsteads could be seen, villages, an occasional factory surrounded by gardens – but nowhere man; the land was empty, livestock run wild, weeds reclaiming the fields. Among them flowed the river, metal-bright in the early sun.

When he looked out the viewports of the flyer where he sat, Heim saw his escort, four Aleriona military vehicles. The intricate, gaily colored patterns painted on them did not soften their barracuda outlines. Guns held aim on the unarmed New Europeans. *We could change from delegates to prisoners in half a second,* he thought, and reached for his pipe.

'Pardon.' Lieutenant Colonel Charles Navarre, head of the eight-man negotiation team, tapped his shoulder. 'Best lock that away, monsieur. We have not had tobacco in the *maquis* for one long time.'

'Damn! You're right. Sorry.' Heim got up and stuck his smoking materials in a locker.

'They are no fools, them.' Navarre regarded the big man carefully. 'Soon we land. Is anything else wrong with you, Captain Alphonse Lafayette?'

'No, I'm sure not,' Heim said in English. 'But let's go down the list. My uniform's obviously thrown together but that's natural for a guerrilla. I don't look like a typical colonist, but they probably won't notice, and if they do it won't surprise them.'

'*Comment?*' asked another officer.

'Didn't you know?' Heim said. 'Aleriona are bred into standardized types. From their viewpoint, humans are so wildly variable that a difference in size and coloring is trivial. Nor have they got enough familiarity with French to detect my accent, as long as I keep my mouth shut most of the time. Which'll be easy enough, since I'm only coming along in the hope of picking up a little naval intelligence.'

'Yes, yes,' Navarre said impatiently. 'But be most careful about it.' He leaned toward Vadász, who had a seat in the rear. 'You too, Lieutenant Gaston Girard.'

'On the contrary,' the minstrel said, 'I have to burble and

chatter and perhaps irritate them somewhat. There is no other way to probe the mood of non-humans. But have no fear. This was all thought about. I am only a junior officer, not worth much caution on their part.' He smiled tentatively at Heim. 'You can vouch for how good I am at being worthless, no, Gunnar?'

Heim grunted. Pain and puzzlement flickered across the Magyar's features. When first his friend turned cold to him, he had put it down to a passing bad mood. Now, as Heim's distasteness persisted, there was no chance – in this crowded, thrumming cabin – to ask what had gone wrong.

The captain could almost read those thoughts. He gusted out a breath and returned to his own seat forward. *I'm being stupid and petty and a son of a bitch in general,* he knew. *But I can't forget Danielle, this sunrise with the fog drops like jewels in her hair, and the look she gave him when we said good-by. Wasn't I the one who'd earned it?*

He was quite glad when the flyer started down.

Through magnification before it dropped under the horizon, he saw that Bonne Chance had grown some in twenty years. But it was still a small city, nestled on the land's seaward shoulder: a city of soft-hued stucco walls and red tile roofs, of narrow ambling streets, suspension bridges across the Carsac, a market square where the cathedral fronted on outdoor stalls and outdoor cafés, docks crowded with watercraft, and everywhere trees. Earth's green chestnut and poplar mingled with golden *bellefleur* and *gracis*. The bay danced and dazzled, the countryside rolled ablaze with wildflowers, enclosing the town exactly as they had done when he wandered hand in hand with Madelon.

Only ... the ways were choked with dead leaves; houses stared blank and blind; boats moldered in the harbor; machines rusted silent; the belfry rooks were dead or fled and a *fauquette* cruised the sky on lean wings, searching for prey. The last human thing that stirred was the aerospace port, twenty kilometers inland.

And those were not men or men's devices bustling over its concrete. The airships bringing cargo had been designed by no Terrestrial engineer. The factories they served were windowless prolate domes, eerily graceful for all that they were hastily assembled prefabs. Conveyors, trucks, lifts were man-made, but the controls had been rebuilt for hands of another shape and minds trained to another concept of number. Barracks surrounded the field, hundreds of buildings reaching over the hills; from above, they looked like openpetaled bronze flowers. Missiles stood tall among them, waiting to pounce. Auxiliary spacecraft clustered in the open. One was an armed pursuer, whose snout reached as high as the cathedral cross.

'It must belong to a capital ship in planetary orbit.' Heim decided. 'And if that's the only such, the other warships must be out on patrol. Which is maybe worth knowing.'

'I do not see how you can use the information,' Navarre said. 'A single spacecraft of the line gives total air superiority when there is nothing against it but flyers. And our flyers are not even military.'

'Still, it's always helpful to see what you're up against. Uh, you're sure their whole power is concentrated here?'

'Yes, quite sure. This area has most of our industrial facilities. There are garrisons elsewhere, at certain mines and plants, as well as at observation posts. But our scouts have reported those are negligible in themselves.'

'So ... I'd guess, then, knowing how much crowding Aleriona will tolerate – let me think – I'd estimate their number at around fifty thousand. Surely the military doesn't amount to more than a fifth of that. They don't need more defense. Upper-type workers – what we'd call managers, engineers, and so forth – are capable of fighting but aren't trained for it. The lower-type majority have had combativeness bred out. So we've really only got ten thousand Aleriona to worry about. How many men could you field?'

'Easily a hundred thousand – who would be destroyed the moment they ventured out of the forests.'

'I know. A rifle isn't much use when you face heavy ground and air weapons.' Heim grimaced.

The flyer touched concrete at the designated point and halted. Its escort remained hovering. Navarre stood up. '*Sortons*,' he said curtly, and led the way out the door.

Twenty Aleriona of the warrior class – lean, broad of chest, hair tight-braided under the conical helmets, faces handsome rather than beautiful, and expressionless – waited in file. The long sunrays turned their scaly garments almost incandescent. They did not draw the crooked swords at their belts or point their guns at the newcomers; they might have been statues.

Their officer stepped forward, making the droop-tailed bow with fingertips lightly touching that signified respect. He was taller than his followers, though still below average human height.

'Well are you come,' he sang in fairly good French. 'Wish you rest or refreshment?'

'No, thank you,' Navarre said, slowly so the alien could follow his dialect. Against the fluid motion that confronted him, his stiffness looked merely lumpy. 'We are prepared to commence discussions at once.'

'Yet first ought you be shown your quarters. Nigh to the high masters of the Garden of War is prepared a place as best we might.' The officer trilled an order. Several low-class workers appeared. They did not conform to Earth's picture of Aleriona – their black-clad bodies were too heavy, features too coarse, hair too short, fur too dull, and there was nothing about them of that inborn unconscious arrogance which marked the leader breeds. Yet they were not servile, nor were they stupid. A million years of history, its only real change the glacial movement toward an ever more unified society, had fitted their very genes for this part. If the officer was a panther and his soldiers watchdogs, these were mettlesome horses.

In his role as aide, Vadász showed them the party's baggage. They fetched it out, the officer whistled a note, the troopers fell in around the humans and started off across the field. There was no marching; but the bodies rippled together like parts of one organism. Aurore struck the contact lenses which protected them from its light and turned their eyes to rubies.

Heim's own eyes shifted back and forth as he walked. Not many other soldiers were in evidence. Some must be off duty, performing one of those enigmatic rites that were communion, conversation, sport, and prayer to an Aleriona below the fifth level of mastery. Others would be at the missile sites or on air patrol. Workers and supervisors swarmed about, unloading cargo, fetching metal from a smelter or circuit parts from a factory to another place where it would enter some orbital weapon. Their machines whirred, clanked, rumbled. Nonetheless, to a man the silence was terrifying. No shouts, no talk, no jokes or curses were heard: only an occasional melodic command, a thin weaving of taped orchestral music, the pad-pad of a thousand soft feet.

Vadász showed his teeth in a grin of sorts. *'Ils considèrent la*

170

vie très sérieusement,' he murmured to Navarre. *'Je parierais qu'ils ne font jamais de plaisanteries douteuses.'*

Did the enemy officer cast him a look of – incomprehension? *'Taisez vous!'* Navarre said.

But Vadász was probably right, Heim reflected. Humour springs from a certain inward distortion. To that great oneness which was the Aleriona soul, it seemed impossible: literally unthinkable.

Except ... yes, the delegates to Earth, most especially Admiral Cynbe, had shown flashes of a bleak wit. But they belonged to the ultimate master class. It suggested a difference from the rest of their species which— He dismissed speculation and went back to observing as much detail as he could.

The walk ended at a building some hundred meters from the edge of the field. Its exterior was no different from the other multiply curved structures surrounding it. Inside, though, the rooms had clearly been stripped, the walls were raw plastic and floors were stained where the soil of flowerbeds had been removed. Furniture, a bath cubicle, Terrestrial-type lights, plundered from houses, were arranged with a geometric precision which the Aleriona doubtless believed was pleasing to men. 'Hither shall food and drink be brought you,' the officer sang. 'Have you wish to go elsewhere, those guards that stand outside will accompany.'

'I see no communicator,' Navarre said.

'None there is. With the wilderness dwellers make you no secret discourse. Within camp, your guards bear messages. Now must we open your holders-of-things and make search upon your persons.'

Navarre reddened. 'What? Monsieur, that violates every rule of parley.'

'Here the rule is of the Final Society. Wish you not thus, yourselves you may backtake to the mountains.' It was hard to tell whether or not that lilting voice held insult, but Heim didn't think so. The officer was stating a fact.

'Very well,' Navarre spat. 'We submit under protest, and this shall be held to your account when Earth has defeated you.'

The Aleriona didn't bother to reply. Yet the frisking was oddly like a series of caresses.

No contraband was found, there not being any. Most of the colonists were surprised when the officer told them, 'Wish you thus, go we this now to seek the Intellect Masters.' Heim recalling past encounters, was not. The Aleriona overlords had always been more flexible than their human counterparts. With so rigid a civilization at their beck, they could afford it.

'Ah ... just who are they?' Navarre temporized.

'The *imbiac* of planetary and space defense are they, with below them the prime engineering operator. And then have they repositories of information and advice,' the officer replied, 'Is not for you a similarity?'

'I speak for the constabulary government of New Europe,' Navarre said. 'These gentlemen are my own experts, advisers, and assistants. But whatever I agree to must be ratified by my superiors.'

Again the girlish face, incongruous on that animal body, showed a brief loosening that might betoken perplexity. 'Come you?' the song wavered.

'Why not?' Navarre said. 'Please gather your papers, messieurs.' His heels clacked on the way out.

Heim and Vadász got to the door simultaneously. The minstrel bowed. 'After you, my dear Alphonse,' he said. The other man hesitated, unwilling. But no, you had to maintain morale. He bowed back: 'After *you*, my dear Gaston.' They kept it up for several seconds.

'Make you some ritual?' the officer asked.

'A most ancient one.' Vadász sauntered off side by side with him.

'Never knew I such grew in your race,' the officer admitted.

'Well, now, let me tell you—' Vadász started an energetic argument. *He's doing his job right well,* Heim conceded grudgingly.

Not wanting to keep the Magyar in his consciousness, he looked straight ahead at the building they were approaching. In contrast to the rest, it lifted in a single high curve, topped with a symbol resembling an Old Chinese ideogram. The walls were not blank bronze, but scored with microgrooves that turned them shiftingly, bewilderingly iridescent. He saw now that this was the source of the music, on a scale unimagined by men, that breathed across the port.

No sentries were visible. An Aleriona had nothing to fear from his underlings. The wall dilated to admit those who neared, and closed behind them.

There was no decompression chamber. The occupiers must find it easier to adapt themselves, perhaps with the help of drugs, to the heavy wet atmosphere of this planet. A hall sloped upward, vaguely seen in the dull red light from a paraboloidal ceiling. The floor was carpeted with living, downy turf, the walls with phosphorescent vines and flowers that swayed, slowly keeping time to the music, and drenched the air with their odors. The humans drew closer together, as if for comfort. Ghost silent, ghost shadowy, they went with their guards to the council chamber.

It soared in a vault whose top was hidden by dusk, but where artificial stars glittered wintry keen. The interior was a vague, moving labyrinth of trellises, bushes, and bowers. Light came only from a fountain at the center, whose crimson-glowing waters leaped five meters out of a bowl carved like an open mouth, cascaded down again, and filled every corner of the jungle with their clear splash and gurgle. Walking around it, Heim thought he heard wings rustle in the murk overhead.

The conqueror lords stood balanced on tails and clawed feet, waiting. There were half a dozen all told. None wore any special insignia of rank, but the light flickered lovingly over metal-mesh garments, lustrous hair, and silver-sparked white fur. The angelic faces were in repose, the emerald eyes altogether steady.

To them the officer genuflected and the soldiers dipped their rifles. A few words were sung. The guards stepped back into darkness and the humans stood alone.

One Aleriona master arched his back and hissed. Almost instantly, his startlement passed. He trod forward so that his countenance came into plain view. Laughter belled from him, low and warm.

'Thus, Captain Gunnar Heim,' he crooned in English. 'Strangeness, how we must ever meet. Remember you not Cynbe ru Taren?'

CHAPTER SEVEN

So shattered was Heim's universe that he was only dimly aware of what happened. Through the red gloom, trillings went among the Aleriona. One bristled and cried an order to the guards. Cynbe countermanded it with an imperious gesture. Above the racket of his pulse, Heim heard the admiral murmur: 'You would they destroy on this now, but such must not become. Truth, there can be no release; truth alike, you are war's honored prisoners.' And there were more songs, and at last the humans were marched back to their quarters. But Heim remained.

Cynbe dismissed his fellow chieftains and all but four guards. By then the sweat was drying on the man's skin, his heartbeat was slowed, the first total despair thrust down beneath an iron watchfulness. He folded his arms and waited.

The Aleriona lord prowled to the fountain, which silhouetted him as if against liquid flames. For a while he played with a blossoming vine. The sole noises were music, water, and unseen circling wings. It was long before he intoned, softly and not looking at the man:

'Hither fared I to have in charge the hunt for you the hunter. Glad was my hope that we might meet in space and love each the other with guns. Why came you to this dull soil?'

'Do you expect me to tell you?' Heim rasped.

'We are kinfolk, you and I. Sorrow, that I must word-break and keep you captive. Although your presence betokens this was never meant for a real parley.'

'It was, however. I just happened to come along. You've no right to hold the New Europeans, at least.'

'Let us not lawsplit. We two rear above such. Release I the others, home take they word to your warship. Then may she well strike. And we have only my cruiser *Jubalcho* to meet her. While she knows not what has happened to you her soul, *Fox II* abides. Thus gain I time to recall my deep-scattered strength.'

The breath hissed between Heim's teeth. Cynbe swung about. His eyes probed like fire weapons. 'What bethink you?'

'Nothing!' Heim barked frantically.

It raced within him: *He believes I took Fox down. Well, that's natural. Not knowing about our meteorite gimmick, he'd assume that only a very small or a very fast craft could sneak past his guard. And why should I come in a tender? Fox on the surface could do tremendous damage, missile this base and strike at his flagship from a toadhole position.*

I don't know what good it is having him misinformed, but – play by ear, boy, play by ear. You haven't got anything left except your rusty old wits.

Cynbe studied him a while. 'Not long dare I wait to act,' he mused. 'And far are my ships.'

Heim forced a jeering note: 'The practical limit of a maser beam is about twenty million kilometers. After that, if nothing else, the position error for a ship gets too big. And there's no way to lock onto an accelerating vessel till she's so close that you might as well use an ordinary 'caster. Her coordinates change too fast, with too many unpredictables such as meteorite dodging. So how many units have you got on known orbits within twenty million kilometers?'

'Insult me not,' Cynbe replied quietly. He stalked to the wall, brushed aside a curtain of flowers and punched the keys of an infotrieve. It chattered and extruded a print-out. He brooded over the symbols. '*Insant* the cruiser and *Savaidh* the lancer can we reach. All ignorant must the others wheel their way, until one by one they return on slow schedule and find only battle's ashes.'

'What are the factors for those two?' Heim inquired. Mostly he was holding at bay the blood-colored stillness. It jarred him – not too much to jam the numbers into his memory – when Cynbe read off in English the orbital elements and present positions.

'Hence have I sent my race-brothers to summon them,' the Aleriona went on. 'At highest acceleration positive and negative, *Savaidh* takes orbit around Europe Neuve in eighteen hours, *Insant* in twenty-three. I think not the Foxfolk will dread for you thus soon. With three warcraft aloft, this entire planet do we scan. Let your ship make the least of little moves, and destruction shall thunder upon her unstoppable. Although truth, when ready for smiting we shall send detector craft all places and seek her lair.'

His tone had not been one of threat. It grew still milder: 'This do I tell you in my thin hoping you yield her. Gallant was that ship, unfitting her death where the stars cannot see.'

Heim pinched his lips together and shook his head.

'What may I offer you for surrender,' Cynbe asked in sadness, 'unless maychance you will take my love?'

'What the devil!' Heim exclaimed.

'We are so much alone, you and I,' Cynbe sang. For the first time scorn touched his voice, as he jerked his tail in the direction of the warriors who stood, blank-faced and uncompre-

175

hending, half hidden in the twilight. 'Think you I am kin to that?'

He glided closer. The illumination played over shining locks and disconcertingly fair countenance. His great eyes lingered on the man. 'Old is Alerion,' he chanted, 'old, old. Long-lived are the red dwarf stars, and late appears life in so feeble a radiance. Once we had come to being, our species, on a planet of seas vanished, rivers shrunk to trickles in desert, a world niggard of air, water, metal, life – uncountable ages lingered we in savagehood. Ah, slow was the machine with coming to us. What you did in centuries, we did in tens upon thousands of years; and when it was done, a million years a-fled, one society alone endured, swallowed every other, and the machine's might gave it upon us a grip not to be broken. Starward fared the Wanderers, vast-minded the Intellects, yet were but ripples over the still deep of a civilization eternity-rooted. Earth lives for goals, Alerion for changelessness. Understand you that, Gunnar Heim? Feel you how ultimate the winter you are?'

'I – you mean—' Cynbe's fingers stroked like a breath across the human's wrist. He felt the hair stir beneath them, and groped for a handhold in a world suddenly tilting. 'Well, uh, it's been theorized. That is, some people believe you're just reacting because we threaten your stability. But it doesn't make sense. We could reach an accommodation, if all you want is to be let alone. You're trying to hound us out of space.'

'Thus must we. Sense, reason, logic are what, save instruments of most ancient instinct? If races less powerful than we change, that makes nothing more than pullulation among insects. But you, you come in ten or twenty thousand years, one flick of time, come from the caves, bear weapons to shake planets as is borne a stone war-ax, you beswarm these stars and your dreams reach at the whole galaxy, at the whole cosmos. *That* can we not endure! Instinct feels doom in this becoming one mere little enclave, given over helpless to the wild mercy of those who bestride the galaxy. Would you, could you trust a race grown strong that feeds on living brains? No more is Alerion able to trust a race without bounds to its hope. Back to your own planets must you be cast, maychance back to your caves or your dust.'

Heim shook the soft touch loose, clenched his fists and growled: 'You admit this, and still talk about being friends?'

Cynbe confronted him squarely, but sang with less than

176

steadiness: 'Until now said I "we" for all Alerion. Sure is that not truth. For when first plain was your menace, plain too was that those bred stiff-minded, each for a one element of the Final Society, must go down before you who are not bound and fear not newness. Mine was the master type created that it might think and act as humans and so overmatch them.' His hands smote together. 'Lonely, lonely!'

Heim looked upon him in his beauty and desolation, and found no words.

Fiercely the Aleriona asked: 'Guess you not how I must feel alone, I who think more Earthman than any save those few created like me? Know you not that glory there was to be on Earth, to lock with minds that had also no horizon, drown in your books and music and too much alive eye-arts? Barren are we, the Intellect Masters of the Garden of War; none may descend from us for troubling of Alerion's peace; yet were we given the forces of life, that our will and fury rear tall as yours, and when we meet, those forces bind us through rites they knew who stood at Thermopylae. But ... when you seized me, Gunnar Heim, that once you ransomed your daughter with me ... afterward saw I that too was a rite.'

Heim took a backward step. Boldness ran down his spine and out into every nerve end.

Cynbe laughed. The sound was glorious to hear. 'Let me not frighten you, *Star Fox* captain. I offer only that which you will take.' Very gently: 'Friendship? Talk? Together-faring? I ask you never betrayal of your people. Well might I order a wresting from you of your knowledge and plans, but never. Think you are a war captive, and no harm that you share an awareness with your captor, who would be your friend.'

My God, it leaped in Heim. The sounds about him came through as if across a barrier of great distance or of fever. *Give me some time and .. and I could use him.*

'Recall,' Cynbe urged, 'my might on Alerion stands high. Well can I someday make a wall for the race that bred you, and so spare them that which is extinction.'

No! Sheer reflex. *I won't. I can't.*

Cynbe held out one hand. 'Clasp this, as once you did,' he begged. 'Give me oath you will seek no escape nor warning to your breedmates. Then no guard shall there be for you; freely as myself shall you betread our camps and ships.'

'No!' Heim roared aloud.

Cynbe recoiled. His teeth gleamed forth. 'Little the honor you show to me,' he whispered.

'I can't give you a parole,' Heim said. *Whatever you do, don't turn him flat against you. There may be a chance here somewhere. Better dead, trying for a break, than—* Something flashed across his brain. It was gone before he knew what it was. His consciousness twisted about and went in a pursuit that made the sweat and heart-banging take over his body again.

Somehow, though every muscle was tight and the room had taken on an aspect of nightmare, he said dryly: 'What'd be the use? I credit you with not being an idiot. You'd have an eye kept on me – now wouldn't you?'

Where a man might have been angered, Cynbe relaxed and chuckled. 'Truth, at the least until *Fox II* be slain. Although afterward, when better we know each the other—'

Heim captured the thought that had run from him. Recognizing it was like a blow. He couldn't stop to weigh chances, they were probably altogether forlorn and he would probably get himself killed. *Let's try the thing out, at least. There's no commitment right away. If it's obviously not going to work, then I just won't make the attempt.*

He ran a dry tongue over dry lips, husked, and said, 'I couldn't give you a parole anyway, at any time. You don't really think like a human, Cynbe, or you'd know why.'

Membranes dimmed those eyes. The golden head drooped. 'But always in your history was honor and admiration among enemies,' the music protested.

'Oh, yes, that. Look, I'm glad to shake your hand.' Oddly, it was no lie, and when the four slim fingers coiled around his Heim did not let go at once. 'But I can't surrender to you, even verbally,' he said. 'I guess my own instincts won't let me.'

'No, now, often have men—'

'I tell you, this isn't something that can be put in words. I can't really feel what you said, about humans being naturally horrible to Aleriona. No more can you feel what I'm getting at. But you did give me some rough idea. Maybe I could give you an idea of . . . well, what it's like to be a man whose people have lost their homes.'

'I listen.'

'But I'd have to show you. The symbols, the— You haven't

178

any religion as humans understand it, you Aleriona, have you? That's one item among many. If I showed you some things you could see and touch, and tried to explain what they stand for, maybe— Well, how about it? Shall we take a run to Bonne Chance?'

Cynbe withdrew a step. Abruptly he had gone catlike.

Heim mocked him with a chopping gesture. 'Oh, so you're scared I'll try some stunt? Bring guards, of course. Or don't bother, if you don't dare.' He half turned. 'I'd better get back to my own sort.'

'You play on me,' Cynbe cried.

'Nah. I say to hell with you, nothing else. The trouble is, you don't know what you've done on this planet. You aren't capable of knowing.'

'*Arvan!*' Heim wasn't sure how much was wrath in that explosion and how much was something else. 'I take your challenge. Go we this now.'

A wave of weakness passed through Heim. *Whew! So I did read his psychology right. Endre couldn't do better.* The added thought came with returning strength. 'Good,' he accepted shakily. 'Because I am anxious for you to realize as much as possible. As you yourself said, you could be a powerful influence for helping Earth, if the war goes against us. Or if your side loses – that could happen, you know; our Navy's superior to yours, if only we can muster the guts to use it – in that case, I'd have some voice in what's to be done about Alerion. Let's take Vadász along. You remember him, I'm sure.'

'Ye-e-es. Him did I gaintell in your party, though scant seemed he to matter. Why wish you him?'

'He's better with words than I am. He could probably make it clearer to you.' *He speaks German, and I do a little. Cynbe knows English, French, doubtless some Spanish – but German?*

The admiral shrugged and gave an order. One soldier saluted and went out ahead of the others, who accompanied the leaders – down the hall, into the morning across the field to a military flyer. Cynbe stopped once, that he might slip contacts over eyeballs evolved beneath a red coal of a sun.

Vadász waited with his guards. He looked small, hunched, and defeated. 'Gunnar,' he said dully, 'What's this?'

Heim explained. For a moment the Hungarian was puzzled. Then hope lit in his visage. 'Whatever your idea is,

179

Gunnar, I am with you,' he said, and masked out expression.

Half a dozen troopers took places at the rear of the vehicle. Cynbe assumed the controls. 'Put us down in the square,' Heim suggested, 'and we'll stroll around.'

'Strange are your ways,' Cynbe cantillated. 'We thought you were probed and understood, your weakness and shortsightedness in our hands, but then *Fox II* departed. And now—'

'Your problem is, sir, that Aleriona of any given class, except no doubt your own, are stereotypes,' Vadász said. 'Every human is a law to himself.'

Cynbe made no reply. The flyer took off.

It landed minutes later. The party debarked.

Silence dwelt under an enormous sky. Fallen leaves covered the pavement and overflowed the dry fountain, where Lamontagne's effigy still stood proud. A storm had battered the market booths, toppled café tables and chairs, ripped the gay little umbrellas. Only the cathedral rose firm. Cynbe moved toward it. 'No,' Heim said, 'let's make that the end of the tour.'

He started in the direction of the river. Rubbish rustled from his boots, echoes flung emptily back from walls. 'Can't you see what's wrong?' he asked. 'Men lived here.'

'Hence-driven are they,' Cynbe answered. 'Terrible to me Aleriona is an empty city. And yet, Gunnar Heim, was this a . a . a dayfly. Have you such rage that the less than a century is forsaken?'

'It was going to grow,' Vadász said.

Cynbe made an ugly face.

A small huddle of bones lay on the sidewalk. Heim pointed. 'That was somebody's pet dog,' he said. 'It wondered where its gods had gone, and waited for them, and finally starved to death. Your doing.'

'Flesh do you eat,' Cynbe retorted.

A door creaked, swinging back and forth in the breeze off the water. Most of the house's furniture could still be seen inside, dusty and rain-beaten. Near the threshold sprawled the remnants of a rag doll. Heim felt tears bite his eyes.

Cynbe touched his hand. 'Well remember I what are your children to you,' he crooned.

Heim continued with long strides. 'Humans live mostly for their children,' Vadász said.

The riparian esplanade came in sight. Beyond its rail, the Carsac ran wide and murmurous toward the bay. Sunlight flared off that surface, a trumpet call made visible.

Now! Heim thought. The blood roared in him. 'One of our poets said what I mean,' he spoke slowly. *'Wenn wir sind an der Fluss gekommen, und im Falls wir die Möglichkeit sehen, dann werden wir ausspringen und nach dem Hafen schwimmen.'*

He dared not look to see how Vadász reacted. Dimly he heard Cynbe ask, in a bemused way, 'What token those words?'

With absolute coolness, Vadász told him, 'Man who is man does not surrender the hope of his loins unless manhood has died within.'

Good lad! Heim cheered. But most of his consciousness crawled with the guns at his back.

They started west along the embankment. 'Still apprehend I not,' Cynbe sang. 'Also Aleriona make their lives for those lives that are to come. What difference?'

Heim didn't believe he could hide his purpose much longer. So let it be this moment that he acted – the chance did not look too bad – let him at worst be shattered into darkness and the end of fear.

He stopped and leaned on the rail. 'The difference,' he said, 'you can find in the same man's words. *Ich werde diesen Wesen in das Wasser stürzen. Dann springen wir beide.* It's, uh, it's hard to translate. But look down here.'

Vadász joined them. Glee quirked his lips, a tiny bit, but he declared gravely: 'The poem comes from a saying of Heraclitus. "No man bathes twice in the same river."'

'That have I read.' Cynbe shuddered. 'Seldom was thus dreadful a thought.'

'You see?' Heim laid a hand on his shoulder and urged him forward, until he also stood bent over the rail. His gaze was forced to the flowing surface, and held there as if hypnotized. 'Here's a basic human symbol for you,' Heim said. 'A river, bound to the sea, bound to flood a whole countryside if you dam it. Motion, power, destiny, time itself.'

'Had we known such on Alerion—' Cynbe whispered. 'Our world raised naked rock.'

Heim closed fingers on his neck. The man's free hand

181

slapped down on the rail. A surge of arm and shoulder cast him and Cynbe across. They struck the current together.

CHAPTER EIGHT

His boots dragged him under. Letting the Aleriona go, he writhed about and clawed at the fastenings. The light changed from green to brown and then was gone. Water poured past, a cool and heavy force that tumbled him over and over. One off – two off – he struck upward with arms and legs. His lungs felt near bursting. Puff by grudged puff, he let out air. His mind began to wobble. *Here goes,* he thought, *a breath or a firebeam.* He stuck out as little of his face as he could, gasped, saw only the embankment, and went below again to swim.

Thrice more he did likewise, before he guessed he had come far enough to risk looking for Vadász. He shook the wetness from hair and eyes and continued in an Australian crawl. Above the tinted concrete that enclosed the river, trees trapped sunlight in green and gold. A few roofpeaks showed, otherwise his ceiling was the sky, infinitely blue.

Before long Vadász's head popped into sight. Heim waved at him and threshed on until he was under a bridge. It gave some protection from searchers. He grabbed a pier and trod water. The minstrel caught up and panted.

'*Kárhoztatás,* Gunnar, you go as if the devil himself were after you!'

'Isn't he? Though it helps a lot that the Aleriona don't see so well here. Contacts stop down the brightness for them, but Aurore doesn't emit as much of the near infrared that they're most sensitive to as The Eith does.' Heim found it calming to speak academically. It changed him from a hunted animal to a military tactician. 'Just the same, we'd better stay down as much as we can. And stay separate, too. You know the old Quai des Coquillages – it's still there? Okay, I'll meet you underneath it. If one of us waits an hour, let him assume the other bought a farm.'

Since Vadász looked more exhausted than himself, Heim started first. He didn't hurry, mostly he let the current bear him along, and reached the river mouth in good shape: so good that the sheer wonder of his escape got to him. He spent his time beneath the dock simply admiring light-sparkles on water, the rake of masts, the fluid chill enclosing his skin, the roughness of the bollard he held, the chuckle against hulls and their many vivid colors. His mood had just begun to ravel away in worry (*Damn, I should've told Endre what I know*) when the Magyar arrived.

'Will they not seek us here first?' Vadász asked.

'M-m, I doubt it,' Heim said. 'Don't forget, they're from a dry planet. The idea of using water for anything but drinking doesn't come natural to them; you notice they've left all these facilities untouched, though coastwise transport would be a handy supplement to their air freighters. Their first assumption ought to be that we went ashore as soon as we could and holed up in town. Still, we want to get out of here as fast as possible, so let's find a boat in working order.'

'There you must choose. I am a landlubber by heritage.'

'Well, I never got along with horses, so honors are even.' Heim risked climbing onto the wharf for an overview. He picked a good-looking pleasure craft, a submersible hydrofoil, and trotted to her. Once below, she'd be undetectable by any equipment the Aleriona had.

'Can we get inside?' the minstrel asked from the water.

'*Ja,* she's not locked. Yachtsmen trust each other.' Heim unslipped the lines, pulled the canopy back, and extended an arm to help Vadász up on deck. They tumbled into the cabin and closed the glasite. 'Now, you check the radio while I have a look at the engine.'

A year's neglect had not much hurt the vessel. In fact, the sun had charged her accumulators to maximum. Her bottom was foul, but that could be lived with. Excitement surged in Heim. 'My original idea was to find a communicator somewhere in town, get word to camp, and then skulk about hoping we wouldn't be tracked down and wouldn't starve,' he said. 'But now – hell, we might get back in person! It'll at least be harder for the enemy to pick up our message and send a rover bomb after the source, if we're at sea. Let's go.'

The motor chugged. The boat slid from land. Vadász peered anxiously out the dome. 'Why are they not after us in full cry?' he fretted.

'I told you how come. They haven't yet guessed we'd try

183

this way. Also, they must be disorganized as a bawdy-house on Monday morning, after what I did to Cynbe.' Nonetheless, Heim was glad to leave obstacles behind and submerge. He went to the greatest admissible depth, set the 'pilot for a south-easterly course, and began peeling off his wet clothes.

Vadász regarded him with awe. 'Gunnar,' he said, in a tone suggesting he was not far from tears, 'I will make a ballad about this, and it will not be good enough, but still they will sing it a thousand years hence. Because your name will live that long.'

'Aw, shucks, Endre. Don't make my ears burn.'

'No, I must say what's true. However did you conceive it?'

Heim turned up the heater to dry himself. The ocean around – murky green, with now and then a curiously shaped fish darting by – would dissipate infrared radiation. He had an enormous sense of homecoming, as if again he were a boy on the seas of Gea. For the time being, it overrode everything else. The frailty and incompleteness of his triumph could be seen later; let him now savor it.

'I didn't,' he confessed. 'The idea sort of grew. Cynbe was eager to ... be friends or whatever. I talked him into visiting Bonne Chance, in the hope something might turn up that I could use for a break. It occurred to me that probably none of his gang could swim, so the riverside looked like the best place. I asked to have you along because we could use German under their noses. Also having two of us doubled the odds that one would get away.'

Vadász's deference cracked in a grin. 'That was the most awful *Schweindeutsch* I have yet heard. You are no linguist.'

Memory struck at Heim. 'No,' he said harshly. Trying to keep his happiness a while, he went on fast: 'We were there when I thought if I could pitch Cynbe in the drink, his guards would go all out to save him, rather than run along the bank shooting at us. If you can't swim yourself, you've got a tough job rescuing another non-swimmer.'

'Do you think he drowned?'

'Well, one can always hope,' Heim said, less callously than he sounded. 'I wouldn't be surprised if they lost at least a couple of warriors fishing him out. But we've likely not seen the last of him. Even if he did drown, they can probably get him to a revival machine before brain decay sets in. Still, while he's out of commission, things are apt to be rather muddled for the enemy. Not that the organization can't operate smoothly without him. But for a while it'll lack direction, as far as you and I are concerned, anyhow. That's the time we'll use to put well out to sea and call de Vigny.'

'Why . . . yes, surely they can send a fast flyer to our rescue.' Vadász leaned back with a cat-outside-canary smile. '*La belle* Danielle is going to see me even before she expected. Dare I say, before she hoped?'

Anger sheeted in Heim. 'Dog your hatch, you clot-brain!' he snarled. 'This is no picnic. We'll be lucky to head off disaster.'

'What – what—' Color left Vadász's cheeks. He winced away from the big man. 'Gunnar, did I say—'

'Listen.' Heim slammed a fist on the arm of his seat. 'Our amateur try at espionage blew up the whole shebang. Have you forgotten the mission was to negotiate terms to keep our people from starving? That's out. Maybe something can be done later, but right now we're only concerned with staying alive. Our plan for evacuating refugees is out the airlock too. Cynbe jumped to the conclusion that *Fox* herself is on this planet. He's recalled a lancer and a cruiser to supplement his flagship. Between them, those three can detect *Meroeth* raising mass, and clobber her. It won't do us any good to leave her doggo, either. They'll have air patrols with high-gain detectors sweeping the whole planet. So there goes de Vigny's nice hidey-hole at Lac aux Nuages. For that matter, with three ships this close to her position, *Fox* herself is in mortal danger.

'You blithering, self-centred rockhead! Did you think I was risking death just so we could escape? What the muck have we got to do with anything? Our people have got to be warned!'

With a growl, he turned to the inertial navigator panel. No, they weren't very far out yet. But maybe he should surface anyway, take his chances, to cry what he knew at this instant.

The boat pulsed around him. The heater whirred and threw waves of warmth across his hide. There was a smell of oil in the air. Outside the ports, vision was quickly blocked – as he had been blocked, thwarted, resisted and evaded at every turn. 'Those ships will be here inside an Earth day,' he said. '*Fox* better make for outer space, the rest of us for the woods.'

'Gunnar—' Vadász began.

'Oh, be quiet!'

The minstrel flushed and raised his voice. 'No. I don't know what I have done to be insulted by you, and if you haven't the decency to tell me, that must be your affair. But I have something to tell you, Captain. We can't contact *Fox* in time.'

'Huh?' Heim whirled to face him.

'Think for a moment. Diego has his big maser set erected near the lake. But morning is well along, and Diane is nearly full. It set for the Haute Garance hours ago. It won't rise again for, I guess, thirty hours.'

'*Satan . . . i . . . helvede,*' Heim choked. Strength drained from him. He felt the ache in his flesh and knew he had begun to grow old.

After a time in which he merely stared, Vadász said to him, timidly: 'You are too much a man to let this beat you. If you think it so important, well, perhaps we can get *Meroeth* aloft. Her own communicator can reach the moon. The enemy satellites will detect her, and the cruiser close in. But she is lost anyway, you inform me, and she can surrender. We only need three or four men to do it. I will be one of them.'

Lightning-struck, Heim sprang to his feet. His head bashed the canopy. He looked up and saw a circle of sunlight, blinding on the ocean surface, above him.

'Are you hurt?' Vadász asked.

'By heaven – and hell – and everything in between.' Heim offered his hand. 'Endre, I've been worse than a bastard. I've been a middle-aged adolescent. Will you forgive me?'

Vadász gripped hard. Perception flickered in his eyes. 'Oh, so,' he murmured. 'The young lady ... Gunnar, she's nothing to me. Mere pleasant company. I thought you felt the same.'

'I doubt that you do,' Heim grunted. 'Never mind. We've bigger game to hunt. Look, I happen to know what the orbits and starting positions of those ships were. Cynbe saw no reason not to tell me when I asked – I suppose unconsciously I was going on the old military principle of grabbing every piece of data that comes by, whether or not you think you'll ever use it. Well, I also know their classes, which means I know their capabilities. From that, we can pretty well compute their trajectories. They can be pinpointed at any given time – close enough for combat purposes, but not close enough for their ground base to beam them any warning. Okay, so that's one advantage we've got, however small. What else?'

He began to pace, two steps to the cabin's end, two steps

186

back, fist beating palm and jaw muscles standing in knots. Vadász drew himself aside. Once more the cat's grin touched his mouth. He knew Gunnar Heim in that mood.

'Listen.' The captain hammered out the scheme as he spoke. '*Meroeth*'s a big transport. So she's got powerful engines. In spite of her size and clumsiness, she can move like a hellbat when empty. She can't escape three ships on patrol orbit. But at the moment there's only one, Cynbe's personal *Jubalcho*. I don't know her orbit, but the probabilities favor her being well away at any given time that *Meroeth* lifts. She could pursue, sure, and get so close that *Meroeth* can't outrun a missile. But she ain't gonna – I hope – because Cynbe knows that wherever I am, *Fox* isn't likely very distant, and he's got to protect his base against *Fox* till his reinforcements arrive. Or if the distance is great enough, he'll assume the transport *is* our cruiser, and take no chances!

'So ... okay ... given good piloting, *Meroeth* has an excellent probability of making a clean getaway. She can flash a message to *Fox*. But then – what? If *Fox* only takes us aboard, we're back exactly where we started. No, we're worse off, because the New Europeans have run low on morale, and losing their contact with us could well push them right into quitting the fight. So – wait – let me think— Yes!' Heim bellowed. 'Why not? Endre, we'll go for broke!'

The minstrel shouted his answer.

Heim reined in his own eagerness. 'The faster we move, the better,' he said. 'We'll call HQ at the lake immediately. Do you know Basque, or any other language the Aleriona don't that somebody on de Vigny's staff does?'

'I fear not. And a broadcast, such as we must make, will doubtless be monitored. I can use *Louchébème,* if that will help.'

'It might, though they're probably on to it by now. ... Hm. We'll frame something equivocal, as far as the enemy's concerned. He needn't know it's us calling from a sub. Let him assume it's a *maquisard* in a flyer. We can identify ourselves by references to incidents in camp.

'We'll tell de Vigny to start lightening the spaceship as much as possible. No harm in that, since the Aleriona know we do have a ship on the planet. It'll confirm for them that she must be in the Haute Garance, but that's the first place they'd look anyhow.' Heim tugged his chin. 'Now ... unfortunately, I can't

187

send any more than that without tipping my hand. We'll have to deliver the real message in person. So we'll submerge right after you finish calling and head for a rendezvous point where a flyer is to pick us up. How can we identify that, and not have the enemy there with a brass band and the keys to the city?'

'Hm-m-m. Let me see a map.' Vadász unrolled a chart from the pilot's drawer. 'Our radius is not large, if we are to be met soon. *Ergo* – Yes. I will tell them . . . so-and-so many kilometers due east of a place—' he blushed, pointing to Fleurville, a ways inland and down the Côte Notre Dame – where Danielle Irribarne told Endre Vadász there is a grotto they should visit. That was shortly before moonset. We, um, sat on a platform high in a tree and—'

Heim ignored the hurt and laughed. 'Okay, lover boy. Let me compute where we can be in that coordinate system.'

Vadász frowned. 'We make risks, acting in this haste,' he said. 'First we surface, or at least lie awash, and broadcast a strong signal so near the enemy base.'

'It won't take long. We'll be down again before they can send a flyer. I admit one might be passing right over us this minute, but probably not.'

'Still, a New European vessel has to meet us. No matter if it goes fast and takes the long way around over a big empty land, it is in daylight and skirting a dragon's nest. And likewise for the return trip with us.'

'I know.' Heim didn't look up from the chart on his knees. 'We could do it safer by taking more time. But then we'd be too late for anything. We're stuck in this orbit, Endre, no matter how close we have to skim the sun.'

CHAPTER NINE

'BRIDGE to stations, report.'

'Engine okay,' said Diego Gonzales.

'Radio and main radar okay,' said Endre Vadász.

'Gun Turret One okay and hungry,' said Jean Irribarne. The colonists in the other emplacements added a wolfish chorus.

Easy, lads, Heim thought. *If we have to try those pop-guns on a real, functioning warship, we're dead.* 'Stand by to lift,' he called. Clumsy in his spacesuit, he moved hands across the board.

The lake frothed. Waves swept up its beaches. A sighing went among the trees, and *Meroeth* rose from below. Briefly her great form blotted out the sun, where it crawled toward noon, and animals fled down wilderness trails. Then, with steadily mounting velocity, she flung skyward. The cloven air made a continuous thunderclap. Danielle and Madelon Irribarne put hands to tormented ears. When the shape was gone from sight, they returned to each other's arms.

'Radar, report!' Heim called through drone and shiver.

'Negative,' Vadász said.

Higher and higher the ship climbed. The world below dwindled, humped into a curve, turned fleecy with clouds and blue with oceans. The sky went dark, the stars blazed forth.

'Signal received on the common band,' Vadász said. *'Jubalcho* must have spotted us. Shall I answer?'

'Hell, no,' Heim said. 'All I want is her position and vector.'

The hollow volume of *Meroeth* trapped sound, bounced echoes about, until a booming rolled from stem to stern and port to starboard. It throbbed in Heim's skull. His open faceplate rattled.

'Can't find her,' Vadász told him. 'She must be far off.'

But she found us. Well, she has professional detector operators. I've got to make do with whatever was in camp. No time to recruit better-trained people.

We should be so distant that she'd have to chase us for some ways to get inside the velocity differential of her missiles. And she should decide her duty is to stay put. If I've guessed wrong on either of those, we've hoisted our last glass. Heim tasted blood, hot and bitter, and realized he had caught his tongue between his teeth. He swore, wiped his face, and drove the ship.

Outward and outward. New Europe grew smaller among the crowding suns. Diane rose slowly to view. 'Captain to radio room. Forget about everything else. Lock that maser and cut me in on the circuit.' Heim reached for racked instruments and navigational tables. 'I'll have the figures for you by the time you're warmed up.'

If we aren't destroyed first. Please ... let me live that long. I don't ask for more. Please, Fox *has got to be told.* He reeled off a string of numbers.

In his shack, among banked meters that stared at him like troll eyes, Vadász punched keys. He was no expert, but the comsystem computer had been preprogrammed for him; he need merely feed in the data and punch the directive 'Now.' A turret opened to airlessness. A transceiver thrust its skeletal head out for a look at the universe. A tight beam of coherent radio waves speared from it.

There were uncertainties. Diane was orbiting approximately 200,000 kilometers on the other side of New Europe, and *Meroeth* was widening that gulf with ever-increasing speed. But the computer and the engine it controlled were sophisticated; the beam had enough dispersion to cover a fairly large circle by the time it reached the target area; it had enough total energy so that its amplitude then was still above noise level.

Small, bestrewn with meteoritic dust, in appearance another boulder among thousands on the slope of a certain crater wall, an instrument planted by the men from the boat sat waiting. The signal arrived. The instrument – an ordinary microwave relay, such as every spaceship carries by the score, with a solar battery – amplified the signal and bounced it in another tight beam to another object high on a jagged peak. That one addressed its next fellow; and so on around the jagged desert face of the moon. Not many passings were needed. The man's-height horizon on Diane is about three kilometers, much greater from a mountaintop, and the last relay only had to be a little ways into that hemisphere which never sees New Europe.

Thence the beam leaped skyward. Some 29,000 kilometers from the center of Diane, it found *Fox II*.

The problem had been: how could a spaceship lurk near a hostile planet from which detectors probed and around which warcraft spun? If she went free-fall, every system throttled down to the bare minimum, her neutrino emission would not register above the cosmic background. But optical, infrared, and radar eyes would still be sure to find her. Unless she interposed the moon between herself and the planet. ... No. She dared not land and sit there naked to anyone who chanced close when the far hemisphere was daylit. She could not assume an orbit around the satellite, for she would move into view. She could not assume a concentric orbit around New Europe itself, for she would revolve more slowly and thus drop from behind her shield—

Or would she?

Not necessarily! In any two-body system there are three Lagrangian points where the secondary's gravitation combines with the primary's in such a way that a small object put there will remain in place, on a straight line through the larger bodies. It is not stable; eventually the object will be perturbed out of its resting spot; but 'eventually' is remote in biological time. *Fox* put herself at the most distant Lagrangian point and orbited in the moon-disc's effortless concealment.

The maneuver had never been tried before. But then, no one had ever before needed to have a warship on call, unbeknownst to an enemy who occupied the ground where he himself meant to be. Heim thought it would become a textbook classic, if he lived to brag about it.

'*Meroeth* to *Fox II*,' he intoned. '*Meroeth* to *Fox II*. Now hear this and record. Record. Captain Heim to Acting Captain Penoyer, stand by for orders.'

There could be no reply, except to Lac aux Nuages. The system, simple and hastily built, had been conceived in the belief that he would summon his men from there. If anything was heisenberg at the other end, he wouldn't know till too late. He spoke into darkness.

'Because of unexpected developments, we've been forced to lift directly, without passengers. It doesn't seem as if we're being pursued. But we have extremely important intelligence, and on that basis a new plan.

'First: we know there is only one capital ship in orbit around New Europe. All but two others are scattered beyond recall, and not due back for quite some time. The sentry vessel is the enemy flagship *Jubalcho,* a cruiser. I don't know the exact class – see if you can find her in Jane's – but she's doubtless only somewhat superior to *Fox.*

'Second: the enemy learned we were on the planet and recalled the two vessels in reach. They are presently accelerating toward New Europe. The first should already have commenced deceleration. That is the lancer *Savaidh.* The other is the cruiser *Inisant.* Check them out too; but I think they are ordinary Aleriona ships of their respective classes. The ballistic data are approximately as follows—' He recited the figures.

'Now, third: the enemy probably believes *Meroeth* is *Fox.* We scrambled with so much distance between that contrary identification would have been difficult or impossible, and also we took him by surprise. So I think that as far as he knows, *Fox* is getting away while the getting is good. But he cannot communicate with the other ships till they are near the planet, and he doubtless wants them on hand anyway.

'Accordingly, we have a chance to take them piecemeal. Now hear this. Pay no attention to the lancer. *Meroeth* can deal with her; or if I fail, she's no major threat to you. Moreover, nuclear explosions in space would be detected and alert the enemy. Stay put, *Fox*, and plot an interception for *Inisant*. She won't be looking for you. Relative velocity will be high. If you play your cards right, you have an excellent probability of putting a missile in her while warding off anything she has time to throw.

'After that, come get me. My calculated position and orbit at the time are approximately as follows.' Again a string of numbers. 'If I'm a casualty, proceed at discretion. But bear in mind that New Europe will be guarded by only one cruiser!'

Heim sucked air into his lungs. It was hot and had an electric smell. 'Repeating message,' he said. And at the end of the third time: 'The primary relay point seems to be going under Diane's horizon, on our present course. I'll have to sign off. Gunnar Heim to Dave Penoyer and the men of *Fox II* – good hunting! Over and out.'

Then he sat in his seat, looked to the stars in the direction of Sol, and wondered how Lisa was doing.

Increment by increment, *Meroeth* piled on velocity. It didn't seem long – though much desultory conversation had passed through the intercom – before the moment came to reverse and slow down. They mustn't have a suspicious vector when they encountered *Savaidh*.

Heim went to the saloon for a snack. He found Vadász there, with a short red-haired colonist who slurped at his cup as if he had newly come off a Martian desert. '*Ah, mon capitaine,*' the latter said cheerily, '*je n'avais pas bu de café depuis un sacré longtemps. Merci beaucoup!*'

'You may not have much to thank me for in a while,' Heim said.

Vadász cocked his head. 'You shouldn't look so grim, Gun – sir,' he chided. 'Everybody else is downright cocky.'

'Tired, I guess.' Heim slumped onto the Aleriona settle.

'I'll fix you up. A *grand Danois* of a sandwich, hm?' Vadász bounced out. When he returned with the food, he had his guitar slung over his back. He sat down on the table, swinging his legs, and began to chord and sing:

> 'There was a rich man and he lived in Jerusalem.
> Glory, hallelujah, hi-ro-de-rung!—'

The memory came back; A grin tugged at Heim's lips. Presently he was beating time; toward the end, he joined in the choruses. *That's the way! Who says we can't take them?* He returned to the bridge with a stride of youth.

And time fled. And battle stations were sounded. And *Savaidh* appeared in the viewports.

The hands that had built her were not human. But the tool was for the same job, under the same laws of physics, as Earth's own lancers. Small, slim, leopard-spotted for camouflage and thermal control, leopard deadly and beautiful, the ship was so much like his own old *Star Fox* that Heim's hand paused. *Is it right to kill her – this way?*

A legitimate ruse of war. Yes. He punched the intercom. 'Bridge to radio. Bridge to radio; Begin distress signal.'

Meroeth spoke, not in any voice but in the wailing radio pattern which Naval Intelligence had long known was regulation for Alerion. Surely the lancer captain (was this his first command?) ordered an attempt at communication. There was no reply. The gap closed. Relative speed was slight by spaceships standards, but *Savaidh* grew swiftly before Heim's eyes;

Unwarned, the Aleriona had no reason to doubt this was one of their own vessels. The transport was headed toward the Mach limit; not directly for The Eith, but then, none of them did, lest the raider from Earth be able to predict their courses; Something had gone wrong. Her communications must be out. Probably her radio officer had cobbled together a set barely able to cry, 'SOS!' The trouble was clearly not with her engines, since she was under power. What, then? Breakdown of radiation screening? Air renewal? Thermostats? Interior gee field? There were so many possibilities. Life was so terribly frail, here where life was never meant to be;

Or ... since the probability of her passing near the warship by chance, in astronomical immensity, was vanishingly small ... did she bear an urgent message? Something that, for some reason, could not be transmitted in the normal way? The shadow of *Fox II* lay long and cold across Alerion.

'Close spacesuits,' Heim ordered. 'Stand by.' He clashed his own faceplate shut and lost himself in the task of piloting. Two horrors nibbled at the edge of consciousness. The lesser one, because least likely, was that the other captain would grow suspicious and have him blasted. The worst was that *Savaidh* would continue her rush to Cynbe's help. He could not match accelerations with a lancer.

Needles wavered before his eyes. Radar – vectors – impulse – *Savaidh* swung about and maneuvered for rendezvous.

Heim cut drive to a whisper. Now the ships were on nearly parallel tracks, the lancer decelerating heavily while the transport ran almost free. Now they were motionless with respect to each other, with a kilometer of vacuum between. Now the lancer moved with infinite delicacy toward the larger vessel.

Now Heim rammed down an emergency lever. At full sidewise thrust, *Meroeth* hurtled to her destiny.

There was no time to dodge, no time to shoot. The ships crashed together. That shock roared through plates and ribs, ripped metal apart, hurled unharnessed Aleriona to their decks or against their bulkheads with bone-cracking violence.

A spaceship is not thickly armored, even for war. She can withstand the impact of micrometeorites; the larger stones, which are rare, she can detect and escape; nothing can protect from nuclear weapons, when once they have struck home. *Meroeth's* impact speed was not great, but her mass was. Through *Savaidh* she sheared. Her own hull gave way. Air puffed out in a frosty cloud, quickly lost to the light-years. Torn frameworks wrapped about each other. Locked in a stag's embrace, the ruined ships tumbled on a lunatic orbit. Aurore flared radiance across their guts; the stars looked on without pity.

'Prepare to repel boarders!'

Heim didn't know if his cry had been transmitted through his helmet jack to the others. Likely not. Circuits were ripped asunder. The fusion reaction in the power generator had guttered out. Darkness, weightlessness, airlessness flowed through the ship. It didn't matter. His men knew what to do. He undid his harness by feel and groped aft to the gun turret he had chosen for himself.

Most of the Aleriona crew must be dead. Some might survive, in spacesuits or sealed compartments. If they could find a gun still workable and bring it to bear, they'd shoot. Otherwise they'd try for hand-to-hand combat. Untrained for space, the New Europeans couldn't withstand that.

The controls of Heim's laser had their own built-in illumination. Wheels, levers, indicators glowed like watchfires. He peered along the barrel, out the cracked glasite, past wreckage where shadows slid weirdly as the system rotated; he suppressed the slight nausea due Coriolis force, forgot the frosty glory of constellations, and looked for his enemy.

It came to him, a flicker across tautness, that he had brought yet another tactic to space warfare: ramming. But that wasn't new. It went back ages, to when men first adventured past sight of land. *Olaf Tryggvason, on the blood-reddened deck of the* Long Serpent.

No. To hell with that. His business was here and now: to stay alive till *Fox* picked him up. Which wouldn't be for a long time.

A weapon spat. He saw only the reflection of its beam off steel, and squinted till the dazzle passed. *One for our side. I hope.* A heavy vibration passed through the hull and his body. An explosion? He wasn't sure. The Aleriona might be wild enough to annihilate him, along with themselves, by touching off a nuclear warhead. The chances were against it, since they'd need tools that would be hard to find in that mess out yonder. But—

Well, war was mostly waiting.

A spacesuited figure crawled over a girder. The silhouette was black and unhuman against the stars, save where sunlight made a halo on the helmet. One survivor, at least, bravely striving to – Heim got him in the sights and fired. Vapor rushed from the pierced body. It drifted off into space. 'I hated to do that,' Heim muttered to the dead one. 'But you could have been carrying something nasty, you know.'

His shot had given him away. A beam probed at his turret. He crouched behind the shield. Intolerable brightness gnawed centimeters away from him. Then more bolts struck. The enemy laser winked out. 'Good man!' Heim gasped. 'Whoever you are!'

The fight did not last long. No doubt the Aleriona, if any were left, had decided to hole up and see what happened. But it was necessary to remain on guard.

In the dreamlike state of free-fall muscles did not protest

confinement. Heim let his thoughts drift where they would. Earth, Lisa, Jocelyn ... New Europe, Danielle ... there really wasn't much in a man's life that mattered. But those few things mattered terribly.

Hours passed.

It was anticlimax when *Fox*'s lean shape closed in. Not that Heim didn't cheer – so she had won! – but rendezvous was tricky; and then he had to make his way through darkness and ruin until he found an exit; and then signal with his helmet radio to bring a tender into safe jumping distance; and then come aboard and get a shot to counteract the effects of the radiation he had taken while unscreened in space; and then transfer to the cruiser—

The shouts and backslappings, bear hugs and bear dances, seemed unreal in his weariness. Not even his victory felt important. He was mainly pleased that a good dozen Aleriona were alive and had surrendered. 'You took *Inisant*?' he asked Penoyer.

'Oh my, yes. Wizard cum spiff! One pass, and she was a cloud of isotopes. What next, sir?'

'Well—' Heim rubbed sandy eyes. 'Your barrage will have been detected from New Europe. Now, when *Inisant* is over-due, the enemy must realize who lost. He may have guessed you went after *Savaidh* next, and be attempting an interception. But it's most likely that he's stayed pretty close to base. Even if he hasn't, he'll surely come back there. Do you think we can beat *Jubalcho*?'

Penoyer scowled. 'That's a pitchup, sir. According to avail-able data, she has more teeth, though we've more accelera-tion. I've computed several tactical patterns which give us about an even chance. But should we risk it?'

'I think so,' Heim said. 'If we get smeared, well, let's admit that our side won't have lost much. On the other hand, if we win we've got New Europe.'

'Sir?'

'Sure. There are no other defenses worth mentioning. We can knock out their ground-based missiles from space. Then we give air support to the colonists, who're already preparing a march on the seaboard. You know as well as I do, no atmos-pheric flyer ever made had a fish's chance on Friday against a nuclear-armed spaceship. If the Aleriona don't surrender, we'll simply swat them out of the sky, and then go to work on their ground troops. But I expect they will give in. They're not stupid. And -... then *we've* got hostages.'

'But – the rest of their fleet—'

'Uh-huh. One by one, over a period of weeks or months, they'll come in. *Fox* should be able to bushwhack them. Also, we'll have the New Europeans hard at work, finishing the space defenses. Evidently there isn't much left to do there. Once that job's completed, the planet's nearly impregnable, whatever happens to us.

'Somewhere along the line, probably rather soon, another transport ship will come in, all unsuspecting. We'll nobble her and send off a load of New Europeans as originally planned. When Earth hears they're not only not dead, not only not at the point of defeat, but standing space siege and doing a crackling hell of a job of it ... why, if Earth doesn't move then, I resign from the human race.'

Heim straightened. 'I'm no damned hero, Dave,' he finished. 'Mainly I want to get home to the pipe and slippers. But don't you think a chance like this is worth taking?'

Penoyer's nostrils flared. 'By ... by Jove,' he stammered, 'yes.'

'Very good. Make course for New Europe and call me if anything happens.'

Heim stumbled to his cabin and toppled into sleep.

Vadász's hand shook him awake. 'Gunnar! Contact's made – with *Jubalcho* – we'll rendezvous inside half an hour.'

Nothing remained of tiredness, fear, doubt, or even anger. Heim went to the bridge with more life running through his veins than ever since Connie departed. Stars filled the viewports, so big and bright in the crystal dark that it seemed he could reach out and touch them. The ship murmured and pulsed. His men stood by their weapons; he could almost sense their oneness with him and with her. He took his place of command, and it was utterly right that Cynbe's voice should ring from the speaker.

'*Star – Fox* captain, greet I you again? Mightily have we striven. You refuse not battle this now?'

'No,' said Heim. 'We're coming in. Try and stop us.'

The laughter of unfallen Lucifer replied. 'Truth. And I thank you, my brother. Let come what that time-flow brings that you are terrible enough to live with ... I thank you for this day.'

'Good-by,' Heim said, and thought, a little surprised, *Why, that means 'God be with you.'*

'Captain of mine,' Cynbe sang, 'fare you well.'

The radio beams cut out. Dark and silent, the two ships moved toward their meeting place.

CHAPTER TEN

A MAN came to New Europe from Normandy in the early days and built himself a house on the sea cliffs. Steeply fell the land, with golden trees and ripples of wind through grasses and wildflowers, until it made its sudden downward plunge: a country of hills that shouldered into the sky, which was clangorous with birds, of glens, lakes, waterfalls, and eastward a salt blueness edged only by the curve of the world. In those times he had little to work with save native wood and stone; he chose them for beauty. The house he fashioned lifted gables like outlined mountains. Within there were spacious rooms, carved wainscoting, great fireplaces, rafters so high that they were often lost in shadows. Broad windows opened upon the land, of which the house had become another part. And the man built well, as folk do who see themselves only one link in a chain of generations.

But Bonne Chance grew from hamlet to city a hundred kilometers south. Colonists sought more the valleys than the heights. Though this dwelling was not distant when one could fly, the man's heirs moved where wealth and people were. The house stood long empty.

It did not suffer much. Strong and patient, it waited. The time came at last, and it was made a gift of honor.

Rear Admiral Moshe Peretz, commanding blastship *Jupiter*, Deepspace Fleet of Earth's World Federation, set his borrowed flyer down on the landing strip and went out. A fresh breeze swayed the nearby garden, clouds ran white, sunlight speared between them to dance on a restless ocean. He walked slowly, a short man, very erect in his uniform, with combat ribbons on his breast that freed him to admire a view or a blossom.

Gunnar Heim came out to welcome him, also in uniform:

but his was different, gray tunic, a red stripe down the trousers, a fleur-de-lis on the collar. He towered over his guest, bent down a face that had known much sun of late, grinned in delight, and engulfed the other man's hand in one huge paw. 'Hey, Moshe, it's good to see you again! How many years?'

'Hello,' Peretz said.

Heim released him, stung and surprised. 'Uh ... anything wrong?'

'I am all right, thank you. This is a nice home you have.'

'Needs a lot of work yet, after all the neglect, but I like it. Want to see the grounds before we go in?'

'If you wish.'

Heim stood for a moment before he sighed and said, 'Okay, Moshe. Obviously you accepted my dinner invitation for more reasons than to jaw with your old Academy classmate. Want to discuss 'em now? There'll be some others coming pretty soon.'

Peretz regarded him closely, out of brown eyes that were also pained, and said, 'Yes, let us get it over with.'

They started walking across the lawn. 'Look at the matter from my side,' Peretz said. 'Thanks to you, Earth went into action. We beat the Aleriona decisively in the Marches, and now they have sued for peace. Wonderful. I was proud to know you. I pulled every wire in sight so that I could command the ship that went officially to see how New Europe was doing, how Earth could help reconstruct, what sort of memorial we should raise for the dead of both planets – because victory was not cheap, Gunnar.'

'Haven't your men been well treated?' Heim asked.

'Yes, certainly.' Peretz sliced the air with his hand, as if chopping at a neck. 'Every liberty party had been wined and dined till it could hardly stagger back to the tender. But ... I issued those passes most reluctantly, only because I did not want to make a bad situation worse. After all – when we find this planet ringed with defense machines – machines which are not going to be decommissioned – when a ship of the World Federation is told how near she may come – what do you expect a Navy man to think?'

Heim bit his lip. '*Ja*. That was a mistake, ordering you around. I argued against it in council, but they outvoted me. I give you my oath no insult was intended, not by anyone. The

199

majority feeling was simply that we'd better express our sovereignty at the outset. Once the precedent has been accepted, we'll relax.'

'But *why*?' His rage flickered to death, leaving Peretz no more than hurt and bewildered. 'This fantastic declaration of independence . . . what kind of armed forces have you? Your fleet can't amount to more than your own old privateer and perhaps a few Aleriona prizes. Otherwise there is just the constabulary. What strength can half a million people muster?'

'Are you threatening us, Moshe?' Heim asked gently.

'What?' Peretz jarred to a stop and gaped. 'What do you mean?'

'Is Earth going to reconquer us? You could, of course. It'd be bloody and expensive, but you could.'

'No – no – did the occupation drive everyone here paranoid?'

Heim shook his head. 'On the contrary, we rely on Earth's good will and sense. We expect you to protest, but we know you won't use force. Not when your planet and ours have so lately shed blood together.'

'But . . . see here. If you want national status, well, that concerns mainly yourselves and the French government. But you say you are leaving the whole Federation!'

'We are,' Heim answered. 'Juridically, at least. We hope to make mutually beneficial treaties with Earth as a whole, and we'll always stand in a special relationship to France. In fact, President de Vigny thinks France won't object at all, will let us go with her blessings.'

'M-m-m . . . I am afraid he is right,' said Peretz grimly. He began walking again, stiff-gaited. 'France is still rather cool toward the Federation. She won't leave it herself, but she will be glad to have you do so for her, as long as French interests are not damaged.'

'She'll get over her grudge,' Heim predicted.

'Yes, in time. Did you break loose for the same cause?'

Heim shrugged. 'To a certain extent, no doubt. The Conference of Château St. Jacques was one monstrous emotional scene, believe me. The plebiscite was overwhelmingly in favor of independence. But there were better reasons than a feeling of having been let down in an hour of need. Those are the ones that'll last.'

'De Vigny tried to convince me,' Peretz snorted.

'Well, let me try in less elegant language. What is the Federation? Something holy, or an instrument for a purpose? We think it's a plain old instrument, and that it can't serve its purpose out here.'

'Gunnar, Gunnar, have you forgotten all history? Do you know what a breakup would mean?'

'War,' Heim nodded. 'But the Federation isn't going to die. With all its faults, it's proved itself too good for Earth to scrap. Earth's a single planet, though. You can orbit it in ninety minutes. The nations live cheek by jowl. They've got to unify, or they'll kill each other.' His gaze swept the horizon. 'Here we have more room.'

'But—'

'The universe is too big for any one pattern. No man can understand or control it, let alone a government. The proof is right at hand. We had to trick and tease and browbeat the Federation into doing what we could see, with our own eyes, was necessary – because it didn't see. It wasn't able to see. If man is going to live throughout the galaxy, he's got to be free to take his own roads, the ones his direct experience shows him are best for *his* circumstances. And that way, won't the race realize all its potential? Is there any other way we can, than by trying everything out, everywhere?' Heim clapped Peretz's back. 'I know. You're afraid of interstellar wars in the future, if planets are sovereign. Don't worry. It's ridiculous. What do entire, self-sufficient, isolated worlds have to fight about?'

'We just finished an interstellar war,' Peretz said.

'Uh-huh. What brought it on? Somebody who wasn't willing to let the human race develop as it should. Moshe, instead of trying to freeze ourselves into one shape, instead of staying small because we're scared of losing control, let's work out something different. Let's find how many kinds of society, human and nonhuman, can get along without a policeman's gun pointed at them. I don't think there is any limit.'

'Well—' Peretz shook his head. 'Maybe. I hope you are right. Because you have committed us, blast you.' He spoke without animosity.

After a minute: 'I must confess I felt better when President de Vigny apologized officially for keeping our ship at arm's length.'

'You have my personal apologies,' Heim said low.

'All right!' Peretz thrust out his hand, features crinkled with abrupt laughter. Accepted and forgotten, you damned old squarehead.'

His trouble lifted from Heim, too. 'Great!' he exclaimed. 'Come on inside and we'll buckle down to getting drunk. Lord, how much yarning we've got to catch up on!'

They entered the living room and settled themselves. A maid curtsied. 'What'll you have?' Heim asked. 'Some items of food are still in short supply, and of course machinery's scarce, which is why I employ so many live servants. But these Frenchmen built big wine cellars.'

'Brandy and soda, thanks,' Peretz said.

'Me too. We *are* out of Scotch on New Europe. Uh ... will there be cargoes from Earth soon?'

Peretz nodded. 'Some are already on the way. Parliament will scream when I report what you have done, and there will be talk of an embargo, but you know that won't come to anything. If we aren't going to fight, to hold you against your will, it is senseless to antagonize you with annoyances.'

'Which bears out what I said.' Heim put the drink orders into French.

'Please, don't argue any more. I told you I have accepted your *fait accompli*.' Peretz leaned forward. 'But may I ask something, Gunnar? I see why New Europe did what it did. But you yourself— You could have come home, been a world hero, and a billionaire with your prize money. Instead you take citizenship here – well, blaze, they are nice people, but they aren't yours!'

'They are now,' Heim said quietly.

He took out his pipe and tamped it full. His words ran on, almost of themselves:

'Mixed motives, as usual. I had to stay till the war was over. There was a lot of fighting, and afterward somebody must mount guard. And ... well ... I'd been lonely on Earth. Here I found a common purpose with a lot of absolutely first-class men. And a whole new world, elbow room, infinite possibilities. It dawned on me one day, when I was feeling homesick – what was I homesick for? To go back and rot among my dollars?

'So now, instead, I'm New Europe's minister of space and the navy. We're short of hands, training, equipment, everything; you name it and we probably haven't got it. But I can see us grow, day by day. And that's my doing!'

202

He struck fire and puffed. 'Not that I intend to stay in government any longer than necessary,' he went on. 'I want to experiment with pelagic farming; and prospect the other planets and asteroids in this system; and start a merchant spaceship yard; and – shucks, I can't begin to tell you how much there is. I can't wait to become a private citizen again.'

'But you do wait,' Peretz said.

Heim looked out a window at sea and sun and sky. 'Well,' he said, 'it's worth some sacrifice. There's more involved than this world. We're laying the foundation of' – he hunted for words – 'admiralty. Man's, throughout the universe.'

The maid came in with her tray. Heim welcomed her not only for refreshment, but as an excuse to change the subject. He wasn't much of a talker on serious matters. A man did what he must; that sufficed.

The girl ducked her head. '*Un voleur s'approche, monsieur,*' she reported.

'Good,' Heim said. 'That'll be Endre Vadász and his wife. You'll like them, Moshe. He was the man who really bailed us out of this mess. Now he's giving his Magyar genes full rein on a 10,000-hectare ranch in the Bordes Valley – and he's still one solar flare of a singer.'

'I look forward.' Peretz followed the maid's departure with an appreciative eye. 'Do you know, Gunnar,' he murmured, 'I observe a very sound reason for you to stay here. The proportion of pretty girls on New Europe is fabulous, and every one of them seems to idolize you.'

A brief bleakness crossed Heim's eyes. 'I'm afraid the mores here are a little different from Earth's. Oh, well.' He raised his glass. '*Skål.*'

'*Shalom.*'

Both men got up when the Vadászes entered. '*Bienvenu,*' Heim said, shook his friend's hand with gladness, and kissed Danielle's. By now, he'd learned how to do that with authority.

It was a surprise, he thought as he looked at her, how fast a certain wound was healing. Life isn't a fairy tale; the knight who kills the dragon doesn't necessarily get the princess. So what? Who'd want to live in a cosmos less rich and various than the real one? You commanded yourself as you did a ship with discipline, reasonableness, and spirit – and thus you came to port. By the time he fulfilled his promise to stand godfather to her firstborn, why, his feelings toward her would be downright avuncular.

No, he realized with a sudden quickening of blood, it wouldn't even take that long. The war was over. He could send for Lisa. He had little doubt that Jocelyn would come along.

Panther Science Fiction – A Selection from the World's Best S.F. List

More Great Science Fiction Books from Panther